Panic in the Panhandle

PANIC IN THE PANHANDLE

Elmo Simpson Mysteries

J.C. Kenney

TULE
PUBLISHING

Dedication

Panic in the Panhandle is dedicated in loving memory to the one and only Jimmy Buffett. His stories enchanted me at a young age, his outlook sustained me over the decades, and his influence on me as a storyteller cannot be overstated. Bubbles up, Jimmy.

CHAPTER ONE

T HE SECOND I saw the arm protruding from the mouth of the alligator, I knew it was going to be one of those days.

"We need to get out of here. Now!" I used my arm to shield Minerva from the gruesome sight. Despite her protests about being manhandled, we made a hurried retreat from the condominium.

Once we were outside and safe from the fearsome alpha predator, I dug out my phone.

"What's the meaning of this?" Minerva Longet, who wasn't accustomed to being told what to do unless it was coming from a director, put her fists on her hips and fixed me with a death stare. "Elmo Simpson, I demand to know—"

I put my index finger to my lips, shushing the woman. When the 911 operator asked me what the emergency was, I bit back a panicky laugh. Sometimes life in Paradise Springs, Florida, was stranger than fiction.

"I need to report an accident, or a murder, or something, at the Sea Breeze Resort."

"Can you be more specific, sir?" The operator's tone was a combination of cross and bored. Paradise Springs was a community filled with oddballs and a head-scratching history, so I was going to have to be 100 percent honest. Honesty, among some folks, is a rare commodity in these parts.

"Um, yeah." I stole a glance at Minerva, who was patting her hair to make sure every silver strand was in place, and swallowed. There was no way she was prepared for what I was about to say. "I think Fran Cohen's been eaten by an alligator."

As I told the operator the address, there was a whoosh of air followed by a *whump* like a sack of potatoes had fallen to the floor. A quick glance in the semiretired actor's direction confirmed she'd fainted.

Yep, definitely one of those days.

A few minutes later, a navy-blue Paradise Springs police cruiser barreled into the parking lot like a scene straight out of an old *Starsky and Hutch* episode. It skidded to a halt mere inches from my feet.

An officer practically leapt from the vehicle. Then almost tripped over himself as he tried to get his gun out of its holster while he marched toward me. "What's this about a gator and someone in danger, Simpson?"

"Morning, Officer Nimoy." I tipped my ball cap to him. "I think it's a little too late for the *someone in danger* part."

"What do you mean?" The cop pointed at Minerva, who was resting on a blanket I'd fetched from my truck while we waited for his arrival. "This woman clearly needs help."

Thomas Nimoy had been on the Paradise Springs Police Force for almost three years. In that time, he'd gone from a rookie who was scared of his own shadow to a semicompetent cop, on most days. He wasn't the sharpest tool in the shed, though. That led to a noticeable lack of respect many folks in the community showed him.

It didn't help that his pale skin, short black hair, and hawklike nose conspired with his last name to give him a look that reminded people of a certain pointy-eared alien from a classic science fiction franchise. While nobody called him "Spock" to his face, whenever the name was uttered in Paradise Springs, everyone knew it was in reference to the officer standing in front of me.

"I think it'd be best if you see for yourself."

After confirming the still-unconscious Minerva wasn't experiencing any breathing problems, I led the way inside. Nobody else seemed to be around, so she'd be okay for a minute.

Using as much stealth as my cat, Oscar, had, which wasn't a lot, I led Spock back through the condo. An unnerving clicking sound emanated from the bedroom. It sent shivers down my spine. I knew the sounds that trapped small animals made.

This clicking was different. It wasn't coming from a frightened rodent. This creature wasn't frightened at all.

Unsure if the sound was coming from the gator's claws or teeth, I tiptoed to the bedroom door and opened it a sliver.

From over my shoulder, Thomas took a look. An intake of breath followed by the rapid *thump, thump, thump* of work boots fading away made me shake my head. The cop had run away. So much for overcoming his own shadow.

A second look at the gator calmed me. From a professional perspective only. Despite the horrific scene, the reptile seemed content. It was situated next to the bed, its eyes were closed, and it was still. An apparently full belly didn't make the animal any less dangerous. It would make it a little easier to wrangle once the police gave me the go-ahead. Thank goodness for small favors.

"Fran, what did you get yourself into this time?" With a heavy heart, I closed the door and speed-walked out of there, relieved I'd brought my tranquilizer gun with me.

When I stepped back outside, Thomas was attending to Minerva. She was seated upright and was breathing normally between sips of water from a plastic bottle. That was good. She was one of my most reliable customers. And made amazing orange scones. I wouldn't want someone like that to get hurt.

Spock flipped open a little notebook with a one-handed flair that could only have come from hours of practice in front of a mirror. "Explain."

"I can't possibly…" Minerva fanned herself with her hand and closed her eyes. I couldn't help thinking that she was taking advantage of the situation to add some acting drama to the mix.

"Minerva called me this morning." I showed the call log on my phone to Spock as proof. "She told me there were noises coming from inside the wall she shares, er, *shared*, with Fran."

"You live next door," he asked her as he took a photo of the call log.

"Yes." She pointed a bony finger toward a seafoam-green-colored door ten yards down the hall. "I've lived there since I retired from the stage. A revival of *Oklahoma* was my final performance. It was a smashing success. I'm sure you read about it."

Spock looked at me, then raised an eyebrow, like he wanted me to verify her claim but didn't want to insult her. All I could do was shrug. I'm more of a *movie on demand* kind of dude.

Before he could ask more questions, another police cruiser arrived. This one lacked identification stickers and the lights and sirens on Spock's vehicle. The hi-gloss black paint job told everyone who was behind the wheel.

The Paradise Springs police chief had arrived.

She emerged from the vehicle like a queen rising from her throne. Dressed in a short-sleeved navy-blue uniform shirt, matching work pants, and black work boots, Susan Eikenberry radiated no-nonsense authority as she glided toward us. With long legs that went on forever, long hair the color of the rising sun, and piercing blue eyes, she also exuded the glamour of a swimsuit model. Which she had been before turning to a career in law enforcement.

"Witness interviews can wait, Officer Nimoy. We need to get the scene secured. Now. Before more evidence gets...eaten."

"Yes, sir, I mean ma'am, I mean Chief." Composure completely gone in the presence of his imposing boss, Spock shot off a poorly executed salute and dashed to his cruiser to call in for reinforcements.

She shook her head and turned toward me. "You mind taking the lead on neutralizing the gator? I don't want Thomas to hurt himself."

"Anything I can do to help." I tipped my cap to her.

"Then get to it."

Sixty sweaty and curse-filled minutes later, the reptile was inside a cage in my truck bed where it couldn't harm anyone. The remains of the arm had been transferred to an evidence kit. According to Spock, it would be used to ID the victim.

A crowd had gathered while we removed the animal from Fran's condo. There were the usual onlookers, shielding their eyes under the cloudless sky. Tourists dressed in garish tropical-style shirts stood shoulder to shoulder with locals who had nothing better to do than see for themselves what the fuss was all about.

Shoot, even Una, the street performer, was in attendance, juggling oranges while she circled the crowd on her unicycle. Every now and then, she'd hold out her top hat to collect tips. P. T. Barnum would have been proud.

Among the throng was the owner of the Sea Breeze Resort, Jolly Roger Raines. The man was friendly enough and, as the largest employer in the Springs, worked hard with other business owners to keep the local economy thriving. Still, with the slicked-back hair and tailored suit, I couldn't get past the fact that he looked like he'd just come from central casting for a *Godfather* reboot as Gangster Sidekick Number Two.

I waved at him, figuring he'd want the scoop. Instead, he

turned and hurried away, followed by two men dressed in black pants and white polos. Apparently, he'd seen enough. As he disappeared into the building, he put his cell phone to his ear. Probably informing his insurance carrier what had happened. I was glad I didn't have to make *that* call.

Weird. He was normally a chatty sort. People responded to stress differently, I guess.

I was checking the cage for potential weak points—one could never be too careful when it came to a ten-foot-long reptile with a taste for human flesh—when Susan strolled up to me. She donned a pair of reflective shades as she leaned against the truck.

A bead of sweat trickled down my cheek. I wasn't sure if it was due to the intensity of the sun's rays or the woman in front of me.

She gave me a disarming smile and shook her head. "Quite the circus we've got thanks to you. Now I have to cancel my spin class."

"Hey, I'm only the messenger."

"True enough. You don't get all offended when I blame you for things, though. I appreciate that." She opened her notebook to a blank page. There was no dramatic flipping it open like her junior officer. Chief Susan Eikenberry didn't need to do something like that.

"I got Minerva's version of what happened. Now I want yours."

A breeze blew in from the Gulf, filling my lungs with salt-tinged air. I'd escaped to this small burg in the Florida Panhandle to put the soul-crushing tech industry behind me and enjoy a simple life. Things like the sound of the waves crashing on the beach, the smell of the salty air in the morning, and some of the best barbeque this side of Kansas City.

Even my current job as a wild animal relocation specialist had a certain simplicity to it. I caught wild animals, removed them from places they shouldn't be, and returned them safely to the wild. Life wasn't complicated.

Until now.

I gave her the same information that I'd given to Spock. "When I got here, I did some checking in Minerva's condo and couldn't find anything. She swore up and down she'd heard something, so I thought I'd talk to her neighbor on the other side of the wall."

"That would be Francis Cohen."

Depending on who you talked to, Mr. Cohen was either a knight in shining armor or a dragon that put fear in the hearts of the town's residents. Originally from Philadelphia, the retired attorney had moved to Paradise Springs so he'd never have to see snow again. Over the years, he'd been a vocal supporter of rezoning undeveloped land to make it attractive to the tourism industry. His outspokenness had rubbed some folks the wrong way.

He was also a history buff and was supposedly writing a book chronicling the town's quirky history. There was concern among the OG crowd—longtime residents and independent businesspeople—that the project would unearth secrets people wanted kept buried.

The man had been a lightning rod of controversy. And,

by all accounts, had reveled in every moment of it.

"Yeah. I knocked on his door but didn't get an answer. Minerva said he liked to listen to audiobooks and probably had his headphones on, so she told me to use his spare key card."

"And did you?" Her voice was as neutral as the Gulf waters on a calm weekday morning. It carried the subtle menace of a shark lurking in the shallows, though. I was glad Minerva had witnessed everything, otherwise her tone would have me quaking in my work boots.

"Yeah. He kept it inside the ornamental Philly Phanatic gnome by his front door. Minerva told me where it was."

Susan raised an eyebrow that would have impressed the fictional Spock. "I see. And did you know a spare key card was kept there before that?"

A bead of sweat trickled down the back of my neck. It wasn't due to the weather. "No. Swear to whatever celestial being you want me to. Scout's honor."

"As if you were ever a Boy Scout."

"I was. Well, okay, I was a Cub Scout for about six months. But I'm still telling you the truth."

She stared at me for a few seconds. With her eyes hidden behind the reflective lenses, I could only imagine what her thoughts were. Eventually, she made a little circular motion with her finger. Continue.

"I opened the door. It smelled awful, like a swamp when the water's low. There was a coppery smell, too. We went in. I was afraid Fran was sick. When he wasn't in the living room or kitchen, we went to his bedroom. I knocked and called his name. Then I opened the door. The gator was by his bed. There was a lot of blood. That's when I told Minerva we needed to get out of there."

A wave of nausea rolled through me. I dropped onto the lowered tailgate with a thud. Susan fetched me a bottle of water from the cooler in the truck cab. I downed half of it in a single gulp.

While she gave me time to pull myself together, I studied the Sea Breeze. It was an impressive building, painted in soothing hues of beige, sky blue, and pale pink. It was also the largest structure in Paradise Springs. As such, it was regularly featured in the community's promotional materials. Ten stories tall, it stood like a sentinel as it stretched the length of two football fields along the beachfront.

The building's hub featured a two-story glass entrance. A coffee shop that served amazing java and a souvenir store were among the amenities located on the hub's first floor. A set of escalators took visitors to the second level, where a lounge that offered live music three nights a week sold overpriced boat drinks to the tourists.

Privately owned dwellings were located to the right of the hub. Many of them were year-round residences for people like Minerva and Fran. The condos on the other side of the hub, in the left wing, were time-share rentals.

At street level, piles of new mulch lay at strategic spots, ready to be spread by the green-clad maintenance staff. Above, contractors were applying fresh coats of glossy white paint to handrails while housekeeping staff pushed hippo-sized linen carts from one dwelling to the next. A few cars exited the parking garage and turned right onto Gulfview Lane, the main east to west drag through town.

Amid a horrible death, life went on. I was left with an unsettling question among all the normalcy not far from where I was sitting. How in the world had a full-grown alligator gotten into someone's home without anybody noticing?

"And you called 911 as soon as you got back outside?"

"Oh yeah. I was on the phone when Minerva passed out." I drained the rest of the water and tossed the crushed bottle into the bed of the truck.

She tapped away on her notebook as she hummed a tune I didn't recognize.

The wait made me want to scream *I didn't do it!* But I held my tongue. Experience had taught me the hard way that discretion was the better part of valor.

"You're the animal removal expert. Any idea how it got in?"

"No clue. It's not like Fran could have brought it home on a leash. I suppose it's not out of the realm of possibility that it wandered in somehow, but that seems unlikely. This close to the beach isn't exactly prime gator habitat."

"That's what I was thinking. You'd think someone would have reported seeing an animal that big wandering around. I did a quick check before coming over here. There are no recent reports of gator sightings."

I started to ask what she meant by no recent reports, then stopped. This was a town that prized itself on its bizarre personality. At least once a year, I heard a story about someone taking a gator on a leash for a walk. A couple of years ago, Drunk Paul ended up in the emergency room one night when he tried to ride a gator home from the Still Waters Pub. To this day, if you buy him a drink, he'll tell you the story.

The current situation was weird, though. Sure, there were alligators in the area, both in the wild and behind a fence at a nearby gator farm, but the idea of one going for a stroll down Gulfview Lane was absurd.

Unless it had occurred under the cover of darkness.

"I suppose it could have gotten in unseen if it happened after dark. The front door was locked, though."

Susan flicked through her notes. "The patio door wasn't."

"Really." I removed my cap and wiped my brow. This bizarre scenario had just taken another step toward something out of a horror flick. "I can't be 100 percent, but I don't remember seeing that door open."

"I didn't say the patio door was open. I said it was unlocked. And undamaged."

Silence hung over us like a wet beach towel as I processed her words. Fran had as many enemies as he had fans. My jaw dropped as the implication hit home.

"Someone put the gator in the condo."

"And used it to kill Mr. Cohen." She closed her notebook. "I think we've got a murder on our hands."

CHAPTER TWO

I N MY EIGHT years as the proprietor of Elmo's Critter Removal, I'd transferred countless animals from hundreds of homes and businesses. The work was great because it was different every day. One morning, I'd be removing a bat from an attic. Later the same day, I'd be setting traps in someone's backyard to stop a pesky mole from damaging the lawn. On one occasion, I'd even been called to corral a gator that had been hanging out by the fifteenth green at Live Oak Golf Club.

I'd never removed a murder weapon from a crime scene, though.

As the yellow crime-scene tape shrank in my rearview mirror, I laughed out loud. It was better than crying. Looking for a silver lining to this insane situation, I imagined adding a page to my website letting people know I was available to remove large reptilian predators. For a premium price, though.

It was still way better than my old job.

A few minutes later, the truck jostled me from side to side as I turned into my gravel driveway. When I bought the property, it had been asphalt. A hurricane washed out the driveway a few years back. Where the water took it all, I still have no idea.

A gravel replacement had been way more affordable. It had seemed like a good idea at the time, too. The annual maintenance I had to perform on it made me second-guess that decision. Like so many decisions from my past, though, what was done was done. There was no going back.

As the truck rolled to a stop beside the front door of Casa Simpson, my roommate let out a big yawn from his perch on the top of the stoop.

I lowered the window. "Got a gator in the back, Oscar. A big one. You want to check it out?"

My gray tomcat gave me a long look, then curled up to go back to sleep. The feline slept more than any animal I'd crossed paths with. Then again, Oscar had been my wingcat for over a decade. Living with me and my ever-changing menagerie, and the sounds, smells, and noises that came with it, I'd say he'd earned every nap he took.

"Next time, then." I pulled into to the backyard, other-wise known as *Corporate HQ.*

Chief Eikenberry had told me that the gator was evi-dence. That meant I needed to leave it in its cage until the authorities came to get it. Since the reptile was ten feet long and weighed around four hundred pounds, I was more than happy to leave it right where it was.

After a quick check to make sure the beast hadn't chewed or clawed a hole in the cage, I headed to the *shop*, a ten-by-sixteen-foot wooden shed I bought online when I got into the animal relocation business. A window provided enough natural lighting that on sunny days, I didn't have to use the overhead LED fixture. The double doors provided enough side-to-side clearance so I could move things in and out with ease. It came with built-in shelving, but I'd added water, electric, and storage crates. With some much-needed and appreciated help from my good buddy Rambo.

Though small, it met all my needs. Nicola Beecham, my sometimes girlfriend, said it was cozy the first time she saw it. The cyan-colored exterior and the planter box filled with herbs under the window probably contributed to her assessment.

When I was finished scrubbing the materials I'd used corralling the gator, I locked the shed and visited the animals in the *quarantine condos*, enclosures they called home until I released them back into the wild. A pair of bats hung from the rafters of one enclosure. A trio of chipmunks was almost invisible among a small pile of wood chip bedding in another.

"I'm springing you all tomorrow morning. Better pack your bags." They ignored me. Oh well, better than them yelling at me about the injustice of being taken away right after they'd settled into their new digs, or something like that.

The backyard was surrounded by a six-foot-high privacy fence, secured by a gate with keypad locking mechanism accompanied by a combination padlock as backup. I made sure the enclosure was buckled up tight on my way to the house. The truck would stay put inside the enclosure until the authorities fetched the gator.

Was it the most secure setup in the world? Of course not,

but over the eight years I'd been in business, I'd never had a break-in nor suffered any vandalism. Then again, the security camera hanging from the corner of the house, the motion-detecting security lights, and the DANGER, WILD ANIMALS sign posted by the road probably helped deter potential criminals.

I eased myself onto the stoop next to Oscar. While I scratched his ears, I told him about my unusual morning. The cat was a great listener. He didn't interrupt me once while I gave him the details. Then again, the only time he opened his eyes was when I stopped scratching him.

When the report was finished, I stood back up. Oscar ignored the popping of my knee joints. I appreciated the way he let me bear the indignity of advancing age without burdening me with his pity. As if a cat would ever do that.

"Who's ready for some lunch?"

That got him up on all fours. His gray coat became a blur as he snaked through a sliver of space as soon as I opened the door.

My home was a far cry from a luxury abode. The abode back in Indianapolis had encompassed three thousand square feet and featured four bedrooms, the same number of full baths, a game room, and a wet bar.

That was luxury.

Now, I lived in an eight-hundred-square-foot modular home with two bedrooms and one bathroom. It was small. It was also easy to maintain, comfortable in the hot, muggy summer, and snug during the chilly nights in winter. There were lots of windows with sills from which Oscar could monitor his surroundings. It didn't look like much, but it was mine, paid for free and clear.

"What'll it be, beef or salmon?" I put a can of each on the floor so Oscar could choose.

He sniffed the beef, then the salmon, looked up at me, then sniffed the salmon again.

"Fish it is." I grimaced as I pulled the tab back to open the can. Oscar needed soft food because of digestive tract issues that had developed in the last few years. I didn't mind taking care of his dietary needs one bit. The salmon smelled revolting, though. His next meal would be beef, which didn't smell half bad. I owed that to my olfactory senses.

I warmed up some leftover veggie pizza, grabbed a beer, and went back outside to dine al fresco. Like the rest of the house, my patio was no frills. A twelve-by-twelve pad of stone pavers big enough for a table, four matching chairs, and a gas grill. Just the way I wanted it.

While I ate, I checked my phone. There were no work requests. I breathed a sigh of relief. While I never wanted to turn down work, I didn't want to go on a run with an adult alligator a stone's throw from my front door.

Social media was a different kettle of fish, altogether.

My Instagram feed was filled with photos I'd been tagged in. There were shots of me, Spock, and two other police officers lugging the gator to my truck. People were freaking out at the size of the creature. Apparently, they didn't realize I'd sedated it and bound its snout before moving it. At that point, it wasn't that much different from hauling a fallen oak tree out of the woods.

I didn't mind the comments extolling my studliness as I led the removal, though. Compliments were rare in my line of work. I'd take them any way I could get them.

The free publicity I was getting was priceless. It was a mixed blessing, though. Being connected with a murder, even only by association, wasn't quite the way I wanted Elmo's Critter Removal to get noticed.

Hopefully, the old line about any publicity being good publicity would turn out to be true.

I was checking my business page on Facebook when the low rumble of a vehicle's engine made me look up. The warm feeling I'd been enjoying for a job well done under difficult circumstances evaporated.

Chief Eikenberry had arrived. I imagined "Ride of the Valkyries" in the background as she made her way toward me.

The woman's stunning beauty left me tongue-tied more than I wanted to admit. Her no-nonsense demeanor and withering glare made me want to confess to crimes I hadn't even heard of. Just to make her happy.

To top it off, she had catlike reflexes that had left untold drunks and troublemakers cuffed and immobilized before they could finish saying, *Hey, baby.*

Fortunately, the chief liked me. Well, tolerated was probably more accurate, but whatever.

Fine, I had a crush on her. She was as far out of my league as Jupiter is from the Earth, though. Which was fine, too. I was a decade and change older than her. It was a big enough gap that it made it easy to remain friendly and keep it at that.

"Welcome to my humble abode." I tipped my cap as I used my foot to push a chair in her direction. "Get you a beer? You look like you could use one."

"Don't be a wise guy, Simpson. You know full well I'm still on duty." She blew out a long breath as she dropped into the chair.

"Then I'll put it in a cup."

A moment later, I was back from the kitchen with a plastic stadium cup imprinted with the logo of the BALL STATE CARDINALS, my alma mater.

"I really shouldn't." She tossed her sunglasses on the table.

I poured the ale with a dramatic flair that would make an advertising exec proud. My years tending bar in college hadn't gone to waste.

"If there's one thing I know, Chief, it's that life is too short to say things like *I really shouldn't*. Besides, you've got Spock leading the on-site investigation, right?" I handed the cup to her.

"No. Jenkins is taking the lead. He's a good detective. I suppose one won't hurt. If word gets out, though…"

"It won't be from me." We clinked cups. Susan had overlooked a few of my errors in judgment over the years. I owed her. That was one of the things I liked about Paradise Springs. A police chief who wasn't above looking the other way if it served the greater good.

The power of doing someone a solid was strong in Paradise Springs.

While we drank, Susan reviewed her notes with me. Now that I'd had some time to separate myself from the scene, the story was turning weirder and weirder. I mean, what kind of person would use an alligator as a murder weapon? It was something out of a James Bond flick.

When we finished, the chief cracked her knuckles. The sounds sent Oscar scurrying from her lap to behind the house.

"Never seen that mangy thing move so fast. Gives a new meaning to fraidy-cat."

"He's a lover, not a fighter. And he's not mangy. He's lived a life of adventure. He's weathered, seasoned. Like his dad."

Silence hung between us as Susan seemed to be debating whether I had said something inappropriate. Evidently satisfied I hadn't, she rose to her feet instead of slugging me. Which was good, because she had a lethal right jab. I'd seen her drop three idiots with it myself.

"Let's have a look at this gator."

She slowed as we approached my truck. When we got within five feet, she unholstered her gun.

"No need for that." I rapped a knuckle against the cage. "Reinforced steel. It'll hold him."

"What happens when it wakes up?" She leaned against the truck as she stared at the creature, which hadn't moved since the tranquilizer took effect. Her eyes gleamed. She may have been as tough as the gator on the outside, but she had a healthy respect for all living things.

It was one of the reasons I liked her.

"Not sure. This is my first time removing a reptile this big. It'll probably be pissed about waking up in a cage. Who wouldn't be? Seriously, though, it's got a full belly, so it won't be in the mood for a midnight run to Taco Bell anytime soon."

"Speaking of its belly, a crew will be here first thing in the morning to euthanize it. A shame, really. It's a magnificent creature. It's a victim almost as much as Mr. Cohen."

"Yeah." I had the same feeling when I had to euthanize a critter. "That's one way to put it."

Most of the time, animals weren't at fault for being in a situation that called for removal. It's not like a group of squirrels got together and said, *Hey, that's Karen's place. Let's go annoy the snot out of her, just for kicks and giggles.*

Humans called all the shots, though. In animal removal world, it was guilty until...nothing, really. A critter was deemed a nuisance. It was my job to carry out the sentence of removal.

Most of the time, removal offered the critter a second chance. That was something I could totally identify with.

When I got involved with euthanizing an animal, extenuating circumstances were involved. The animal needing removal was injured or sick. The best option available was to have a veterinarian friend put the thing to sleep. It hurt my heart every time. It was better than turning the animal loose and sentencing it to a slow and possibly painful death, though.

"What's that supposed to mean?" Susan fixed me with her famous death stare. It was more intimidating than having a seventy-year-old nun with a ruler in her hand glaring at you after you pulled the fire alarm when you were in fifth grade. Or so I had been told.

"This animal didn't *choose* to commit murder by devouring Fran. Someone used it for that purpose. When someone shoots someone else, who then dies, you don't destroy the gun, do you?"

"No, of course not. But guns don't kill people. Someone has to pull the trigger."

"Gators don't kill people, either. They follow their instincts. And their instincts don't include waddling up to someone's patio door and asking to come in like a twenty-first century version of Land Shark."

She took a step back. "Point taken. So, is there any way you can tell whether this guy is wild or domestic?"

"Just by looking at him, no. I don't see any evidence of a livestock tag. It's possible it's been PIT tagged."

"Explain."

"An electronic transponder is injected under the skin. Kind of like when pet dogs and cats are microchipped. I think Rambo does that with his herd. You might ask if he'd be willing to scan for a tag."

"Thanks for the idea, but I'll ask the Animal Control people to do that." She scratched her shoulder. "You see, the gator Rambo reported missing hasn't been found."

"Uh-oh." I rubbed the muscles at the base of my neck. The plot had just taken a turn down a dark boulevard. "Yeah, I can see how that would be a problem."

A few weeks ago, the town had spent a couple of days in

panic mode when Rambo reported one of his adult gators was unaccounted for.

While tourists freaked out, locals did one of two things. One group helped the police search for the reptile. They were concerned that a farm-raised gator on the loose might put itself, and others, in harm's way. I was part of that camp.

The OG crowd shrugged and went about their business. Alligators were part of life in the Florida Panhandle. If you wanted to live here, you got used to existing side by side with them.

When it didn't turn up, the attention of the town was diverted to the latest shiny thing. In this case, it was the rescue, and subsequent jailing, of a drunken tourist who jumped from a tour boat in an attempt to ride a dolphin.

While most everyone else forgot about the wayward reptile, the chief hadn't. And now she seemed to have a murder suspect.

Waldo Quigley, known to one and all as Rambo.

CHAPTER THREE

I KEPT IT together until the chief left. Then, I broke out in a sweat and started shaking all over. It didn't help that before she got in her SUV, she mentioned with a smile that failure to keep the gator secured might be seen by some people, especially in law enforcement, as aiding and abetting the commission of a crime.

If the parting shot was meant to scare me, it worked. If it was meant as a joke, it still scared me. Rambo and I hung out from time to time, helped each other with odd jobs, but weren't super close. More like got along well and were friendly with each other. Heck, I was convinced that the only things he was actually friends with were cold-blooded and walked on four legs.

Something Susan, apparently, was well aware of.

So, I did my usual thing when I was freaking out. I grabbed my battered copy of *Leaves of Grass* and a bottle of my favorite Dew—Tullamore, not Mountain—and spent the rest of the day in *escape from reality* mode. I'd played my role in capturing the gator and keeping it in a safe place. My involvement with the whole awful episode was concluded.

The following morning, I was jolted awake by a thunderous, rapid pounding on my front door. I winced as the world swam before me when I sat up. That fourth whiskey on the rocks had proven to be one too many.

"Hold on. I'm coming," I hollered at the impatient visitor.

At that moment, I decided that banging on people's doors on Sunday morning should be designated a criminal offense. If the person who wanted to see me was a cop, I was going to let Susan have a piece of my mind. I didn't deserve to be harassed like this.

I yanked the door open. "What do you..." The words died in my throat as my gaze landed on my visitor.

At six-five and three hundred pounds, Waldo Quigley was a mountain of a man. When you factored in his shoulder-length shaggy brown hair and a beard bushy enough that a bird or two could be living there, the man's appearance became borderline terrifying.

"Need your help, Simpson." His normal loud, commanding voice was wavering like a fiberglass post in a hurricane-force wind. "Can I come in?"

With memories of yesterday's conversation with Susan fresh in my mind, I looked around. No cop cars were to be seen. I didn't want anybody jumping to conclusions that I was conspiring with a killer. Especially with the murder weapon still in my truck.

"Um, yeah." I stepped aside. "I was gonna have a cup of coffee. Want some?"

"That would be great, thanks." He settled his massive frame onto a chair at the kitchen table.

I paused filling the coffee filter in midpour, fearful the

secondhand piece of furniture would collapse under his weight. The chair held. I took that as a positive sign.

"So, ah, what brings you by? Do you have a job for me?" I got most of my work on a referral basis. Since Rambo raised gators, many people considered him the local expert on all things reptile. They often called him when they wanted a lizard or a snake dealt with. Without fail, he sent them my way.

"No." The coffee cup I offered him practically disappeared in his giant mitts. He took a sip, then nodded toward the door. "The gator still here?"

"Yep." I glanced at the digital clock on the microwave. "Animal Control's supposed to be here around noon."

"Detective Jenkins paid me a visit last night. They think it's the one I reported missing." His voice was like a rumble of thunder. It almost made the window blinds vibrate.

While I'm admittedly no Albert Einstein, I'm no dummy. Rambo's comment about the police suggested whoever had talked to him hadn't mentioned the chief's visit with me. That was a relief. Until I had a handle on what, exactly, Rambo wanted, I was going to keep that tidbit to myself.

"What do you think?" I stirred some creamer into my coffee. Evasive responses were the way to go. For now, at least.

For all I knew, I had the murderer sitting in my kitchen right this minute. I sure didn't want him to get mad and turn me into the gator's second human meal in as many days.

"Seems like a mighty big coincidence for one of my gators to disappear and then one shows up a couple of weeks later having a human for breakfast." He drained his coffee cup. My eyes watered as the steaming drink went down his gullet.

"If it's one of mine, it'll be chipped. I brought my scanner. You mind if I check? It would be a load off my mind to have proof it's not."

Great. He was making the very suggestion Susan had shot down. If he was offering to do the scan, that suggested he wasn't involved in Fran's murder. Rambo was a decent enough dude. He might look scary, but he wasn't a bad guy once you got to know him. He just didn't give many people that chance.

"Why not?" We headed outside. I noticed Oscar was nowhere to be seen. Couldn't blame him. He was probably hiding so he wouldn't have to be added to a witness list if things went south in the next few minutes.

While I unlocked the fence gate, he jogged to fetch his scanner. For a human version of an alp, he was quick on his feet. Upon his speedy return, he was breathing like he'd just gotten out of his chair instead of sprinting thirty yards. Evidently in good shape, too. Apparently, raising carnivorous reptiles was good for one's physical health. Go figure.

He wasn't strong enough to wrangle an adult-sized alligator by himself, though. Was he? As big as he was, the reptile had to outweigh him by a hundred pounds.

The second he stepped up to the truck, Rambo started rubbing his chest, as if his heart was aching. "That's him. Butkus. A tough bugger."

His scanner was still in his hand. It hadn't been turned on. "How can you tell?"

"I know my gators, Simpson. When you live with someone as long as me and Butkus have, you learn to recognize them on sight." His hard as granite gaze softened and he even grinned.

"How old is he?" Animals fascinated me and I enjoyed spending time with other animal lovers. The affection Rambo had for Butkus was as obvious as the colorful alligator tattoo that ran the length of his right arm.

"Almost twenty. He was one of my first hatchlings. I remember the day he was born." He looked away and wiped one of his eyes, like there was dust in it. Or maybe a tear. "Well, might as well make it official."

The scanner in his hand looked like a futuristic ping-pong paddle. The handle was about six inches long and was wrapped in red grip tape. An LED screen was in the center of the round scanner section. A few controls were situated below the screen.

He pressed a switch, then walked the length of the cage and back, keeping the scanner as close to the animal as possible. When he was finished, he showed me the display. A numerical sequence was displayed.

"That's my code for Butkus. Not that I had any doubt about it." Rambo chewed on his upper lip as he turned toward his reptilian companion. "They're going to send you to the next adventure, buddy. I want you to know they're the monsters, not you."

"I'm sorry, man." I really was. I'd read too many stories

to count about some clueless dude bro getting himself into some place he shouldn't be. Then a predator came along, followed its instincts, and went after the idiot human. Inevitably, the dude bro got rescued and a huge Instagram following while the animal got a death sentence.

"Thanks, Simpson. I don't care what they say about you. I think you're okay."

I knew what a lot of people said about me. I was a slacker, a burnout, a fool who walked away from a career and lifestyle most people only dreamed about.

They weren't wrong.

The thing was, I didn't care what people said about me. Well, most people. I was happy with the clarity and simplicity of my current life. It was enough for me. The haters could take a long walk off a short pier, for all I cared.

"That means a lot, Rambo. Do you want a few minutes alone with Butkus? You know, to have a chat?"

"I want to stay with him until Animal Control gets here. He shouldn't have to face that all alone."

A lump formed in my throat. Oscar and I had been together for almost as long as I'd lived in Paradise Springs. The bond people formed with their nonhuman companions was as real as the scar on my forehead I got when a woman's boyfriend hit me with a beer bottle years ago.

There was a problem, though.

"I don't think you should be seen with Butkus. It might raise questions."

Rambo spun toward me, his fists balled into massive sledgehammers. "What do you mean? He belongs to me. I have…" His mouth formed an O as reality slapped him across the face. "They think I had something to do with Cohen's murder."

"Afraid so. I hate to say this, but if you're here when they arrive, there's a chance you could be accused of tampering with evidence."

"But I didn't do anything. You gotta believe me." He held his hands out in a pleading fashion. "Simpson, you're smart. You can help me get out of this mess."

"Me?" I looked around to make sure someone else hadn't crept up from behind me and filmed the request. "What can I do?"

"Sneak around. Get information. Ask questions. Come on, man. You come and go all over the place, and nobody pays you any mind. Someone's bound to blab something, and you might hear it. You can prove I got nothing to do with Cohen getting killed."

"I dunno." I wasn't opposed to eavesdropping. While I didn't gossip, I did adhere to a lesson my mom taught me at an early age. Keep my eyes and ears open and my mouth shut.

"Come on, man." He pointed a beefy finger at me. "You made me a promise. Remember?"

"Oh yeah. That." I scratched my chin as images from a fateful encounter a decade ago came to me. The culmination of a series of life-changing events.

When I arrived in Paradise Springs, I didn't know a soul. All my possessions were contained in a backpack, gym bag, and a half dozen moving boxes strapped down in the bed of my 2005 Ford F150 pickup.

For months, I'd been on the run from my old life. The journey, one I hoped naturalist John Muir would be proud of, had brought me to this little town nestled on the Gulf of Mexico halfway between Pensacola and Panama City. With no place to be, I walked into a little cinderblock dive with a tin roof and an outdoor bar called the Riptide Barbeque Shack.

The beer was cold and the brisket tender and smoky. In other words, perfect. I'd just ordered a lager from a local brewery when the largest man I'd ever seen live and in person sat down at the bar two stools down from me.

"The usual, Rambo?" the bartender asked.

"Make it a double. The kids were in a nasty mood today."

My beer bottle came to a stop halfway to my mouth. "Kids? Are you a teacher?"

The man froze me with a long stare, not even breaking it when the bartender placed a tumbler containing a brownish liquid in front of him.

"You're not from around here, are you?" He sucked down half of his drink in one swallow and wiped his mouth with the sleeve of a black T-shirt that was fraying at the edges.

"No. I'm from Indiana. Visiting the area for a few days." I took a slug of my beer and stared at my plate. The last thing I wanted was to get beaten to a pulp for saying something stupid to a lookalike of reality TV star Rupert Boneham.

"Well, then." He slapped me on the back so hard I almost spit out my drink. "Welcome to Paradise Springs. That's Wendell. He's the proprietor of this fine establishment. And I'm Rambo. I raise alligators. That's who my kids are."

"Benjamin Simpson. Everyone calls me Elmo." We shook hands while I complimented Wendell on the meal. I had no idea what to say to someone who worked with dangerous reptiles for a living.

They were a friendly duo, so I spent the evening at the bar, trading stories with them. I kept quiet about my past. There was no need to ruin a nice night by spilling about the ghosts I was trying to outrun. Like the fact that everyone called me Elmo because of my life-long adoration of the Sesame Street character, for instance.

Before I knew it, Wendell barked out last call. I got up. My legs were wobbly from a few too many beers. As I got out my wallet, Rambo wrapped a beefy paw around my forearm.

"Tonight's on me, friend."

Friend. Nobody had used that term with me in ages. I grinned. Even if it was alcohol induced, it felt good to use those muscles.

Still, the offer left me a tad uneasy. "I appreciate it, but I don't know when I'll be able to return the favor."

Rambo moved his hand to my shoulder and gave it a friendly squeeze. "A man with integrity. I like that. Tell you what. Someday down the road, if I need your help, you can return the favor then. Deal?"

Back then, I had no intention of sticking around Paradise Springs any longer than a few days. Just long enough to do some laundry and get some sun. I didn't want to insult the man. If the chance to repay him never came up, that wasn't my fault.

"Sure. If you ever need a favor, I'll be happy to help."

Now here we were. Rambo stared at me. It was time to pay up. We'd done a lot for each other over the years, but this was the first time he'd actually mentioned that promise made all those years ago. The desperation in his eyes was impossible to miss.

The man could be gruff. He was impatient with folks he thought were fools. But he'd always been a straight shooter and his advice was rock-solid. That, and he'd helped me find a place to hang my hat.

I liked the guy. I trusted him. He'd never once lied to me or screwed me over.

Those factors didn't change one key fact. The logical answer was no. Murder was serious business. If Rambo wanted a private investigator, he should hire one. And a good defense lawyer.

"This is insane." I threw up my hands. "You know that, right? I relocate animals. Looking for killers isn't exactly in my skill set."

He grinned. "Think of it as adding another line to your résumé."

My phone buzzed. I dropped a cuss word as I read the message.

"What's wrong?"

"Animal Control's on their way. That means you need to get out of here. Now. I'll come by your place later."

"Thanks, Simpson. I knew I could count on you." After saying goodbye to Butkus, Rambo took me into a bone-crushing hug, then headed out.

Once I was alone, Oscar wandered up to me. As he wound himself between my legs, he let out a meow, as if asking if I had the slightest clue how to deliver on the promise I'd just made.

"I don't know, bud. But Rambo's innocent. I can feel it. Now all I gotta do is figure out how to prove it."

CHAPTER FOUR

THE ANIMAL CONTROL team arrived minutes after Rambo split. Dressed in matching green polos and tan khaki shorts, they looked more like employees of Gulf Coast Zoo instead of the local animal impound.

After exchanging mundane pleasantries about how warm it was going to be later in the week and that maybe the winter chill was behind us, I led them to the truck.

"Wow. That's a whopper," the youngest of the three men said as he reached for his phone.

"No photos allowed." Spock ran toward us, waving his hands over his head like he was practicing communication via semaphore.

His PARADISE SPRINGS ball cap flew off his head as he skidded to a stop inches from the team leader. As he retrieved his cap, a pen fell out of his breast pocket. After what seemed like a century, he finally gathered himself together.

"Officer Thomas Nimoy, PSPD." He hooked his thumbs on his belt. "I'm here to supervise the transfer of an adult reptile for examination as evidence—"

"Give it a rest, will you, Spock?" The team leader, a Black man named Louis, who looked like he should be playing linebacker for the New Orleans Saints, rolled his eyes. "We all know why you're here. Did you bring the chain of custody paperwork?"

"The chain of—" His eyes went wide as he patted his back pockets. "Right. Be back in a sec."

The young man sprinted to retrieve the forgotten paperwork. God love him, he was trying. In more ways than one.

"How do you want to handle this, Mr. Simpson?" Louis patted the cage. Butkus raised his snout in response. "I see the tranq's worn off."

"Are you going to, you know"—I cocked my head to the side—"do it here?"

"No. We'll do that at our facility." Louis's dark eyes softened. Apparently, he wasn't without feelings when it came to animals.

"In that case, let's just move the cage with Butkus still in it. I can fetch it later."

All three heads of the team nodded in unison. While we were discussing the best ways to accomplish our task, Spock returned. He held the form out to me. It was used to ensure a record was kept for when a piece of evidence—Butkus, in this case—changed hands. Since Butkus was going from me to Animal Control under the direction of the police, use of the form made sense. If the gator went missing, the chances of finding the real killer could take a massive hit.

"Elmo, I need you to sign here." Spock pointed toward a line at the top of the page.

Louis ripped the paper from his hands and gave it to me. "We're all adults here. Let's get this done."

I didn't know Louis, so his hostility toward Spock puzzled me. Sure, the cop was a bit of a doofus and we all tended to lose patience with him, but the obvious contempt the Animal Control agent had for the cop was at another level.

Who knew, maybe Fran's murder was connected somehow.

Louis and his team were pros and as strong as oxen, so once we convinced Spock to just stay out of the way so he didn't get himself hurt, we got the still-caged Butkus moved to their truck in no time at all. Before the cop could open his mouth, Louis signed the form confirming transfer from me to Animal Control.

We said our goodbyes, and a few minutes later, it was me and an empty truck bed. And Oscar. He'd kept an eye on the whole event from his spot on the stoop. When I looked at him, he yawned and put his head down to take a nap.

Man, at times like this I wouldn't mind the life of a housecat.

That evening, after giving the bats and chipmunks their freedom, I picked up some barbeque from the Riptide and headed for Rambo's place. On my way there, I put a Bob Marley CD into the player. The reggae legend's music always put my mind at ease. As the sign for Quigley Farms came into view, I was pretty sure I was going to need all the brainpower I had to get Rambo out of the fix he was in.

The enterprise was located on a two-hundred-acre plot of scrub and marsh land on the outskirts of Paradise Springs. This far inland, palm trees were nowhere to be found. Instead, slash pines towered above pockets of crabgrass and man-made lagoons. A twelve-foot-high stainless-steel chain-link fence surrounded the gator enclosure, which took up over half of the property.

Rambo told everyone the barbed wire strung along the top of the fence helped keep the gators from escaping. He'd confided in me that it was used more to deter fools from trying to enter than preventing the residents from getting out.

A gravel driveway led to a two-story clapboard farmhouse. A parking lot large enough to accommodate two dozen vehicles was situated in front of the building. The first floor served as the farm's welcome center and business office. Rambo lived on the second floor.

My muscles started aching as my mind drifted back to the weekend Rambo, Wendell, and I had spread a new load of gravel to level out the parking area. That's what friends were for, though.

There was no Mrs. Rambo or little Rambos. The man lived and breathed for his farm's only commodity—alligators. One time, while I was helping Wendell load a new supply of hickory for his smoker, he told me that Rambo had been engaged to a beauty originally from Barbados. After a while, the woman realized, no matter what, she would always be second fiddle to Rambo's gators. Rather than compete with a group of reptiles for the man's love and attention, she returned to her island home.

The man had been single ever since, content with his status as the fourth generation in the Quigley family to run the enterprise.

I found him in his pole barn. He was mixing up a concoction of fishmeal and oil that he fed to his livestock. In the background, Alicia Keys sang about celebrating being on fire. My musical preferences leaned toward reggae. Rambo loved his pop.

With the music so loud, the only way I could get his attention was to hit Pause on the CD player sitting on a nearby shelf. It was either that or tap him on the shoulder and risk getting stabbed with the Crocodile Dundee–style knife he was using.

Prioritizing my personal safety, I went with the Pause-hitting route.

"Simpson." Rambo wiped the enormous blade with a towel as he turned toward me. "Was beginning to worry you might not make it."

"Never fear." I held out the bag containing dinner. "Elmo is here, or at least food is."

He laughed—a sound like a bunch of whiskey barrels rolling down a hill. Or what Santa Claus would sound like if he said *ha, ha, ha* instead of *ho, ho, ho.*

"A sense of humor in the face of impending doom. Proof you're the man for the job. Give me a few minutes to give the kids their dinner."

While Rambo attended to his congregation, I spread the meal out on a folding card table in the corner of the barn. As far away from the gator food prep area as possible. Thankfully for me, the aroma of the smoked ribs and chicken overpowered the not awful, but not exactly pleasant, odor of the gator food.

I went to my truck to fetch a growler of pale ale I got at the Riptide. When I returned, Rambo was washing his hands in the barn's utility sink. Between the fridge, microwave, and sink, about the only amenity the barn lacked was a bathroom. When I'd mentioned that fact to Rambo once, he glared at me and suggested I go outside and find the nearest tree.

I never brought it up again.

We got seated across from each other and tore into dinner. The only words exchanged involved sharing barbeque sauce and refilling empty cups with beer. The meal was glorious, but it couldn't mask the tension radiating off of Rambo like a gas grill turned on high.

He seemed to be waiting for me to address the elephant in the room. I wasn't relishing the task. At five feet eleven and one hundred and ninety pounds, I wasn't a small guy. Still, compared to my dinner companion, I was a pipsqueak.

Even though he needed me, I didn't want to say the wrong thing and make him mad. I'd never seen the man truly angry. I'd heard stories, though. I didn't need to experience it firsthand.

My plate was half cleared when the silence became too much.

"So, what do you think happened to Fran?"

"I don't know, Mr. Obvious. Maybe he was eaten by an alligator?" He gave me a little snarl, then went back to gnawing on a rib until the last scrap of meat was gone.

Okay. Not my best opening line ever. And Rambo was under a ton of pressure. Still, he didn't need to be a jerk about things.

"Duh. Butkus didn't get magically transported from here into Cohen's bedroom. How did he get there? Who hated Fran enough to want him dead? Did Fran fight back or try to escape?" I chewed on a cornbread biscuit. "Better?"

He slapped me on the shoulder hard enough I almost went tumbling out of my chair.

"Way better." He tossed a stripped rib onto a growing pile in the middle of the table. "Why don't you get your newest toy, and we can do some brainstorming."

"It's not a toy. It's the latest two-in-one laptop. I can do all of my critter-removal work from it. Send estimates and invoices, receive and process payments. I'm like 90 percent paperless. Efficient and saving trees at the same time."

I removed the computer from my backpack. Its glossy silver finish sparkled like diamonds in the light cast by the overhead florescent bulbs.

"What about Wi-Fi, Mister Genius Ex-IT Guru? I expect you want the farm's password." Rambo wasn't averse to tech. Like almost everyone else in their forties, he'd come of age in a world connected by the internet. He had a laptop and a cell phone, but it was because he needed them to do business. Not because he enjoyed using them.

"Nope. Got it covered. I'll use the hot spot on my phone."

He shook his head. "I'll never understand why you walked away from all that."

"No need to. It's in the past." I rarely talked about my former career as IT director for a post-dot-com-bubble tech start-up with anyone in the Springs besides Nic. Given the way things ended, it was something I didn't like to think about, much less discuss.

I pulled up a blank spreadsheet on the computer. "Let's start with a list of suspects. Who had it in for Fran?"

"About half the town, depending on what day it was." Rambo swallowed a biscuit in one bite.

"Not helpful, dude. Seven thousand people makes for an awfully long list. Can you be more specific, even a little?" My sarcastic tone wasn't productive, but Rambo had asked for my help. That, and he'd helped himself to an extra serving of baked beans so I didn't get as much. And baked beans were my favorite side dish at the Riptide.

He eyed me as he slurped down the last of the baked beans. The man could be heartless when he wanted to.

"I'd start with The Vampire."

"What about him?" A female voice came from parking area outside the barn. It was Nic. "Come on, nerds. Fill me in."

She grabbed a folding chair from against the wall and helped herself to the last biscuit. At this point, I was going to have to stop for some takeout on the way home.

"Haven't been graced with your presence here in a while, Nicola." Rambo offered her the last two ribs and the remaining green beans. "To what do we owe the honor?"

"I heard about yesterday. Since Elmo handled the big lizard, I went by his place after this afternoon's cruise. When he wasn't there, I figured you'd know something, Rambo."

"Like what?" He gulped down the last of the beer in his

cup. With hands that had the slightest tremble to them, he refilled it. And took another big drink.

She rolled her eyes and looked at me. "Are you going to play games? Or are you going to give me the scoop?"

While we were currently in an off-again phase of our relationship, thanks to my reluctance to make a long-term commitment to her, we both knew I couldn't lie to Nic. She was the one person in the Springs who knew the whole story about my past. Well, her and Oscar.

They were equally impressive in their unwillingness to share that information with anyone else. And I appreciated it.

"The cops think Rambo used his gator Butkus to kill Cohen. I'm gonna try to prove he didn't do it."

"And did you?" She looked at Rambo. I didn't consider antagonizing someone more than twice her size to be a wise move. But then, Nic had once told me wisdom was for old people.

Except for when she was on the water.

"Hell, no." Rambo pounded his fist on the table with enough force to make the dinnerware bounce. His chest heaved like he was a bull ready to charge a matador.

"Good enough for me." She wiped her hands on a paper napkin. Her bright-yellow nail polish matched the shade of her closely cropped hair perfectly. They complemented her brown, sun-kissed skin like peanut butter complemented jelly. "Who did it, then?"

"That's what we were talking about when you got here," I said. "Rambo thinks The Vampire should be a suspect."

"Okay, I'll bite, pun totally intended. Why do you think The Vampire killed the dearly departed Philly Fran?"

"Well." Rambo cleared his throat. "I know Cohen's been—er, was—pushing the city to adopt a curbside recycling program. The Vamp spends his nights collecting aluminum and steel. Then he sells it to Big Baby."

"And you think that's motive enough to kill someone? Come on, man. You're smarter than that." Nic was a tough customer. She wasn't going to let Rambo make an accusation as serious as murder without good reason. Evidently, losing out on recycling income wasn't a good enough reason for her. I agreed with her. For now, at least.

"What do we really know about the guy? He keeps all to himself in that monster of a house. He only goes out at night. He listens to that weird music from the seventies. And he only wears black. That might have worked for Johnny Cash, but for anyone else, it's weird."

"Maybe he just likes the goth look," I said.

I wasn't defending the guy everyone in Paradise Springs knew as *The Vampire.* I didn't like the idea of listing someone as a suspect based on nothing more than their appearance, though. That was way too close to profiling to me.

"He's been rocking that look long before it was called goth. For as long as I can remember, in fact." Nic took a drink from my cup.

"Same here." Rambo pointed his finger at me. "The guy's lived here for years and nobody really knows anything about him. Besides, there was no evidence that my gate lock was tampered with. How did a normal person get in and out without leaving a trace? Fly over the fence? Put him on your list. If nothing else, we can always tail him one night. See if he might have crossed paths with Fran."

Nic snorted at the implication that The Vampire was, well, a vampire. If, for no other reason than to keep the conversation moving, I added his name to the list. If I was going to get any investigating done, I needed people to investigate. Debating the eccentric lifestyles of whoever might have held a grudge against Fran Cohen would keep us here all night.

And for days afterward.

"Who else?" I kept my fingers on the keyboard, hoping that I could keep the duo focused.

"I wouldn't put it past Minerva. From what I've heard, she couldn't stand the guy." Nic leaned forward, like she wanted to share a secret. "Fran tried to put the move on her a few months ago. It was when they were on my New Year's Eve cruise. She didn't respond kindly. By the time I got there from the ship's helm, it was all over, but supposedly, it was quite the scene."

Rambo drummed his fingers on the tabletop. "Fran didn't like not getting his way. If he pulled something like that in public, can you imagine what he might have tried living next door to her?"

A shudder coursed through me as I typed Minerva's name into the spreadsheet. The thought of living next door to someone who had, at the very least, attempted to sexually assault you totally creeped me out. If Cohen had done that, I wouldn't blame the woman for retaliating.

But murder? If she thought she was in fear for her own safety, why not go to the police? The crime scene was too bizarre. It was one that begged a pretty big question.

How did the murderer pull off getting a fully grown alligator into Fran's bedroom so it could eat the guy? That took some planning, resources, and smarts.

Whoever the murderer was, they weren't going to be easy to corral. I'd have to tread lightly to make sure I didn't take a wrong step and end up the next victim.

CHAPTER FIVE

A LOT OF benefits came from having Oscar as my roomie. The only mice or chipmunks I ever saw in my house were deceased ones he brought to me as presents. I hadn't needed an alarm clock in ages, either.

For years, every morning, between six thirty and seven, Oscar's leapt onto my bed and walked on top of me. He always started at my ankles, then strolled up my legs, with a stop to knead my belly, then continued up my torso until he was perched on my shoulder.

Then he'd start talking to me.

It always started as a quiet *mow*, as if he didn't want to startle me. If I failed to respond, it would progressively get louder into a full-throated *meow* with a few bats at my ear for good measure. At that point, I'd surrender to the inevitable and get up. At least he's always allowed me the accommodation of going to the bathroom before I feed him.

That's Oscar. He's always been a giver.

Being forced into rising early isn't without its benefits. I never tired of watching the sun rise. With a cup of coffee, I'd sit on the patio and revel in the start of a new day as the giant orb ninety-three million miles away warmed me and my surroundings. In a way, it was my favorite form of meditation.

The skies were overcast this particular Monday morning. As I served Oscar a beef and chicken combo, I lamented the lack of sun. Life in the Panhandle didn't include all sun, all day, especially in February. Still, I could have used some rays as a sign that helping Rambo was the right thing to do. Such was life. I'd just make my own positivity instead of relying on the sun to create it for me.

With Oscar provided for, I whipped up some oatmeal. The temps were in the low fifties. For a native Hoosier like me, fifties in February was practically balmy, so I added a sweatshirt to my usual breakfast attire of gym shorts and a T-shirt and headed outdoors.

The brisk conditions invigorated me. With my brain kicking in, I planned my day. Sybil the Seer had texted me asking to bring some traps to her place. She also mentioned, in rather cryptic fashion, that she had information I needed.

I'd learned that when dealing with the local fortune-teller, it was best to go with the flow. Her predictions did have an uncanny habit of coming true, but I was a skeptic. She had a thriving business, though, so she must have been doing something right.

My Monday rounds needed to be taken care of first, so I replied that I'd come by in the early afternoon. The lack of a specific time for my arrival would annoy her as she loved to claim her appointment book was always full. I didn't buy it. If she really had the *gift*, she'd know exactly when I'd be arriving.

All was calm in Paradise Springs as I made my way through the downtown area. I had service agreements with a half dozen businesses that required I check traps and for other evidence of nuisance critters weekly. Most were single-story buildings painted in a variety of pastel shades. With flat roofs and slabs for foundations, the structures didn't provide a lot of places for a critter to hide. There was always a nook or cranny that allowed something small unauthorized entry, though.

If I came across an animal that had been caught, I removed it and checked the premises for evidence of possible infestation. If there was none, I moved on. If I uncovered a possible problem, like a gap in caulking, I had a word with the client. When my business was completed, I moved to the next stop on my route.

It had taken some trial and error, but over time I learned Monday was the best day to do my regular checks. Paradise Springs was like a lot of tourist towns in that during the offseason, many businesses were closed on Monday, especially restaurants. That made it easier for me do to my work without bothering customers.

Diners lost their appetites in no time when they saw Critter Guy poking around. Go figure.

After the downtown district, I headed to the tourist district. Palm trees lined the streets in case visitors needed reminding that they were literally only a stone's throw from the Gulf of Mexico. Many of the buildings were older in this area. The two- and three-story wood-framed structures that had survived hurricanes contained a lot of character to go along with their respective histories. The resorts, restaurants, and bars attracted almost as many critters as they did people due to the presence of garbage. In this part of town, fifteen businesses relied on me to keep the customers coming through the doors by making sure nothing uninvited did.

I concluded my rounds at a fifties-style diner called Sue's Place. It was furnished with red vinyl booths, a working jukebox, and more chrome than a classic car. I often ate lunch there, partly because it was one of the few restaurants open on Monday and partly because the owner let me eat there for free for life when I cured the place of a persistent vole problem.

"What'll it be today, Elmo?" The manager on duty, a woman about my age with flame-red hair styled in a beehive reminiscent of Amy Winehouse, poured me a cup of coffee.

"How about a bowl of chili with extra onions and a side salad, Nadine. Trying to watch the old waistline." I patted my belly.

"You got it. Can I interest you in an appetizer of alligator poppers?" She winked as she pulled a pen from a hiding place somewhere in her massive pile of hair. "Heard about your adventure the other day. Couldn't resist."

Once Nadine had turned away from me, I placed my palms on the counter. The smooth Formica surface was cool to the touch. Just the thing I needed to calm my rattled nerves. I didn't want word getting out about me helping Rambo too soon. There was no doubt that eventually it would. I wanted to make progress between now and then, though.

On the other hand, since Nadine had broached the subject, I could get her take on the situation. The diner was only a quarter mile down Gulfview Lane from the Sea Breeze. She knew a lot of people and no doubt heard a lot of things.

"That was insane," I said when she returned with my order. "Still trying to wrap my head around who'd want to kill him. Especially that way."

"Rumor has it the cops have Rambo Quigley dead to rights. Something tells me you don't think so. Am I right?"

"Busted. Something doesn't make sense. If Rambo wanted to kill Cohen, why use one of his prize gators? You can't tell me he was planning on fetching it after it finished gobbling up Fran. No. Whoever came across the scene first was supposed to find the gator there."

Nadine raised her eyebrows. "The killer sets up Rambo, so everyone's supposed to think he did it. Interesting theory. Who do you think did it, then?"

I downed a spoonful of chili. It was seasoned to spicy perfection. The beans were tender but not mushy. While I chewed, I figured out how to answer without showing any of my cards.

"I think whoever did it had it in for both Cohen and Rambo. Kill two birds with one stone. Anyone like that come to mind?"

"Reverend Jackson." She laughed. "I've been told he's never forgiven them for that fight that broke out at that community meeting his church hosted. Not that I'm suggesting he actually did it, mind you."

"Of course not. We're just making conversation while I enjoy this wonderful meal." I smiled. And hoped I didn't have a chunk of chili bean caught between my two front teeth.

Nadine went to attend to other customers. I took the time to mull over her suggestion, as far-fetched as it seemed. The Reverend Maynard Jackson, head of the Church of the Sacred Light, could be a poster boy for what I thought was wrong with organized religion. He wore custom suits made by a high-end tailor in New Orleans. The diamond-studded rock he sported on his right pinkie finger was bright enough to blind any member of his flock. To top things off, he lived in a gated community by the bay and had a chauffeur drive him around in his silver Cadillac.

Despite my misgivings, his congregation loved him. The church offered free day care to families dealing with financial challenges, regardless of religious affiliation. It also ran a food bank that was open Tuesday evenings. It was hard to argue with the good things the reverend's following did for the community.

I didn't trust him, though. For my money, he was a little too good to be true.

And, from what I'd heard, the postfight repair bill had been enormous, as in five figures. What if insurance hadn't covered the damage? That would have meant a lot of money coming out of the church coffers. Perhaps he'd decided to take a pound of flesh out of both men in retribution.

While I made a note in my phone to follow up about what locals loved to call The Blowup at the Barbeque, Nadine returned with a coffee in a to-go cup.

"Anything else, darlin'? I've got pecan pie fresh out of the oven."

My stomach growled at the suggestion, but I shook my

head. The last time I'd eaten a slice of the diner's signature sugary dessert, I'd gotten dizzy from the sugar rush and slipped off my stool. It took three months before I got over my embarrassment and returned to the diner.

With a full belly, and a lengthening list of murder suspects, I headed for Sybil's place for a visit with the baffling and entertaining fortune-teller.

Depending on who you asked, Sybil was anywhere from sixty-three to one hundred and seven years old. All anybody could agree on was that her birth certificate, if one existed, was guarded more closely than the crown jewels in England.

It was fact that she came to Paradise Springs from New Orleans in the aftermath of Hurricane Katrina. One evening in September of that year, she simply showed up on the lawn in front of the mayor's office. Using only a battered camp chair, she began telling people their fortunes. A week later, she moved into a bungalow on Palm Road, only a block off Gulfview Drive, around the corner from the Springing Dolphin coffee shop.

That she paid for in cash.

My truck's brakes squeaked as I came to a stop in front of that same house. The salt, sand, and humidity made a witch's brew that was hell on the exposed components of my truck. Which, to be fair, had already seen its better days in the rearview mirror by the time I arrived on the Gulf Coast.

The clapboard dwelling, which wasn't much bigger than my place, was painted in lavender with dark violet trim. A wooden sign was planted in the front lawn letting visitors know they were at the residence of SYBIL THE SEER. Fortunes could be told. Long-lost loved ones who were beyond the veil could be contacted.

BY APPOINTMENT ONLY. CASH PAYMENT DUE IN ADVANCE.

I gave the front door three loud knocks, a little put out that Sybil hadn't opened the door the moment I stepped on the first stair leading to the front porch. She didn't answer, so I knocked again. When there was no response, I slipped a business card into the storm door screen to let her know I'd stopped by. I could set the outdoor mouse traps without her.

The second I turned around, she came into view. Her multicolored muumuu billowed in the wind along with a few stray strands of silver hair as she piloted her Vespa up Palm Road at breakneck speed. She gave me a wave as she came to a stop in her driveway.

"I've got groceries in the top box and under the seat." She removed a pair of goggles that made her look like a pilot from World War I and tossed me her keys. "After you help me put them away, I have things to tell you."

With a bag in each hand, I followed her into the house. The essential oil diffusers were on full blast in the front room. The overwhelming scent of peppermint made my eyes water. Things were much better in the kitchen. Since clients never ventured back here, the only smell was a fresh pine scent emanating from the stainless-steel sink, which gleamed in the afternoon sunlight.

Once everything was put away, Sybil put a tea kettle on the stove. It suddenly occurred to me that I'd done all the work while she'd plopped into a chair, content to scroll through her phone while pointing out to me where things went.

"You have a lot on your mind. A blend of chamomile and jasmine tea will help clear it." She smiled. It was a kind smile that made her coal-black eyes dance and took ten years off her dark-brown complexion. Or maybe forty years. Given her uncertain age, it was tough to tell for sure.

I followed the old woman into the front bedroom, which she'd made into her consultation area. A ceiling fan with wooden paddles covered with dust spun at a lazy pace above us. The walls, which were painted a flat gray, were covered with various pieces of artwork depicting fortune-tellers from all over the world and from all periods of history. Sunlight coming through the lone window was obscured by a curtain of multicolored beads that called to mind a Mardi Gras parade I'd watched during a trip to New Orleans.

What I could remember of that trip, at least. According to my credit card statement, I'd downed enough hurricanes to last the rest of my life.

Sybil remained silent while she poured the tea. She had a slightly forward stoop, like so many elderly ladies, but her eyes were sharp. Her gaze darted this way and that as she eased herself into the chair across from me. It was covered in a floor-length purple felt tablecloth. She placed a crystal ball and a deck of tarot cards in the center of the circular table to complete the scene.

"I'm not here for a reading, Sybil. You called me, remember?" I sipped my tea. The warm fumes were soothing. Had to give her that.

"The spirits have told me you're investigating Fran Cohen's murder. You think the police are wrong in suspecting Waldo Quigley."

Thanks to years of playing cards with the likes of Wendell and Rambo, I knew how to maintain a poker face. Rambo had laughed in Sybil's face when she offered to give him a palm reading a while back, so it was unlikely he'd be confiding in her now.

She was bluffing. The question was why. Another one was why she'd brought me here.

"If the spirits told you this, why didn't they tell you who killed Fran? Seems like they could save us all a lot of time and energy."

"The spirits' ways are mysterious. I do not question them." She took a drink from a small teacup made of white bone china. "Nor should you."

"Fair enough. Let's say I am asking around. Just for argument's sake. Why am I here? Do the spirits have information they want you to pass on to me?"

Beyond watching reruns of *The Rockford Files*, I had no experience with conducting a murder investigation. It couldn't hurt to ask for some otherworldly help, right?

She closed her eyes and put her hands on the table, fingers splayed out wide. Gaudy rings featuring a lot of silver, jade, and amethyst adorned every finger. Delicate bands of silver encircled her thumbs. The woman sure knew how to dress the part.

"I am in danger. I'm being pursued by a man." She took in a sharp breath. "The man is Fran Cohen. He wants to do me harm."

"Are you saying he wanted to kill you? But he can't now, so you're safe. Do you have any idea why he wanted to harm you? Some secret, perhaps?"

"The spirits say you need to go to the source. There is where you will find the answers."

"The source? What's that even mean?"

After another sharp intake of breath, she opened her eyes. They were unfocused, but after a couple of blinks, Sybil's sharp gaze returned.

"I'm sorry, Elmo. The spirits will share no more until you earn their trust."

"All righty, then." I rubbed my hands together. "I guess we're done here. Do you want any mousetraps set here inside the house?"

I debated the weird visit with Sybil the whole drive home. She knew I didn't buy her act, yet she went through the whole seer rigmarole anyway.

Why?

If she knew something, it would have been a whole lot easier if she'd come right out and said it instead of being all mystical. On the other hand, Sybil wouldn't take up valuable time that could have been filled by a paying client without a good reason. That meant she must have been trying to tell me something while she maintained a level of secrecy. Something important.

Now it was up to me to figure out what, exactly, that was. Good times.

CHAPTER SIX

SINCE I HAD bills to pay, I spent the rest of the afternoon doing the company's financial work. While I wasn't exactly a numbers person, I enjoyed solving puzzles. Making sure all of the figures fit together so I got paid, my vendors got paid, and I didn't end up in the red was like a puzzle.

Problem-solving was what drew me to the IT world as a kid. I loved the way tiny chips and thin wires allowed us to do everything from talk to someone halfway around the world to monitor weather conditions so people could respond to developing tropical storms.

Now that I lived on the Gulf of Mexico, I appreciated that ability to model storms more than ever.

What I didn't miss was the business end of the work. Too many decisions to be made without enough information. Too many sleepless nights. Too much money for my own good. Too many fake friends who were willing to let me spend that money on them.

That's not to say if I had to do it all over again, I'd take a different path. Those years and those experiences, as damaging as they ended up being, brought me to the wonderful and weird Paradise Springs. To Oscar. To Nic and so many other friends.

No. I wouldn't change a thing. Even losing my daddy when I was only three years old helped make the person I'd become. It was like a great storyteller once said. I've experienced the most magic of moments. Some of it's been filled with tragedy. But when I put my head on the pillow at the end of the day, I have to admit, I've had a pretty good life. And wouldn't change a thing.

Except maybe for agreeing to root out Fran's killer.

Still, despite the fact that I felt like a blindfolded man trying to find his way out of a pitch-black forest, under a starless sky, at night, Rambo had asked me to do him a solid. I'd agreed. He'd helped me out plenty of times in the past without so much as a grumble. I owed the guy. There was no turning back once you'd promised you'd do someone a favor. To do so was to risk angering the gods.

I wasn't sure which gods, exactly, but I didn't want to take any chances.

All the memories and philosophizing kept my mind so occupied, I was finished with the books before I knew it. It was only six o'clock and the skies had cleared. Prime conditions for dining out on the patio.

"What'll it be tonight, Oscar?" I snapped my fingers. "I know, how about some chicken, right off the grill?"

A couple of chicken breasts had been in the fridge for almost a week, and I needed to do something with them. I had some asparagus, too. That would make for a tasty evening meal. A healthy one, too. My cholesterol was at a level that made my doctor happy. I wanted it to stay that way.

Oscar seemed to agree with the suggestion. He let out a loud *meow* and paced back and forth in front of the door while I gathered my things.

The grill was one of the few luxury items I owned. It was a top-of-the-line model that allowed me to cook using either gas or wood. When I'd mentioned to Wendell one time that I wanted to get a gas grill, his eye started twitching as he glared at me.

"Don't you dare commit such an abomination. I'll help you find a proper grill."

Within forty-eight hours, I was the proud owner of a grill that had more bells and whistles than the latest video game console. The sticker price had almost given me a heart attack, but Wendell insisted it was an investment worth every penny.

And he'd been right.

I cued up some Jimmy Buffett on my phone and sang along as I made dinner. Cheeseburgers may not have been on the menu, but it was still paradise. My Bermuda grass lawn, while not massive, was healthy and soft to walk on barefoot. I even had a couple of palm trees on my property. I'd strung a hammock between them to complete the idyllic scene.

A guy could do a lot worse in life.

As soon as a tiny section of the chicken was cooked, I cut it up into little chunks and served Oscar.

"Your dinner, sir. May I suggest a fine bowl of water, fresh from the tap, for your beverage?"

Oscar stared at me as I put the dinner plate and water bowl in front of him. He looked at them for a moment, then back at me. It was like he was telling me his dinner was acceptable.

"Bon appetite." I kissed my fingers like an Italian gourmet chef, then bowed to him.

He gobbled up his meal before I'd even finished slathering my chicken with Wendell's barbeque sauce. Then he spent the next five minutes licking his face. I think he wanted to make sure he got every last morsel.

When my cat approved of my cooking, that meant one thing. I'd made it to the big time. Of what, I had no idea, but making my cat happy made me happy, so it was all good.

With his dinner finished, Oscar wandered off. I basked in solitude while I dined. The chicken was tender, the asparagus crisp, and the water cool in my throat. My kind of dinner.

A little while later, after cleaning up, I was back on the patio plucking away on my ukulele when the low-throated purr of a familiar engine caught my attention. It was the powerhouse for a black 1964 Lincoln Continental that was motoring by. The four-door was the most famous vehicle in all of Paradise Springs, my town's answer to the Green Hornet's legendary ride, Black Beauty.

I sprinted to the road so I could follow the car. It was owned by an individual who was tough to track down when it suited them. A person shrouded in more mystery than Sybil could ever hope to attain. A being on my suspect list.

The car belonged to The Vampire.

He was making his rounds, picking up aluminum and steel cans for recycling. The constant stop, get out, retrieve the quarry, get back in the car, and move to the next stop made it easy to follow on foot. Which was good, since I'd given this mission of tailing him absolutely no thought at all.

It also opened my eyes to how many aluminum cans the good folks of Paradise Springs went through in a day. Holy smokes, these people drank like fishes.

The man was meticulous as he made steady headway through the neighborhood. A black trench coat slowed his progress as he had to constantly swish the bottom portion underneath him when he reentered the vehicle. The evening temperature was cool, but far from cold. I was in a sweatshirt and shorts. The conditions made me wonder why someone would need a long coat on a night like this.

Then I remembered his nickname. I pushed the thought away as I began to wonder if real vampires got cold. The guy behind the wheel couldn't be a real vampire. They didn't exist, right?

That's what I told myself.

After a while, I clued into the fact that folks left their aluminum and steel out for him to pick up. A lot of the time, all he had to do was empty the contents of a cardboard box into one of his plastic trash bags. Whether he was simply an eccentric or a horrific supernatural being didn't matter at the moment. He had a good gig going and was helping save the planet, too. One can at a time.

I had to tip my hat to him.

As my surveillance proceeded, we traveled from my neighborhood filled with bungalows and modular homes to the tourist district. The bars, restaurants, and variety stores that sold everything from T-shirts to costume jewelry to tiny vials of genuine white Florida Gulf Coast sand sent through an enormous number of cans, too.

The area was a gold mine for my aluminum hunter.

I studied him from the shadows as he rifled through a trash container behind the One Love Jamaican restaurant. He was tall, six-three or so, with the lean build of a basketball player. His hair was short and, while the surrounding darkness made it tough to tell, looked to be black that was graying at the temples.

A flash of red on one of his fingers caught the light as he stuffed a bag into his trunk. At that point, I had no idea whether the ring carried any significance. All I knew was it must have been humongous for me to be able to see it from so far away. The guy, whose name I was ashamed to admit was unknown to me, sure had style.

Not my kind of style, but with my wardrobe consisting chiefly of jeans and T-shirts, who was I to judge?

The pace picked up when The Vampire turned onto Gulfview Lane. The condos and hotels took up large swaths of space, and I almost lost him between a Marriott and a Fairfield Inn due to folks checking in. When I caught up, his car was parked at the Sea Breeze.

Things had suddenly gotten interesting.

The resort had a number of communal gathering spaces on the ocean side of the building. Among swaths of green space, charcoal grills and picnic tables were the most common amenities. There was a beach volleyball court and a mini-golf course, too. Trash bins were strategically placed in out-of-the-way spots throughout the grounds. The patio door to Cohen's condo was only a few yards away from one of the grills.

And The Vampire, who was now on foot, had just rounded a corner of the building and was only a few feet from that door. With my heart beating like I'd just finished an ocean swim, I closed in on him.

So far, the man hadn't done anything suspicious. If driving around town in the dead of night, stopping at any number of homes and businesses didn't bother you, that is. Yet, he'd gone practically right to the murder victim's back door. Maybe the whole aluminum collecting effort on this night was merely an excuse to get him back to the scene of the crime.

I peeked around the corner The Vampire had rounded when he disappeared from my sight. He was nowhere to be seen. I was undeterred, though. With his need to stop to collect whatever he could find, he couldn't be far.

Sweat had formed on my brow as I crouched down and continued my pursuit. The sound of waves crashing against the beach filled my ears now that I was fully on the ocean side of the building. I hoped the sound was loud enough to drown out the hammering of my heart against my chest.

I was in the open, vulnerable to a surprise attack. The Vampire wasn't going to escape me, though. Maybe I had a knack for this kind of thing, after all. As I crept along the edge of Cohen's patio, an issue reared its ugly head.

The man was still nowhere to be found.

I scanned the area from the building to the beach. It was

too dark to make out any movement beyond the flapping of a CHICAGO CUBS flag hanging from someone's third-floor balcony.

He'd gotten away. I dropped a few French cuss words Nic had taught me as I straightened up. So close to Fran's condo and he'd disappeared into thin air.

Like a vampire transforming into a bat and flying away.

The thought of the night ending up a bust was unbearable, so I decided to have a look around. Especially with a thirty-minute walk home ahead of me. Maybe I'd come across something Spock and company had missed.

I turned on my phone's flashlight. It illuminated the surroundings and helped settle my nerves. Instead of monsters and murderers lurking in the shadows, my gaze fell on aluminum patio railings and plastic lawn furniture. A spatula lay on top of the nearest grill, apparently forgotten by a resident.

Fran's condo appeared as unremarkable on this back side of the building as it was from the front side. No bite or claw marks were to be seen. The screen door slid open without a sound. A promising sign. I pushed down the door handle and leaned forward. My hopes were dashed when the door refused to open.

Hmm. What now?

With an air of resignation, I waved the flashlight back and forth across the nearby grassy area. Other than a cigarette butt a discourteous smoker had left behind, there was nothing.

"It's been a fun chase. Can't wait to tell Rambo about

it." I let out a sigh of defeat.

Just for kicks, I swept the patio a final time. Something metallic was half hidden underneath a decorative bush. Upon closer examination, the item turned out to be a pin, the kind I adorned my backpack with back in my college days.

It was round with a touch of rust on the backside. I got the feeling the rust wasn't because it was cheap, though. The rust was from age. The face of the pin was black with a red pentacle. The profile of a man viewed from behind was at the center of the five-pointed star. A whisper of a memory spoke to me. I'd seen the graphic before. It was a logo. For something sinister, perhaps?

My first clue.

While I was uncertain about the pin's origin, my gut told me it belonged to The Vampire. Assuming I was correct, it might have fallen off mere minutes ago. A logical enough conclusion. Logical enough for me, at least. I wasn't exactly an expert at this sleuthing thing, after all.

Then a thought came to me. Could it have fallen off The Vampire's coat when he was wrangling Butkus into the condo? While he struggled to maneuver the animal inside, the pin may have been jostled loose and ended up hidden under the plant. At the time, he probably didn't even notice it was gone. After all, the task couldn't have been an easy one.

At least not for a normal human being.

The ocean breeze sent chills down my spine. Yeah, the wind was the culprit. I wasn't getting freaked out and suddenly buying into all the talk about The Vampire's alleged true nature.

I mean, if he was a real vampire, why would he choose to live in Paradise Springs? New Orleans would be a lot more fun for a creature of the night. He could hang out with all of those creatures from the Anne Rice books. Or even Wellington, New Zealand, if *What We Do in the Shadows* was actually a legit documentary and not a comedy as it claims to be.

Goose bumps that broke out on my arms and legs prompted me to get moving. Regardless of whether he was human or something else, I didn't want to be around if The Vampire returned. I'd give him the pin when it was safe to do so.

Like at high noon on a sunny day. In the middle of town. With gobs of onlookers milling about.

I jogged back home, glancing over my shoulder from time to time to make sure I wasn't being followed by bats or any other shadowy creatures. Yes, I was quite susceptible to the power of suggestion. Why bother denying it?

That openness to ideas, no matter how outlandish, was one of the traits that helped me become a successful game designer. That it also contributed to my downfall couldn't be denied, either. For better or for worse, it was part of me. Made me who I was. And all in all, I was pretty content with the current version of Elmo Simpson.

Oscar was lounging by the front door when I got home. He let out a low *mrrwow* to let me know he didn't approve of my nighttime adventure.

"Sorry, buddy. Gotta follow the leads wherever they take me." I picked up the uke that I'd left on the patio table and followed him inside.

My cat made a beeline for the cabinet where I kept his provisions. Given the late hour—it was almost eleven—he didn't want dinner. I needed to make amends for keeping him out so late. He wanted the good stuff.

"Kitty treats coming up." Among the dozen brightly colored pouches in the cabinet, Oscar's favorite was the red one, the beef and turkey combo.

I dropped a half dozen of the goodies in his food bowl and scratched his right ear. It was missing a chunk near the top, thanks to a tussle with another clawed critter a half dozen years ago. Before that, he used to spend his nights on the prowl. Since then, he'd found being a homebody quite appealing.

With experience comes wisdom, and all that. I could totally identify.

A few minutes later, I was staring at an image on my computer screen. It was the same artwork that was on the pin, a graphic in the gatefold of the album *2112* by the progressive rock band Rush. Was there something that connected the symbol, which was commonly known as the Starman logo, and The Vampire? I set that question aside for the time being. A more urgent one popped into my head.

Was there a way I could use the pin to connect The Vampire to the actual crime instead of merely the scene of the crime?

CHAPTER SEVEN

I T WAS A good thing Tuesdays were my day off, because I stayed up way too late surfing the Web in search of some deep, hidden meaning behind the symbol on The Vampire's pin. It was almost two when I reached the conclusion a normal person would have reached hours earlier. Without losing out on a lot of quality shut-eye.

The Vampire was a fan of the band. Nothing more, nothing less.

My searching did uncover one intriguing fact, though. It appeared the red and black pin had been manufactured around the time the *2112* album came out, way back in 1976. That made it over forty years old. So, it was vintage. Which meant it was valuable, though more likely in a sentimental way than a monetary one.

And The Vampire would want it back. Assuming people of his kind were into keeping things with sentimental value.

It would be the perfect reason to pay the man a visit to find out where he was the night Fran Cohen was murdered. If I could work up the guts to actually approach the man.

Oscar was unsympathetic to my sleep-deprived state and was pawing at my head seemingly as soon as my head had landed on the pillow. With my own growl, I threw back the sheet.

"I was doing real work last night, dude. You could let me sleep in once in a while, you know."

As if to tell me to get over myself, he flicked his ears back, leapt from the bed, and marched out of the room. At times, that cat had about as much sympathy for me as Liam Neeson had for the bad guys in all those *Taken* movies.

Since I was awake, and the case was still fresh in my mind, I got cleaned up and headed for the beach. There was a sword-wielding woman I wanted to talk to.

Three days a week, Chief Eikenberry spent an hour on the beach in meditation. Her words, not mine. The method of meditation was the most intimidating I'd ever seen. And made me that much more fearful of the woman.

She was in her usual spot, a quiet stretch of sand so soft and white that some folks called it sugar sand, far from the hustle and bustle of the marina or pier. As I approached, she was swinging a three-foot-long katana in long strokes in between graceful footwork that looked like a dance as much as a sword fight move.

I watched her for a while as the sandpipers dashed back and forth along the beach in reaction to the tide. She was totally absorbed in her workout routine, as if she and her imaginary opponent were the only things in existence. The combination of lethal ferocity and ethereal beauty on display left me awestruck.

Eventually, she let out an animalistic howl and stabbed the sword straight into the sand. It went all the way down to the hilt.

"You going to be a creeper and watch me all morning or do you have something to say?" She pulled the sword out of the sand with the same effort I put into pulling a knife from my utensil drawer and pointed it at me.

Even though I was twenty yards away, I still took a step back.

"I was wondering how the case is going. Feel like I have a bit of a vested interest since, you know, I kind of found Fran."

"Or what was left of him." She wiped her forehead and her arms with a towel. She was dressed in a gray tank top and black workout shorts, and the definition of her muscles was eye popping. Anyone who tried to take her on in a fight would be on the ground in seconds.

"Touché."

She laughed. "Good one, what with me working out with my swords. Now, are you going to let me get back to what I was doing or are you going to keep bugging me?"

"I know your time's valuable, Chief. I wanted to know if you've learned anything new."

"The rest of Mr. Cohen was found inside the gator. No big surprise. We're waiting on the results of a toxicology screen to see if there was anything in the man's system that shouldn't have been there."

It took me a few seconds to catch up. When I did, the inference made my jaw drop.

"You think someone drugged him, which made it easier for the gator to have him for dinner. That's diabolical."

"It is. And in case you were wondering, I'm telling you

this because it's in line with my theory that Rambo's the guy. And I know you and Rambo were hanging out Sunday night."

She gave me a smile that made me think she was a barracuda and I was a poor clownfish about to meet my doom.

"Since you're here, care to tell me why you were hanging out with a murder suspect?"

"The guy's a buddy of mine. I was being a friend. That's not a crime." I swallowed as the hair on the back of my neck stood on end. "Is it?"

"Depends." She picked up a second sword. With one in each hand, she executed a lightning-fast spinning move and came to a stop, inches from me. Her arms were crossed. A blade lay on each of my shoulders. One wrong move and she could cut me as easily as a pair of scissors slices through a piece of paper.

"On"—I squeezed my eyes shut—"what?"

"Whether you're guilty of conspiracy to commit murder. Either before or after the fact." She lowered the swords, keeping just enough pressure on my chest to make me relieved I was wearing a shirt.

"Why would I do that?"

Despite the panic in my voice, it was a legit question. I'd done nothing wrong. The vibe coming from Susan made it loud and clear that she hadn't ruled out the possibility that I might have.

"Two things." She withdrew one sword. "The first is that, like Rambo, you've been clear you don't like the commercial developments Mr. Cohen supported." She lifted the other sword. "The second is that whoever pulled this off couldn't have done it alone.

"For most people, I think it would have needed a group of at least three or four. You and Rambo could have pulled it off by yourselves."

"Um, thanks, I guess?" The sand beneath my feet was getting hot. Or maybe I was just wilting under the chief's pressure.

"I wouldn't take it as a compliment."

"Oh, come on, Chief. Sure, Fran drove me up the wall, but he did that to half the people in town. I value life. Do you really think I'd get involved with some murder plot just because I disagreed with his commercial development ideas? And especially one that would end up with an innocent animal being euthanized? Get real. It's my job to save animals, for crying out loud."

The back of my head started throbbing. The classic sign of an Elmo Simpson stress headache. I closed my eyes and massaged the area with my fingertips. It relieved some of the pain but was only a temporary fix. Once this conversation was over, I needed to find someplace out of the sun where I could get an ice-cold glass of water.

She tilted her head to the side for a moment, staring at me like I was a space alien from Andromeda. Then a small smile appeared as she shook her head.

"Color me shocked. Some folks have said you didn't have it in you. It's good to see they're wrong."

"Don't have what in me?" I ran my tongue over my teeth in a vain search for a few rogue grains of sand that got in my mouth during my diatribe.

She took a beach towel from her bag and spread it out on the sand. With a little wave she invited me to join her as she lowered herself to a seated position. I was envious of her grace in motion.

If I had tried to lower myself to the ground from a standing position with my legs crossed and without using my hands for support, I'd have fallen over like a drunken sailor on his first night of shore leave. Sure, I had a few years on her, but that didn't make up for the fact that the words *Elmo Simpson* and *graceful* had never been uttered in the same sentence.

"You and I have something in common," she said when I finally got seated.

I had a tough time believing her. Her first career had been in modeling while mine was in IT. She was drop-dead gorgeous. I was physically fit but about as average as they came. When she wanted to, she could reduce arrogant men to quivering puddles of tears. I was easygoing and some people thought of me as a bit of a pushover. My days as a source of intimidation were in the past. Okay, they'd never really existed.

"Other than occupying the same space on this beach, I don't think we have much of anything in common."

"Where are you from?"

She nodded when I told her Indianapolis.

"In case you didn't know, I'm from Asheville, North Carolina."

I did know. Some of the locals had made a fuss about her

not being from the Springs area when she was hired. When Nic had asked me about it, I said I didn't care. What mattered was whether she was the best candidate for the job.

Then it hit me.

"We're both outsiders. That's what we have in common."

She touched her index finger to the tip of her nose and pointed at me. "You win the grand prize. Which is a peek behind the curtain, so to speak. You see, I didn't know what would happen if I leaned on you hard about this case. Would you crumble and maybe cop to something? Would you lie? Or would you stand up for yourself? People around here like you, Elmo, but some think you're a little too easygoing for your own good."

"How I choose to conduct my life is nobody's business but my own." I traced a rudimentary outline of my cat in the sand. "And maybe Oscar's."

"Sure, it is. But in my line of work, it pays to know peoples' stories. I know more about you than most. I get the feeling that only a handful of people around here know your story. I can probably count them on one hand and have two fingers left over."

"Your point being?" She was right, but I wasn't going to give her the satisfaction of telling her that. I had my pride, after all.

"There's more to you than meets the eye." She picked up a tiny seashell and tossed it toward the water. "You're up to something. I'm not sure what it is, but it isn't covering up a murder."

Given her tone earlier in the conversation, I was relieved. Being accused of murder was no laughing matter. Especially when the police chief was the one doing the accusing. I was a little ticked off, though. After all, if she didn't think I was involved in Fran's murder, why play these games?

"Fine. I'll level with you. I was at Rambo's place because he asked for my help. He says he had nothing to do with Fran's murder. I believe him, so I'm doing some investigating."

She barked out a laugh and shook her head.

"It's a free country. I appreciate your candor. Saves me the trouble of having to haul you down to the station for a formal interview. I'd keep my distance from Quigley, though. I get that you guys are friends, but everything points to him in this case. I don't want to see you get sucked into a situation you can't get yourself out of."

I got to my feet. Since I'd been living in the Springs, the toughest decisions I'd faced usually were deciding between chocolate chip or vanilla ice cream. Now, I couldn't escape the thought that the chief was backing me into a corner. I had a choice. It was a simple matter. Fight or flight.

I chose to fight.

"I appreciate the advice, Chief. And I understand at this point the evidence points to Rambo doing it." I brushed sand from my palms. "Looks like I'm going to have to prove you wrong."

After a tip of my hat, I made a hasty exit. I tried to be casual about it, but I wanted to put space between me and the chief before she hollered at me. Despite the bravado I hoped I had shown, reality was a different matter.

She could have stopped my investigation with a few well-chosen words like *interfering with an official police investigation*. At heart, I didn't want to deal with conflict. The important thing was that I was well aware of that fact.

I'd bet she knew it, too. Yet, she didn't stop me. The gambler in the old Kenny Rogers song of the same name would be proud of me. I'd picked the right time to walk away.

My showdown with the chief hadn't gone like I'd hoped. We'd never gotten around to discussing my suspects. Without credible alternatives or evidence, there was little incentive for the cops to investigate anyone other than Rambo. The opportunity to bring up The Vampire, Minerva, or even the reverend had been right there. And I'd botched it.

Ugh.

Then again, I'd brought the whole thing down on myself by allowing her to sidetrack the conversation. On the other hand, I kind of liked the idea of being able to tell people about interrupting the police chief during one of her sword workouts and living to tell about it.

It was important to find the positives whenever possible, after all.

On the walk back to my truck, I decided I needed someone to help me talk my way through the recent case developments. It made sense to heed the chief's warning and steer clear of Rambo. Or, at least, give the appearance that I was doing so. That meant there was only one person I could turn to and keep the whole investigation thing under wraps.

It was time to jump from the frying pan right into the fire.

CHAPTER EIGHT

NICOLA BEECHAM WAS an enigma wrapped in a riddle with a bow tie of a mystery on top. She was a lifelong resident of the Gulf Coast. A true child of the water, Nic grew up helping her parents with their charter fishing boat business. It had been her dad's hope that when they retired, she'd take the helm, literally and figuratively.

Nic had her own plans.

Once she got her business degree from the local community college, she said goodbye to Pascagoula, Mississippi, and made a run to Paradise Springs. When I arrived on the scene, she was the captain and sole proprietor of a charter boat that took customers on sightseeing cruises. A woman for whom the sea truly ran through her veins, she knew every cay, inlet, and lagoon from New Orleans all the way east to Cedar Key, Florida. For her, navigating by the stars was easier than getting out of bed in the morning was for me.

She had a spellbinding smile and was quick with a laugh. Her gift for storytelling was a thing of legend, too. Many clients booked their excursions with her a year in advance so they could listen to the yarns she spun during a cruise. If someone got out of line during one of her trips, though, she was quick with discipline. And slow to forgive foolish acts committed while on the water.

I'd fallen head over heels for her the first time I crossed paths with her.

Goob's Fish Market, a tiny diner next to the fuel station and convenience store at the Paradise Springs Marina, was the room where it happened. I'd been eying the menu board when a soft voice came from behind me.

"Go with the blackened grouper. It's a can't-miss."

I turned to the voice. A woman was standing there. A pair of Ray-Bans were propped on the top of her head to reveal the most captivating eyes I'd ever seen. They were a shade of ice blue that reminded me of a calm sea under cloudy skies.

Her hair was midnight black highlighted with purple and green streaks. She wore a necklace with a gold pendant that I recognized. Which finally unloosened my tongue.

"That's a St. Christopher medal."

"Point for the guy at the head of the line."

"I've got one, too." I dug the medal out of my pocket and showed it to her with pride. And the hope that I'd made a connection with her.

"Good for you, buddy. Around here, we all need all the help we can get. Now, are you going to order anytime this decade? I gotta get back to work."

Chastened by her failure to see our connection in the same strong way as me, I ordered the blackened grouper and told the man behind the counter that I wanted to pay for the woman behind me. To say thank you for the suggestion. Nothing more, nothing less.

"Thanks." She gave me a friendly elbow bump to my upper arm. "You're new around here, aren't you? I'm Nicola."

"I'm Elmo. And yes, I am."

She raised an eyebrow. It was a reaction I got a lot when I told someone my name. Then she smiled.

"Welcome to Paradise, Elmo. If you ever want to take a cruise around the bay, come see me. It'll be an experience you'll never forget." She winked, grabbed the paper bag containing her lunch, and was gone before I could formulate a response.

With my head spinning from the encounter, I took a seat at a picnic table in front of the diner. Boats anchored at the pier rocked side to side like they were keeping time to the reggae song emanating from the diner's outdoor speakers. Paradise, indeed. I took a bite of the blackened grouper Nicola had recommended.

And almost gagged.

Back in Indiana, where beef, pork, and chicken are plentiful and affordable, fish had never been a big part of my diet. I'd had my share of fried fish fillets during my school years, but never acquired a taste for seafood.

Evidently, that included blackened grouper. Since Nicola had recommended it, I took another bite. And had to force it down. Yep, I was going to have to try different kinds of the local cuisine to avoid a life of frozen pizzas and ham sandwiches.

Despite my best efforts, a decade had passed and I still hadn't acquired a taste for seafood. Such were the trials and tribulations of life. Thank goodness for barbeque.

With the memory of my first exchange with Nic fresh in my mind, I entered Goob's. You know the old saying that the way to a man's heart is through his stomach? I found the saying applied every bit as much to her.

The store hadn't changed much since my arrival in the Springs. The exterior was still white vinyl siding with a red tin roof. The bin where you could get a bag of ice was still a few feet to the right of the entrance, though the price had gone up fifty cents over the years.

Inside, coolers where you could purchase your favorite beverages, both soft drinks and not-so-soft drinks, lined one wall. Two small rows of shelving fixtures were located in the center of the store. On one, you could find all sorts of snacks and other edible items. The other was where you went for sunscreen, bug spray, and other household and vacation items. On the opposite wall, the coolers were stocked with all kinds of fishing supplies and equipment.

The deli counter took up a large portion of the store. There was a section for hot foods like fish, sausage, and baked beans. Next to it, was a section for breads and cookies. A third one was home to refrigerated items like cheeses and cold cuts.

"Elmo, my boy. What can I do for you?" The elderly bald man behind the counter was Goob himself. He was going on ninety but was as fit and energetic as a man half his age. He was wearing a new pair of glasses with round fluorescent-orange frames. They matched the band on his smart watch.

I inhaled. The glorious aroma of Caribbean spices filled me up and reminded me to take time to slow down and enjoy a moment.

"How about some of your incredible jerk chicken with a side of slaw. Also, I'd like the blackened grouper sandwich with potato wedges."

"Off to see your lady friend, I see." He chuckled as he prepared my order. His swollen knuckles may have betrayed his arthritis, but he had the dexterity of a chef at an Asian steakhouse. "What are we in trouble for this time?"

I looked at the ceiling fan above me to avoid making eye contact. The man could read me like a paperback novel.

"I'm not in trouble…this time. We're taking a break. That's all." I had to admit that I had a history ordering the same thing from Goob whenever I was on my way to Nic's to attempt to bribe my way back into her good graces. Sometimes it worked. Sometimes it didn't.

This time, things were different.

As a true queen of the sea, she lived on the water. Her home was a small pleasure craft she'd bought at auction. In a story right out of an Elmore Leonard novel, its original owner was an oilman who'd been caught leaving the Bahamas in an attempt to smuggle a trio of Dominican beauties into the States. It turned out the women were actually undercover federal agents running a sting operation. He went to jail, they went back to Freeport for their next assignment, and Nic got a place to live literally right next door to where she worked. Or one berth over, to be more accurate. Sometimes I still struggled with the maritime lingo.

On my way, I strolled along the wood-plank dock, past berths that served as home bases for crafts ranging from decades old, wooden-hulled sailboats to sleek multilevel yachts that carried price tags in the millions of dollars. The kind of craft where if you had to ask how much it cost, you couldn't afford it.

Nic's home was a ten-minute walk from Goob's. Nestled between a forty-foot fishing boat and her seventy-foot cruise ship, it was like a baby gosling hidden between two adult Canada geese.

I knocked on the side of the hull. This time of year, she didn't run cruises on Tuesdays. If she was home, she'd be in her cabin, reading a giant tome of Russian historical literature or something similar. She loved the intellectual challenge.

Her face appeared in a round port hole. When I showed her the bags from Goob's, she waved me aboard, then met me on deck, eying the bags with furrowed brows.

"What's this for?" Despite her distrust, she accepted her bag without complaint.

"I want to pick your brain about this thing with Rambo."

"And by *this thing* you mean the murder investigation." At my nod, she turned to go inside. "I think this conversation requires alcohol. Come on."

The living quarters were small, but every inch of space was put to use. We passed the head, which consisted of a sink, shower stall, and commode. All function, no frills, as Nic liked to say. Next was the galley, which had a dorm-room-sized fridge, a small cook stove, and a microwave. Despite the bare-bones appliances, Nic made the most of what she had and was a whale of a cook.

While she got a beer from the fridge, I made an Irish whiskey on the rocks. We'd been in an *off-again* state for three months, but she had an unopened bottle of my beloved Tullamore Dew.

She still cared.

Which was lucky for me. The reason for our current off-again status was a serious conversation we had not long ago. Nic wanted to know where our relationship was going. Did we have something long-term or was she just a glorified booty call? I objected to the characterization but told her I didn't know what kind of future we had.

In turn, she accused me of being incapable of being in a long-term committed relationship. She was right. My mom had done an amazing job raising me, but without my dad around, I didn't get to grow up around two adults in a healthy relationship. Then, the way my friends and colleagues abandoned me when I was at my lowest. Well, that was about the most bitter of pills to swallow.

In the end, we agreed that if I was unable or unwilling to make a commitment to her, we needed to be done.

"People care about you, Elmo," she told me then. "I care about you. But until you're ready to step outside the bubble you've built around yourself and make an effort to build something with someone else, you're going to be alone."

This was my first visit to her boat since that painful conversation at my house.

The cabin was a tiny room farthest forward. Like the rest of the living quarters, every space served a function. There was room for a full-size bed and a square dining table that could accommodate two, barely. A flat-screen TV was mounted on one wall.

I was proud to say that I'd helped Nic install it. And set up both of her boats with high-speed internet functionality.

"What's on that little mind of yours?" She was teasing me. Another sign she cared.

"Suspects not named Rambo."

While we ate, I recapped the events of the last twenty-four hours. I didn't leave anything out, from the odd chat with Sybil to my late-night escapade to my contentious chat with the chief.

"A lot of people didn't like Cohen. It's more than that, though. I just don't know what. You're smart and you know a lot of people. I wanted to get your take."

She licked ketchup from her fingers before she spoke. When she was finished, she gave me a long look.

"If it was me, I'd leave this alone. Let the cops do their job. Some of them are dunces, but Susan knows her stuff. And it wouldn't look good if she sees you doing the meddling-kid thing after she told you to step off and Rambo turns out to be the killer."

"I know." I took a big gulp of my whiskey. It was a good thing I wasn't driving. "But if you could have seen Rambo with Butkus, you'd be as convinced as me that he didn't do it. It was like he was saying goodbye to an old friend on their deathbed. He wouldn't put one of his prize gators as risk."

She took a sip of her beer. "You know what one of the things about you is that drives me crazy?"

Before I could ask her how much time she had, because the list was long, she waved me into silence.

"You've got a big heart. Rambo's not exactly Mister Congeniality, but you manage to see the good in him. I don't know how you do it."

We'd had too many versions of the same conversation to count over the years. She was worried that I took Rambo and Wendell at their word too readily. That in my desire to have a few friends I could really count on, I gave them the benefit of the doubt that I rarely gave anyone else. This time, her tone was different. Instead of aggravation, there was a smidge of respect.

"Does this mean you'll help?"

"Only because I agree with you." She tapped the tabletop with her index finger for emphasis. "Rambo might be a lot of things, but he's not a killer."

A charge went through me. Nic saw things I didn't. While I was an expert with computer systems and code, she was an expert at dealing with people. Fifteen years running her own cruise ship had taught her a lot.

We rehashed everything we knew about the case. Nic asked a few questions, but mostly let me do the talking. I was in my IT problem-solving mode. It felt good to put the old skills to use. Kind of like how I felt the first time I turned the pedals of the secondhand cruiser I bought when I decided to make Paradise Springs home. I hadn't been on a bike since high school, but it came back. After a wobbly start. And a crash into a stand of sea grass. I preferred to not think about that, though.

When we reached the end, she asked me pointed questions about Sybil and The Vampire. The best I could offer were theories.

"Sybil's a fraud. Harmless, yes, but still a fraud. We all know it. She must have wanted to talk to me for a reason, though. The way she was going on about danger makes me think Fran had concrete evidence that she was up to something shady."

"I could see that." She twisted the emerald stud earring in her right ear. "But does that make her a murderer? After all, I'd wager most people know the majority of fortune-tellers are fakes."

"True enough. If her secret's big enough, she might. What if she's got a pile of cash stashed somewhere and he found out about it? If so, that would help her finance a murder for hire."

"If that's true, for the sake of argument, why drag Rambo under with Fran?"

That was a good point. And the very reason I wanted to talk this through with Nic.

"You know Rambo. He says what's on his mind. He doesn't think much of Sybil and he won't hesitate to say it. I'll ask him to be sure. If it's true, she could get rid of a critic along with a threat to her secret. What do you think of that?"

She nodded as she munched on the last bite of her sandwich. "It's got possibilities. Sybil can be a real witch to people she doesn't like. I've seen her ream people out at the grocery store over the smallest thing."

"I'll keep her on my list. What about the reverend?"

"He does a lot of good in town. Do you really think he'd resort to murder just because of a fight?"

I shrugged. "Dunno. I heard he was pretty worked up about all the property damage and blamed Cohen for the whole thing."

Nic drummed her fingers on the table. "Broken chairs, busted-up walls. I totally see him being mad, but to kill a guy?"

Times exactly like this were why I loved talking with Nic. She made me think. Challenged me, but never made me feel like a dummy. "You're probably right. I still don't trust him. Do me a favor and let me know if you hear anything about him, okay?"

"Sure. What about Longfellow?"

"Who?" Other than the American poet, that name didn't register.

"Abe Longfellow. You know, The Vampire, as you and your cronies like to call him."

"Wait, what? Do you mean to tell me The Vampire's name is Abraham Longfellow? As in the same as two famous Americans from the eighteen hundreds?"

"The guy's eccentric. So what? Twice a year he books a dinner cruise for himself and a few friends. They're friendly and tip well. What more can you ask?"

"Do they actually eat the meal?"

She rolled her eyes before answering. "Of course they do, you doofus. And before you even ask, they tend to drink hard liquor. No red wine and no Bloody Marys. Satisfied?"

I ignored the question. To me, the man's habits were too bizarre to ignore.

"The Vamp...Longfellow does all this recycling, right? Maybe Fran wanted to put a stop to that, so Longfellow killed him."

Nic frowned. "That doesn't sound like much of a motive to me."

"Sure, but do you know if he does anything else to make money? Besides, what about the pin I found on Fran's patio? How do you explain that if he was just making recycling rounds?"

"I can't explain it. Maybe the little clasp thing came loose and it fell off. Then again, it's not my job to. If you want to know, talk to Abe yourself. Unless you're too afraid he'll bite your neck."

"Very funny." She was right, though. I was going to have to confront the man. "Okay, I'll go see him. Maybe you can come along since he already knows you?"

"For the love of Neptune, Elmo, I will never understand how bugs and rodents don't bother you but talking to someone can turn you into a walking jellyfish."

"What can I say? Bugs and rodents don't lie. It's one of the reasons I went into IT. Computer code doesn't, either. But back to the investigation. The chief brought up some great points. Regardless of who's responsible, this was planned. At least three people had to have been involved in wrangling Butkus. That's what makes me think this thing was set up to frame Rambo, too. Whoever was the mastermind behind it must be methodical, have cash to hire others to help carry out the plan, and have something against Sybil since she says she's in danger."

"Not bad, Sherlock. Seriously." Nic gestured like she was tipping a hat to me. "But why go to all the trouble with the gator? It would have been way easier to cap him and toss the gun in the ocean. No muss, no fuss."

I cringed at her blunt assessment. But that was Nic. She was straightforward. I could take what she told me at face value. After having to deal with the game playing and backstabbing from my past, her honesty was a ray of sunshine after a thunderstorm.

"The killer wanted both of them out of the way. Using Butkus amounted to a two-for-one," I said.

"But why? Rambo and Fran ran in completely different circles. Where's the connection?"

"That, my dear Nicola, is what I aim to find out."

CHAPTER NINE

THE NEXT DAY, I was up with the dawn. Living on the Gulf Coast, it was an amazing thing to watch. Kind of like that scene in *Running Scared* when people gathered together to applaud the sunset. I liked to applaud the sunrise.

"The view never gets old, does it, buddy?" I sipped my coffee with one hand while I scratched my feline's ear with the other.

He'd already gobbled up his breakfast of canned fish and had jumped onto my lap for a postmeal groom and scratch. After cleaning the side of his face with a paw, he stared at me for a minute, then lifted his chin an inch.

It took it as a sign he agreed with me.

"I'm glad you concur. In appreciation, I'll see if I can get you some real fish while I'm out today. Maybe some grouper I can put on the grill. Sound good?"

Oscar stretched, then leapt to the ground. After a quick look around, he climbed the stairs and began pawing at the trailer's door.

"Ah, yes. You need to head inside so you can build up some energy with a nap. That way you'll be ready for dinner. I get it. Good plan."

We made our way indoors. Today, the first stop on my

rounds was at one of my least favorite clients. The highest maintenance client in the history of high maintenance. Oscar needed to start napping. All things considered, I wouldn't have minded changing spots with him.

That first stop was the Bayside Inn, the swankiest restaurant this side of New Orleans. It was my best paying gig. Despite the indigestion it produced, I didn't want to lose the contract. I gave Oscar a knuckle bump for good luck, and headed back outside to start the workday.

The Bayside is a two-story wooden structure situated right on the beach a mile or so down the road from the pier. The site's original building had been built in the early fifties. The rusty tin roof and clapboard siding had created an atmosphere that welcomed customers of all stripes, from state senators to bootleggers.

When Hurricane Opal flattened that structure in 1995, the original owner took the insurance proceeds and retired to the relative safety, weather-wise, of Santa Fe, New Mexico. The lot remained a sand-covered wasteland until a world-famous chef to the stars bought it five years later.

She sunk hundreds of thousands of dollars into the new restaurant. The exterior was painted robin's-egg blue with white trim. And had a steel roof that didn't rust. The interior featured polished hardwood floors, strategically located fireplaces to ward off the chill during the winter, and three private dining rooms on the second floor that could be converted into a single reception area.

Diners were treated to linen tablecloths and napkins that changed colors every month to coincide with the calendar, from red in February to blue in July to nutmeg in November. The front-of-the-house staff wore white dress shirts and black bowties.

And took orders without writing them down. That never ceased to amaze me.

Even the beachside bar leaned toward the classy end. The live music every weekend featured contemporary jazz or show tunes. There were no specials that featured cocktails in garish plastic containers or beers in thirty-six-ounce mugs, either.

It was also the only restaurant where I could get Redbreast. I'd treat myself to the top-shelf Irish whiskey on super-special occasions. So, not very often.

The restaurant was a hit from day one. Diners came from all over the world to experience the unique menu, which featured Cajun, Creole, and Continental fare with a twist that was unique to Chef Claudine. The fish of the day was literally pulled from the Gulf of Mexico each morning. Talk about fresh.

The restaurateur had no last name. I mean, I'm sure she was born with one, but by the time she arrived in Paradise Springs, she was a one-name force of nature, right up there with Akwafina, Rihanna, and Banksy.

Without the sense of humor of those superstars.

She worked eighteen hours a day, six days a week. And expected the same level of excellence from her staff that she demanded from herself. From what I'd heard, the pay was good and helped make up for Claudine's periodic eruptions when something didn't meet those expectations.

Her temper was a thing of legend. She didn't discriminate with it, either. Suppliers, employees, even customers weren't spared her wrath when they'd done something to make her unhappy. She was quick to forgive her suppliers and staff. Not so much with customers or high-society big shots, especially when they were jerks to her staff. Innocent mistakes happened. Rudeness was a choice. And the wrong one in her establishments.

There were rumors that one time she even made Chef Gordon Ramsay cry.

I didn't know if the story was true, but I believed it. You didn't mess with Claudine. Which was why I was on my way to the Bayside in plenty of time to arrive at eight A.M. sharp, my scheduled time. And not a minute later.

I piloted the truck down Gulfview Drive with the windows rolled down. Two- and three-story apartments and condos dominated the street on my left, the side nearest the ocean. Every now and then, I passed an empty lot, a remnant of the most recent hurricane and the havoc it wreaked. On the other side of the street, businesses were beginning to open. A breakfast café had put chairs and tables under a palm tree to maximize the shade. The breeze coming in from the Gulf brought with it the familiar taste and smell that reminded me why I'd come to love this odd community so much. Paradise Springs worked its way into your bones, then into your heart.

Jolly Roger was out for his usual morning walk. Dressed in pink pants and a yellow polo shirt, he was impossible to miss. I slowed down so we could exchange greetings and a wave. The poor guy smiled, but couldn't hide a haunted look in his eyes, as if he hadn't slept since Fran's remains had been discovered. Shoot, even his handlebar mustache was drooping on one side. Who could blame him? One of his residents was dead. That was bad enough. The sensational nature of the crime had made regional news. That couldn't be good for business.

Especially with spring-break season kicking off in a month.

"Hang in there, man. I'm sure the cops'll find the murderer," I said as a car grew larger in my rearview mirror. Roger gave me a thumbs-up and shouted a response I couldn't quite make out as I rolled away.

For a second, I wondered whether he was the evildoer. I shook my head and turned on some Ziggy Marley. Having one of your residents offed, especially in such a gruesome way, couldn't be good for his bottom line. Besides, it didn't seem like Jolly Roger's style. He seemed like someone who'd drop something lethal in your glass of wine.

A lot less publicity that way. And a lot less to clean up, too.

My thoughts turned from the resort owner as Ziggy started to sing about being lonely on a beach in Hawaii. A man could have a worse fate. Like being stuck lonely in Indianapolis in January with the temperature hovering around fifteen degrees and the sky a solid sheet of slate-gray clouds.

It had been a long time since I'd been in that situation. I had good memories of my hometown, but as I gazed out at the pier while I waited for a traffic light to turn green, I had zero interest in going back for more than short visits to see my mom. Life on the Florida Panhandle suited me.

A few minutes later, I turned into the Bayside's parking lot. I'd been providing service to the place for five years. Every single time, my pulse quickened the microsecond I shut the engine off.

It wasn't that I was afraid of Claudine. It was more that I was intimidated by her reputation, but I'd given her top-notch work without causing her any indigestion. My price increases had been minimal, and I always stayed out of her way. Over the years, I'd become part of the background, like the pigeons that strutted along the beach in front of the restaurant's bar. It had gotten to the point that she barely paid me any attention. Which meant I was allowed to show up, do my job, and get out of there without much more than a wave or nod.

I'd put that freedom to my advantage today.

The first thing I did was check the traps I'd hidden among the decorative grasses that tourists loved to ooh and aah over while they waited outside for their turn to be seated. Beach areas, like so much of North America, were home to small rodents like squirrels and the occasional chipmunk. Mice could be the big problem, though. And it didn't take long for an infestation to take hold.

At the Bayside, my job was to make sure the only creatures diners laid eyes on were the birds flying about in the area. If I found so much as a single mouse dropping, I needed to go on full Ghostbusters-style alert.

That hadn't happened. Yet. A check of the outdoor traps confirmed that was still the case. I ticked off a checkmark on my tablet and went to the service entrance to begin my interior inspection. Before I knocked, I scanned the parking lot. Claudine's Bentley was parked in its usual spot, under a wooden canopy reserved just for her. The vehicle was dark red. One time, I'd made the mistake of referring to it by that color. Claudine was quick to point out, in a tone that made Maleficent seem like a kitten, that the color was Dragon Red.

I refrained from commenting that the car color was befitting the owner. Discretion being the better part of valor.

After greeting the back-of-the-house manager with the customary fist-bump exchange, I began my rounds. Normally, the indoor inspection didn't take a lot of time. Since I wasn't an exterminator, I wasn't on the lookout for spiders, ants, or creepy-crawlies like that. Claudine had another company provide that service.

The vast majority of my job was focused on the exterior area. It was kind of like building a force field that the little buggers couldn't get through. If there was no evidence of them outside, odds were in my favor that they weren't getting inside.

When Claudine was your client, you never played the odds on anything, though. Ever. Thus, the indoor walk-through.

With my handy-dandy penlight, I checked the perimeter of each dining area, scanning the baseboards for signs that something had penetrated my force field. Not that it was any surprise, there were none.

I was headed for the kitchen area, where rodents were more likely to be found at a restaurant, when raised voices coming from the second floor caught my attention. The words were coming from too far away to make out, but the voices were unmistakable. One had the familiar low-throated timbre of the Hollywood film legend Lauren Bacall.

That was Claudine.

The other voice belonged to her executive chef, Renee. The two had worked together for years. How Renee had put up with Claudine's temper tantrums was beyond me. It could be because she was an amazing chef in her own right. And had the guts to yell back. Behind closed doors, of course.

Two fiery personalities who were brilliant at their jobs. When you got through the shouting matches, there was a ton of mutual respect there.

My usual routine took me through the kitchen before moving upstairs. With the restaurant's top people deep in discussion, curiosity suggested I alter my route. I ascended the stairs as quietly as my rubber-soled work boots would allow.

With each step, the words became clearer. I stopped at the top step. The door to Claudine's office was open.

"I'm just saying it would be a nice gesture to have some sort of acknowledgment," Renee said. "He wielded a lot of influence and spent an awful lot of money in this place, after all."

"So do a lot of other people. It never ceases to amaze me

how people determine their own self-worth by being seen in my fine dining establishments."

"I'm not talking about tourists and celebs. The locals here in Paradise Springs matter, too. We could have something on a Tuesday night and post it on social media. That way we can increase traffic flow on the slowest day of the week without spending any advertising dollars. What have we got to lose?"

"My self-respect." There was a clicking of someone working on a computer keyboard. "The man was a parasite. We're all better off with him gone."

This was getting good. To avoid being accused of eavesdropping, I completed my ascent and began checking the baseboards like on the first floor. I did it at a snail's pace, though, and in close proximity to the office so I wouldn't miss the rest of the conversation.

"This isn't about you, Chef. It's about him. I agree he was a pain in the neck, but he treated the staff well and tipped generously, especially around the holidays."

Claudine barked out a laugh. "Of course he tipped generously. With the way he propositioned the servers, his credit card was the only thing that kept him from getting slapped across the face and getting kicked out of there on his backside."

Wow. From what I'd heard, the circle of people Claudine tolerated was smaller than my watch face. Most folks, like me, she dismissed as irrelevant. We weren't worth the energy of giving us any thought.

She seemed to have an unmistakable dislike for Fran,

though. Was it deep enough to commit murder? I pretended to make notes on my tablet so I could hang around for more.

"Fine." Renee let out a sigh. "Let's make it about you, then. We could spin it as a charitable event. Ten percent can go to a charity. Of your choosing."

"Hmm. I might be open to that. Provided we can drive enough traffic to make sure we end up with a large enough donation that doesn't embarrass us."

"I'll make sure that happens." A chair squeaked, as if someone had gotten to her feet.

I scurried behind one of the movable partitions to remain out of sight. But could still hear.

"Be honest with me, Chef. You don't look happy with this idea, either. What did you have against the guy? Was it something personal?"

"No. I wouldn't allow something like that to happen." A pause that seemed to go on forever held me in suspense. "It was purely professional."

"What's that mean? Did he back out on an investment deal or something?"

"No. Way worse." Claudine cleared her throat. "A number of years ago, this was before your time, he came in for lunch. Just like normal. He ordered shrimp cocktail for an appetizer. Again, just like normal."

Acting against my better judgment, which happened way more than I cared to admit, I edged closer to the office doorway. I broke into a sweat. Holy cow, investigating was proving to be scary and exciting at the same time.

"Wait. Are you sure?" A few seconds went by. The only

sound was the *tick, tick, tick* of the clock on Claudine's wall. I had a feeling the boss was giving her main employee a stare down that could turn her into a human icicle. "Of course you're sure. My apologies. I don't remember him ever ordering shrimp cocktail."

"That's because he doesn't. Not here. Not anymore." She sighed. It was the one and only time I'd ever heard her sound anything less than 110 percent in control.

I twirled my index fingers in a circle to urge her to hurry up. I had a murderer to catch. And another appointment in twenty minutes.

"Anyway, the next day, he barged into my office, shouting that he got food poisoning from the shrimp cocktail and threatening to sue."

"Seriously? There wasn't anything to it, was there? I mean, assuming he actually got sick, it must have been from something else he ate that day."

"My thinking exactly. So, I asked for proof. He showed me a discharge order from the local med check. Said he wanted ten thousand dollars or he'd go to the press. I didn't want to take the chance of the negative publicity, so I paid. The restaurant hadn't been open very long and I'd sunk too much money into it to risk taking a financial hit. He came back five more times, and I paid each time."

"Wow. How much did you pay him?"

The figure seemed like an awful lot of cash for a single case of food poisoning. Ten grand? Claudine might pay close to that in legal fees fighting the claim. Beyond that, though, making more payments made her seem like a pushover.

If there was one thing I knew about her, it was this. She

was no pushover.

"He upped the ante each time. I paid that cockroach a total of one hundred thousand dollars. The last time, I said we were done. So, I hope you'll excuse me for not being excited about doing something in honor of him."

"I'm sorry. I didn't know."

Renee's response sounded a lot more diplomatic than asking Claudine why in the world she so willingly coughed up so much cash. Something else was going on. I could sense it. It was like those times I'd trap a handful of chipmunks that had been hanging out in someone's crawlspace but could feel it in my bones there was one more hiding from me, a rodent version of that doctor from *The Fugitive*.

"It's all right. We kept the matter between ourselves."

"Well, at least you don't have to deal with him and his crazy demands anymore."

"Very true," Claudine said. "With that thought in mind, go ahead with your little memorial event. I like the idea of making money off Fran Cohen after everything he took from me."

The conversation continued, but I made my way to the stairs as fast as I could without making a sound. I'd heard enough.

It was all I could do to finish the inspection without dropping something or jumping out of my skin when someone from the kitchen staff said *hi*. Against the odds, despite my initial doubts that I could do it, I'd found another clue to Fran's murder.

And now I had my first serious suspect. And boy, was she a whopper.

CHAPTER TEN

I MIGHT HAVE been new at this sleuthing thing, but that didn't mean I lacked at least a little common sense. Along with the excitement that came from overhearing Claudine's conversation came a ton of anxiety. The first step in dealing with the sailor's knot that had twisted itself up in my gut was to write everything down.

As soon as I got back to my truck.

Taking time to jot down my notes about a murder suspect while still inside her business didn't seem like a bright idea. Especially when the business had dozens of razor-sharp knives and other potential instruments of torture within arm's reach.

Once I was finished with that task, I headed out for my next appointment. During the drive, I called Rambo. He needed to know about this new development.

"Quigley," he answered on the first ring. You had to hand it to the man. He didn't mince words.

"Dude, you are not going to believe what just happened." I was so excited, I had to jam on my brakes to avoid running into the back of an old codger driving ten miles an hour below the speed limit.

"The sun rises in the east and sets in the west? What do

you want, Simpson? I've got a congregation of baby gators that needs fed and if I don't give them something to eat right now, they might eat me."

I told him what I'd learned at the restaurant. The line was silent for a while, the only sound coming from Rambo's breathing. Then he laughed.

"Holy Toledo, Simpson. That's the best news I've heard all week. To be honest, I didn't know if you had it in you to do this cloak-and-dagger stuff."

"I didn't, either." Rambo's upbeat tone made me smile. It felt good to help out a friend. Especially one who was twice as big as me. "I'll swing by the Riptide for some takeout and come by your place later. We can figure out what's next."

Rambo thought my suggestion was a great idea. I ended the call and cranked up the radio. Elmo Simpson, Private Eye. It had a certain ring to it. Or even better, Elmo Simpson, International Consultant. I let out a laugh.

This snooping-around gig, and the adrenaline rush that came with it, was something I could get into.

That afternoon, I closed the file on my last appointment of the day. It had been a good day in the critter-removal business. All of my traps had been empty. On top of that, I'd detected no scat or other *gifts* that had been left behind on my clients' properties.

With no feathered, furry, or reptilian friends to relocate, I was free to take off my day-job hat and put my sleuthing one back on.

I pulled up to Rambo's barn wondering if Rick Castle

felt as positive midinvestigation as I currently did. Things were moving. And in the right direction.

Rambo was waiting for me, a big grin on his face. The man had even put on a clean shirt. That was something he'd never done for me in the past.

"Elmo, my man." He gave me a high five the moment I closed my truck's door. "There's a cold beer in the fridge with your name on it. We need to celebrate."

He slapped me on the back hard enough to loosen my molars. I knew the man was dangerous when he was angry. I never thought he'd be lethal when happy. Chalk it up to learning something new every day.

"Slow your roll, man." With my free hand, I checked my teeth. Just to make sure they were still solidly in place. Once I was satisfied I wouldn't be visiting my dentist in the near future, I handed him the food. "It's not like I found a smoking gun or anything like that."

"I know, I know." He led me into the barn. "It feels good to know that I'm not on my own in this mess. It would have been easy to tell me to get lost when I asked you to help me out."

"Happy to help. It's my turn to step up. Us small-time businesses need to stick together."

That was the truth. I loved Paradise Springs and its bizzarro vibe. I'd lived here long enough to see the town change, though. Some of it was for the better, like when a new causeway was built, or the pier was renovated.

A lot of it was for the worse, though. From my perspective, at least. For example, the colorful, quaint mom-and-pop inns that had been a staple of the area for decades kept closing for good. The flashy hotels and condos that replaced them offered tourists every amenity under the sun. Except for one.

The new, corporate businesses lacked the soul of the longtime places.

Sticking up for the little guy was important to me. Maybe it was because I ran my own one-person operation. There was a good chance it was because other small business proprietors, like Rambo and Wendell, took me under their wings when I was a Paradise Springs newbie. It was also a good possibility because I'd fallen for another person who ran her own business.

God help me if Nic ever heard me say that out loud. Especially since there appeared to be no *on-again* stage for us in sight.

"Well, I appreciate it." He handed me an ice-cold 30A Bleach Blonde from Grayton Beer Company, my favorite. "And I'll never forget it."

We clinked glasses and tore into the barbeque. As far as the two of us were concerned, we could eat Riptide fare every day of the week.

When you had dinner with someone as massive as Rambo, it took a while. He plowed his way through two whole chickens, a full serving of mac and cheese, the same of green beans, and half a dozen cornbread biscuits. I'd had a full workday and my meal was a quarter of my dining partner's.

I shuddered at the thought of the size of Rambo's grocery bill.

By the time we finished, we had a pile of plates, napkins, and utensils a foot high. It was an impressive effort.

"I'll clean up. Least I can do since you bought." He swept the remains of our feast into a trash barrel with a single swipe of an arm. "There's a new Caribbean place in town I want to try, so I'm buying next time."

"Works for me." I put my feet up on a cooler and ran my thumb around the label on my beer bottle. "What do you think? Is Claudine the murderer?"

He dropped into his chair with a grunt. I gritted my teeth for a second, fearful that the steel frame was going collapse.

"Maybe. I mean, if someone was blackmailing me, I'd sure want it to stop." He put his hands up. "Nobody's been blackmailing me. Wanna be clear about that."

"I'll make a note of that. Since, you know, that's what a real PI would say. I think." I opened my phone's Notepad app and added that piece of information. Mostly just for show, but you never knew when something might turn out to be important. "Now, back to Claudine."

"She's a chef. Seems to me, if she wanted someone dead, she'd poison 'em or chop 'em up and toss the pieces in the ocean." He wrung his hands and looked up at the ceiling. "I'm gonna let you in on a little secret. I know I can be intimidating and some people might be scared of me."

I started to bark out a laugh. When Rambo glared at me, I covered my mouth and tried to hide it by coughing. The man scared almost everybody within a fifty-mile radius. Including the gators.

"Anyway, comes with the territory when you look like me and do what I do. I'll tell you, though. Claudine is one scary broad."

I almost spit out the drink I was in the middle of at the admission.

"Scared? You? And what's up with the *scary-broad* thing? What, are we characters in a Raymond Chandler novel? This is the twenty-first century, dude. With language like that, no wonder you're still single."

"Yeah, well, maybe you're right. Tell you what." He pointed a finger as big as a sausage at me. "You get me out of this, and I promise to cut back on all the classic movies I watch and try some new stuff. Except *The Maltese Falcon*. That one is nonnegotiable."

"Fair enough." We shook to seal the deal. "So, if Claudine's our murderer, how'd she do it?"

He scratched his beard. "Good question. A lot of times, the gator that's on her menu comes from the stock I raise and sell to my processor. A few years back, she paid me a visit. Said she wanted to get a look at my operation to make sure I treat the animals humanely. At first, I thought it was pretty nervy. Then I realized she was just doing her due diligence. Anyway, I gave her a complete tour, the outside pens, the indoor facility. All of it. She had me on edge the whole time, lemme tell ya, but thanked me when we were done."

"I see where you're going with this. Seeing your big boys must have made an impression. And when it came time to do the dirty deed, she remembered her trip here."

"Maybe she did." He got to his feet, his knees cracking as he rose. "The question is how she pulled off the heist. I mean, it ain't easy wrangling an adult gator, even if you know what you're doing. And that's on top of getting through the gate. That's an expensive digital security system I use."

"She's rich enough to own a small country. Maybe she's got connections to organized crime on account of her restaurants in New York. I don't think the price of some hired specialty help would be a problem for her. The question is, how do we prove it? Do you have any security cameras?"

He shook his head. "Between being out here all by my lonesome and the barbed wire fence, never thought I'd ever need one."

We were debating possible scenarios with Claudine's involvement when Chief Eikenberry's SUV pulled up.

Rambo and I exchanged a glance, then I shrugged. "Maybe they're here to tell you they caught the murderer."

She emerged from the vehicle like a cobra rising from a woven basket. Her expression was unreadable, neither a smile nor a frown, as she donned a pair of reflective sunglasses. A moment later, Spock got out of the passenger side.

My Spidey senses told me this wasn't a social call.

"Am I correct in assuming you aren't expecting a visit from Paradise Springs' finest?" My heart rate ticked up a notch. After a trip to the hospital to treat a blockage, I'd learned to pay attention to my ticker. The pulse was strong and steady. But too rapid, nonetheless.

"Aye. The chief said she'd be in touch. That was it." He used the last of the napkins to wipe his hands. As he strode toward the cops, he tossed the wad into a trash can. It was a smooth move, but I had a feeling my old friend wasn't feeling as relaxed as the move made him look.

"Evening, officers." Rambo came to a stop at the edge of the barn. "Simpson and I were having a beer after a hard day's work. Care to join us?"

"Afraid we're here on official business, Mr. Quigley." The chief stopped a few feet from him and extended her hand. "Mind if we have a word with you? Alone?"

While they shook, Spock drifted to their right. His hand went toward the holster of his Taser. It took him three attempts to release the snap. God love the poor kid, he was not meant to be on the front lines of law enforcement. If he had to use the Taser, odds were good that he'd neutralize himself before he took down a criminal with it.

Regardless of the junior officer's ineptitude, the fact that he had a service weapon at the ready couldn't be a good sign. I double-timed to Rambo's side, inserting myself between him and Spock. The chief's request for a private conversation be damned.

"There's no need for a show of force, Chief." I nodded toward her young counterpart. "We're both law-abiding citizens who don't want trouble."

"In this town, law-abiding can mean different things to different people." Spock widened his stance. It didn't help his cause since his voice had cracked halfway through his retort.

The chief clenched her jaw as she removed her sunglasses. She shot Spock a hard look that would have left me six feet under.

"Officer, take your hand off that weapon. There's no need to escalate the situation." She let out a long sigh. "Sorry, guys. At times I think he'd be better off with a single bullet in his breast pocket."

Spock's cheeks turned pink as he put his hands on his hips, then crossed his arms, and eventually settled with hooking his thumbs on his belt.

"What situation?" Rambo asked.

I put my hand on his shoulder and took a step forward. It was a move I'd learned from Wendell at the Riptide. It didn't take much for Rambo's temper to surface if he felt he was being wronged. A hand on the shoulder was a signal to the bear of a man to take a deep breath and let someone else do the talking.

It was okay for him to glower and look frightening, but nothing else.

"Are we really going to have to do this, Elmo? It's been a long day." She reached for a set of handcuffs.

Rambo put up his hands in front of him like dual stop signs. "Now hold on a minute, boss lady. Those cuffs can only mean one thing. Before you do something you'll regret, my good friend Elmo and I were about to call you."

"We were?" I shot a look at Rambo. "I mean, yes, we were. We've got a line on Fran's murderer."

She looked at Spock, then let out another sigh as she shook her head.

"Officer Nimoy, please make sure your bodycam is on."
The chief returned her focus to us. "While my associate does
that, tell me what you mean by *got a line on Fran's murderer*
and be quick about it. I would really like to be home in time
to watch some *Downton Abbey* before I call it a night."

I stepped between Rambo and the chief. Smart enough
to know watching *Law & Order* reruns didn't make me an
expert on the law, it still made sense that the less my buddy
said at the moment, the better.

After a deep breath to buy some time to get my thoughts
in order, I laid out our theory involving Chef Claudine. As I
spoke, the scratching of Spock's pencil against notepad paper
calmed me. If nothing else, there would be a record of my
attempt to keep Rambo out of the slam.

I mean, I was convinced he wasn't the murderer. Right
now, I was fighting an uphill battle, though. And the hill was
made of sand. For every two steps I took, I slid back one.
Still, I'd fight the good fight.

When I finished relating our theory to the chief, I put
my hand back on Rambo's shoulder. "Thanks for coming by,
officers. We don't want to delay your investigation of Chef
Claudine. Have a great evening."

"Not so fast, Simpson." To her credit, she actually
smiled. "That's a good story. Awfully convenient that you
just happened to hear these things today when your friend is
under the microscope, though. Enough with the games.

"Waldo Quigley, you're under arrest for the murder of
Francis Cohen." She cuffed Rambo as she read him his
rights.

Once the handcuffs were secured, Spock leapt from his position so he could guide Rambo into the vehicle.

"Come on, Chief." I clamped my mouth shut for a few seconds. Verbally abusing a police office would just get me a ride to the same place Rambo was going. "You and I both know this isn't right."

She turned on her heel and marched back to the SUV. Before grasping the door handle, she stopped for a moment, then looked me in the eye.

"What I know, Mr. Simpson, is that there is credible evidence linking Mr. Quigley to the murder of Mr. Cohen. I suggest you stop trying to play Magnum P.I. and let the justice system do its job."

Before I could get a response formulated, she was behind the wheel and heading down the driveway.

Things had gone from bad to worse in no time at all. Now, not only did I still have a murderer on the loose, but my client was also on his way to a stint behind bars. It was time for some quick thinking and even quicker action.

CHAPTER ELEVEN

RAMBO WAS A proud man. A classic individualist. Not the kind to ask others for help.

That's why I found myself wearing a suit that was a little tight around the waist and a tie that hadn't seen the light of day in half a decade. As I walked toward the entrance to the county courthouse, I tried to reassure myself that making a good impression in front of the judge would be good for Rambo.

I was pretty sure the bail money I had in my pocket carried more goodwill than a suit and tie, though.

Didn't matter. My one and only goal this morning was to make sure I'd be walking out of the courthouse with Rambo by my side. And the sooner, the better.

I hadn't attended a bail hearing in decades. To be honest, the only other one I'd witnessed firsthand was my own. Back in my college days, some buddies of mine and I had a little too much to drink and decided it would be a good idea to prank the mean old dude who lived next door. He'd yelled at us for playing the B-52's "Rock Lobster" too loud.

The plot had involved a live lobster, some fishing line, and a smoke machine we *borrowed* from the Performing Arts Department. Well, one thing led to another, and instead of pulling off the greatest prank in the history of humankind, me and my crew ended up behind bars for the night. On an animal cruelty charge, among others. Since the old man had the last laugh, we got off with a fine and community service. The lobster? It ended up being the main course in the guy's dinner the following night.

I broke out in a cold sweat just thinking about that misadventure.

The judge presiding over Rambo's hearing was a tiny man with about six wisps of white hair who looked to be about a million years old. He glowered at the parties through massive square glasses that called to mind the legendary announcer for the Chicago Cubs, Harry Caray.

I kept my mouth shut during the hearing and noted a few of the prosecutor's comments in case it came in handy later.

The judge knew everybody in the courtroom but me. And he seemed to like Rambo a whole lot more than the prosecutor. When the attorney asked that Rambo be held without bail, the judge laughed.

"Your case is circumstantial at best, Counselor. Mr. Quigley may be a little rough around the edges, but I know his family." He turned his gaze on Rambo. "Son, I play cards with your grandfather every Tuesday night. If I grant you bail and you so much as think about taking a step outside the county, I will personally ask him to hunt you down and teach you a lesson you won't forget. Do you hear me?"

There was an audible intake of air from the assembly at the mention of Rambo's grandfather. George Washington

Quigley, known to one and all as *Patton*, was widely considered the most fearsome man in three counties. He distilled his own whiskey, rolled his own cigarettes, and was rumored to have helped hundreds flee the Castro regime. On his ninetieth birthday, he wrestled one of Rambo's fully grown gators.

And won.

It didn't matter that Patton Quigley was nearing ninety-five years of age. You didn't cross the man. Even if you were a blood relation.

"Yes, sir. Your Honor, sir." Rambo's voice quavered. Something told me it was a reaction to the mention of his grandfather more than anything else.

"Good. I'm satisfied the defendant isn't a flight risk." The judge set the bail amount and brought the hearing to a close with a solid *whack* from his gavel. "Next case."

A little while later, I was waiting in the hall for Rambo to be released when Wilhelmina Crabtree, the mayor of Paradise Springs, approached me. Dressed in her usual attire of blue jeans and solid color polo shirt, with a pair of sunglasses atop her head, the woman radiated laid-back confidence. Born in Paradise Springs, she'd grown up giving air boat tours. She parlayed that work ethic into a master's degree in public administration from an Ivy League school.

Wil Crabtree was a sharp woman. Nic had once referred to her as a shark hiding inside a dolphin suit. I leapt from my chair to greet her.

"There's no need to get up," the brown-haired woman said as we shook hands.

"In that case, that chair may be the most uncomfortable chair ever made. Your arrival gave me another reason to stand."

She laughed. It was an easy, friendly response that made her hazel eyes sparkle. Not something manufactured, like a lot of phony politicians produce.

"Given where we are, I'd bet they were designed to discourage people from lingering."

"It works. That chair must have been designed by someone who wanted people to look at it but not sit in it." I rubbed my hip to drive the point home.

We chatted for a bit, then she asked what brought me to the courthouse.

"I'm here for Rambo. As soon as he's released, I'm taking him home."

"Good for you." She took a step closer to me. "You deserve a tip of the hat for sticking by your friend. Are you sure you want to be seen associating with someone who has a murder charge hanging over them, though? I'm thinking of your business. Wouldn't want to see it suffer due to misplaced loyalty."

I gave my head a scratch. Mayor Wil was a master of the high-wire act. While she was a well-versed in the art of BS, she was fair and did her best to keep in mind the varying interests in Paradise Springs. That wasn't an easy job. On one hand, she had to support the hospitality industry. The hotels, resorts, and dining establishments kept a ton of people employed.

On the other hand, there were the OG folks, like Rambo

and Goob. They valued the fact that the community hadn't been overrun by tourists. They had nothing against Destin, Panama City Beach, and other places like it. They preferred the laid-back lifestyle and slower pace here.

They liked to say that the town didn't have Paradise in its name by accident.

The mayor had to balance those competing interests every day. Unlike Chief Susan Eikenberry, she tried to play nice with everyone. Well, most folks. Jerks got nowhere with her. It couldn't be an easy job.

I didn't envy her.

That didn't mean I took everything she said as gospel.

"I appreciate your concern, Mayor. Rambo's done a lot for me over the years, so I owe him. Besides, he's not the murderer."

She stepped back and crossed her arms. Then she gave me a head-to-toe once-over. I'd seen this move before. She did it when she thought someone was challenging her. Which I wasn't, but that didn't seem to matter now.

"Chief Eikenberry doesn't agree with you. Do you know something she doesn't? If so, you have a duty to report it. After all, we all owe it to Mr. Cohen's memory to bring his murderer to justice."

The shark's razor-sharp teeth were showing. I had a rodent removal contract with the city. She could terminate that with the stroke of a pen. It didn't seem like a good idea to test her level of tolerance.

It also didn't seem like a good idea to mention the fact that I was conducting my own investigation. Why tempt fate? I could still tell her what she wanted to hear.

"That's why I told the chief everything I know about the matter when she arrested Rambo last night."

Somewhere down the hall, a door slammed closed, yet Wil didn't flinch like I did. She stood still for a moment, like she was contemplating my answer. Apparently, it wasn't what she was expecting.

"That's good to hear. We should all be on the same side of the law."

"Agreed." That was true. I'd told Susan everything she was willing to listen to. "I know Rambo. Sure, he can be as approachable as an angry badger, but he's not a murderer. I mean, everyone's been so focused on the gator, I haven't heard anyone talk about what motive Rambo would have. If any."

Sure, the prosecutor had mentioned a few things about motive during the hearing, but I wasn't going to tell Wil that. If she knew something, I wanted to know what it was.

Man, it was like I was turning into a secret agent. I was trusting no one.

"I realize you may not be as up to speed as other citizens about recent developments, so I'll help you out. Mr. Cohen was a leading voice in an effort to establish ordinances regarding livestock operations located within city limits."

I didn't like the sound of that. "What kind of ordinances, exactly?"

"We need to set boundaries on operations that raise animals…like reptiles, for example." Before I could object, she put her hands up. "You need to understand, tourism is the future of our community. Whether people like it or not, it's the truth. Without proper zoning ordinances, people like Mr. Quigley can run their businesses with virtually no local government oversight."

"What's wrong with that? The state keeps tabs on Rambo's farm. As far as I know, he's never been cited."

"He's been a good corporate citizen. Be that as it may, right now there's nothing to stop him if he wants to expand his operation. The land bordering his property could be valuable to developers. But not with dozens of large predators in the vicinity."

My jaw dropped as the implication made it through my skull. It was one I didn't like.

"Cohen wanted to put restrictions on Rambo's farm." I nodded. "Pretty clever. It's a classic squeeze play. You cut him off, then you choke him to death."

"That's a rather simplistic assessment—"

"But it's not wrong, is it?" My blood began to boil. I'd always be a newcomer to Paradise Springs. That was okay, though. The OG crowd knew me. They'd looked after me. They didn't have the spit-shined, glossy finish of the new money, but they were the area's soul.

And I was lucky to know them.

Sure, they were scruffy and a little rough around the edges. They were also honest, hard-working, and reliable. People like Rambo, Nic, Goob, and Wendell were the real deal. Their lives were here. They had no interest in moving to or being forced to relocate to the next shiny location on the Gulf Coast.

They and their businesses had survived everything from hurricanes to oil spills to economic implosions. They'd done that by having their fellow member of the OG crowd's backs. They didn't abandon each other when things got tough.

That was an ethic sorely lacking in my former career. Colleagues and so-called friends were constantly searching for the proverbial brass ring. Back then, the ethic among people I knew was simple. Whoever died with the most toys won.

It was completely different now. The people I knew, and knew me, looked out for each other. No, I would not turn my back on Rambo in his darkest hour. Because it was the right thing to do.

I didn't want to think of what the consequences would be if his grandfather ever found out I left him high and dry. There was that tiny factor, too, to be completely honest.

"Look." The mayor ran her manicured fingers through her hair. She was as tall as me and took advantage of that fact by giving me a stony stare. "I get it. In your view, underneath that rough exterior, Rambo's got a heart of gold. He'd never hurt a fly. Probably cries whenever he sees that Sarah McLachlan commercial about the stray animals. He and I are both Paradise Springs born and bred, though. I may know him a little better than you do."

"I'll give you that, but he's never mentioned any zoning dispute to me. If it was such a problem, I'm sure he would have mentioned it."

She shook her head as she smiled. Then she patted me on

the shoulder.

"He probably never mentioned it to you because he thought he didn't need to."

"Why not?" Her condescending behavior had made me mad. Now, though, I was confused.

"Because he made his feelings crystal clear at the council meeting when the proposal was presented." She showed me her phone. She'd pulled up a report from the *Paradise Springs Palladium* about the meeting in question.

I scanned the article. It portrayed Fran as a visionary whose only desire was to see his adopted community thrive. Rambo wasn't treated nearly as well.

"The reporter forgot to mention the horns on Rambo's head and his forked tail."

"Grow up, Elmo. Democracy can get messy at times. What's the big deal?" She reached for her phone but I had stepped away so I could read the article in detail.

I was halfway through when the bells went off in my head. And they weren't playing a happy melody.

"Says here that Fran was there on behalf of a group that wants to develop some land in the area." I returned the phone to her. "Let me guess. They want that scrub land by Rambo's place, but don't want the headache of having live alligators living next door."

"I can't comment on what potential capital projects may or may not be in the works."

A laugh escaped me. It carried a bitter tone to it. "Of course you can't. Doesn't take a genius to put two and two together and get four, Mayor. If I was a conspiracy theorist,

I'd say these are the first two steps in driving Rambo out of business. All under the boring cover of zoning hearings."

"Don't be such a drama queen." She did a little flick of her wrist, as if batting away my accusation like she'd bat away a bug. "As long as Mr. Quigley's business remains in compliance, he has nothing to worry about."

A door at the end of the hall opened. Rambo emerged. After spending the night in jail and then sitting in a court room on a murder charge, the man looked like the proverbial horse that had been ridden hard and put away wet.

His hair kept falling over his eyes. His clothes looked like they'd been wadded up into a ball and left in a corner. For a week. My friend needed me.

"Thanks for the chat, Mayor. I appreciate the info. The whole thing seems like a game of dirty pool, though."

"That's one of the great things about America, Elmo. We're all entitled to our opinions." She leaned in close again. "Remember this. The wheels of progress cannot be stopped. You'd be wise to make sure you don't get caught under those wheels. That outcome wouldn't be pretty."

She plastered on a smile as my friend approached. "Rambo, I'm so happy to see your stay was brief. If there's anything I can do to help, let me know."

"Thank you, Wil. I mean, Mayor. I appreciate the support."

She gave him a quick pat on the back, then walked away, the heels of her suede oxfords tapping away on the tile floor with each step she took.

I kept my focus on Rambo as his attention was 100 percent focused on Wil. He had a glazed look and a goofy half smile on his face.

"Did you see that, Elmo?" He poked me with an elbow. "She said to let her know if I needed anything. That's the most she's said to me in, like, forever."

"That's great, man. Let's get out of here. You hungry? I could use something to eat."

"Yeah, sure. You think I should take her up on her offer? Couldn't hurt, right?"

God help me, Rambo had a crush on the mayor. I'd never seen him act like this. Ever.

And it just happened to involve someone who was more interested in the female gender than the male one. And who was also more interested in driving him out of business than actually helping him.

CHAPTER TWELVE

I TOOK US through a drive-through for breakfast. While we waited for our order—a breakfast sandwich and iced tea for me; three sandwiches, three sides of hash browns, a cinnamon roll, and a Diet Coke for Rambo—I gave him a report on my attempt to feed the gators the previous night.

It amounted to dropping some chunks of meat in strategic locations and then running away as fast as my legs would carry me. He laughed when I told him I had no interest in becoming dessert for one of his reptiles.

After breakfast, I dropped Rambo off at home and made a quick exit. God love the poor guy, it wasn't his fault. After his night in the slam, he smelled like he'd gone on-on-one with one of his gators in a dank, mosquito-ridden lagoon. And lost.

It would take days for my truck to air out.

The things we did for friends.

After the events of the past day, I needed time to think. And eat again. In the scramble to get my hands on enough cash to post the bail bond, I'd skipped dinner the night before. Breakfast with the big guy hadn't filled the tank sufficiently. My stomach growled loud enough to drown out Jimmy Buffett's "A Pirate Looks at Forty" that was playing through the speakers.

With no critter-removal emergencies on the docket, I had the rest of the day to myself. Normally, that meant getting lost in a Mark Twain novel or going for a long walk on the beach. Today, things were so much different. I needed guidance to go with some sustenance.

That meant a visit to the Riptide.

The barbeque joint's parking lot reminded me of my driveway. To be honest, in its current state, it wasn't much more than a gravel-covered expanse the size of a soccer pitch. Every year, Wendell paid someone to spread a few truckloads of gravel and level the lot out.

Then, every few years, a serious storm would smack the area. In its wake, the weather event would leave behind downed trees, damaged buildings, and washed-out parking lots. Usually, the Riptide's was among them since it was situated on the water, with only a row of seagrass separating the building from the beach.

One star-filled Sunday night, I was seated at the outdoor bar adjacent to the restaurant with one too many Irish whiskeys in my belly. Wendell's daughter, Amelia, better known to one and all as Seven, was behind the bar. I asked her why they didn't have the lot paved instead of spending so much time and money on the current arrangement.

She pulled herself up to her full five-foot, ten-inch height, leaned forward, and gave me a death stare with her iridescent green eyes.

"Are you questioning my father's judgment?" Her low, sultry tone, which normally carried a flirtatious lilt, had an edge sharp enough to cut steel.

"No. Um, sorry. Never mind." In the blink of an eye, a bead of sweat had broken out on my brow. Despite the fact that the windows were open and a cool breeze was coming in from the Gulf. In that instant, I came to understand how she'd earned the nickname. It was in honor of the *Star Trek* character, Seven of Nine, who was one intimidating, kick-butt character.

"Then why did you bring it up?" She placed her hands on the bar top, looming over me like a gator hovering near an unsuspecting bird that had wandered too close to the water.

"I was just wondering, I guess." I rubbed my palms, which had become as clammy as my forehead had become sweaty, against my cargo shorts. "Seems like a lot of work y'all have to over and over again."

She didn't move a muscle as she stared at me. The seconds seemed to stretch into decades. Eventually, I grabbed for my drink.

And proceeded to knock it over.

With the quickness of a cat, she caught the bottle before it landed on its side to pour its contents all over the wooden bar top and placed it back upright in front of me. Not a single drop was spilled.

If I'd been intimidated by this woman before, I was downright afraid of her by then. She was so unlike her affable father. I managed to croak out a thanks and took a long swig from the bottle. Using both hands.

In response, she let out a long laugh. "You're funny, Mr.

Simpson. I like you."

Unsure if I was free of the minefield that was Seven Banderas, I kept my response brief. "Thanks."

She laughed again as she placed another Irish whiskey and water in front of me. "And smart, too. A man who knows when brevity is a virtue."

Since she was smiling, I decided to try my luck at saying something that involved more than one syllable. "I thought silence was a virtue."

"That, too. Though, my bar, my rules, so brevity gets virtue classification."

"Your bar?"

"Yes. If Pops had his way, we'd have never built this. I convinced him to let me oversee the project. He agreed on the condition that I take responsibility for it."

"Seems to be working out." Unless it was raining, Seven's bar always had customers keeping the stools warm. And that didn't include Callie, the cat who'd adopted the bar as her home a few years ago. The calico feline even had her own cat bed next to the bar's ice maker, courtesy of Seven.

Callie was the reason the Riptide wasn't a client. The establishment didn't need critter control. She was an accomplished mouser.

"It is. And as to your question about the parking lot, when Pops bought the place it was paved. Looked real nice. The parking spaces marked with new bright-yellow striping paint. A hurricane wrecked the whole thing beyond repair. Insurance wouldn't cover replacement, a total rip-off, so he decided to go the gravel route. It can be a pain sometimes, but it's still way less expensive than a full-blown resurfacing."

Since that night, Seven and I had remained on friendly terms. Not as close as I was with her father, but she hadn't left me fearing for my life again.

In the present, as I navigated a series of potholes that were close to attaining small lake status, I couldn't help wondering if Wendell and Seven needed to revisit their parking lot maintenance plan. I could have sworn one pothole could swallow one of those Fiat subcompacts whole. Since discretion was the better part of valor, though, I decided to keep that thought to myself.

It was a pleasant enough afternoon with endless blue sky to keep my face warm even though my spirits were down as I strode to the bar. Why ruin it with shop talk?

"Why the frown, Elmo?" Seven asked as I dropped onto my favorite stool.

"Things aren't looking good for Rambo." I told her about the arrest and hearing.

"The police chief's a smart woman. I'm in book club with her. She wouldn't arrest him without a good reason."

"Does that mean you think he did it?"

She tapped a black-painted fingernail on the bar top while she considered my question. One thing I'd learned about the woman was that she took her time answering questions she thought were good ones. Apparently, I'd succeeded on that score.

"Could he have done it? Sure, especially if he felt threatened by the whole development thing. But Rambo's OG. That's not our style. If you got a problem with someone, you hash it out over a beer or five. If that doesn't work, there's the court of public opinion. But murder? No, that's a coward's way of doing business. Especially if you're not willing to look your adversary in the eye when you're committing the act. Leaving it to an animal? No."

I took a sip of the ice water she'd gotten for me. While she hadn't answered my question, she'd freed an idea that had been lodged in the junk pile part of my brain.

"There's no way he could have done it. At least, not without an accomplice. At some point, he could have needed help moving the gator."

"And by that I assume you don't think he put it on a leash and walked it into Mr. Cohen's condo." One corner of her mouth curved up for a moment. It was her tell that she was joking.

"I'd pay good money to see Rambo do that. But, no, I don't think he did. He doesn't have the personality to take on something that required as much planning at this did."

"I agree." She shook her head. "Rambo didn't do it. To be honest, I couldn't stand Cohen. If Rambo walked up to the bar right now, I'd shake his hand and buy him a drink."

"If you don't mind me asking, why didn't you like Fran?"

"He was smug and pushy and thought he was smarter than everyone in town just because he had a law degree from some Ivy League college. I've got my master's in aeronautical engineering. I am literally a rocket scientist, but you don't see me acting all high and mighty about it."

For a second, I wanted to ask why, with a degree like

that, she was tending bar at her father's restaurant. Then I remembered it was Seven I was chatting with.

"Fair enough." I ran through my list of suspects. "Does anyone seem more likely to be a murderer than the others?"

"Dude, you're going about this the wrong way. Depending on who you ask, any of your suspects could be a murderer. Personally, I think the reverend is as trustworthy as a real-life pirate. When he's around, lock up your daughters and your cash. That's just me, though. Put your tech background to use. Instead of wasting time thinking about human emotion, follow the observable evidence."

"That's the problem. Claudine could say her conversation never mentioned murder. So far, the only thing I have is the pin I found. I think it's The Vampire's, but I haven't confirmed that yet."

She closed her eyes as she shook her head. "Tell you what I'm going to do. I don't have time or energy to lead you around like a tour guide. But since Pops likes you, here's a suggestion. Go talk to Big Baby. If anyone's got the skinny on The Vampire, it's them."

"Seriously? I heard that place is scary." It wasn't that I was afraid of Big Baby, the unforgettable soul who everyone in the Springs knew preferred to use gender-neutral pronouns, or didn't like them. It was that the recycling station they owned gave me the creeps. In fact, the term *junkyard* seemed to be a whole lot more accurate for a name.

Seven put up her hands, as if in surrender. "Hey, if you're too chicken or too lazy to do the work, far be it from me to try to force you into something. Just don't come crying to me if Rambo finds out your commitment to his cause wasn't as strong as you claimed."

"I'm not a chicken. I just don't want to step on a rusty piece of metal and get lockjaw or something like that."

"Wear work boots, then." Her eyes went wide. "Besides, think of the rodents that are living there. You could make a fortune off Big Baby."

"That's a good point." It would be a mistake if I chose to leave stones unturned.

I'd never paid a visit to Gulf Coast Reuse & Recycling. My animal removal business was motivated by a desire for something helpful to do rather than a need to make a bunch of money for my retirement years. Because of that, I didn't aggressively seek out new clients. I'd steered clear of the business run by Paradise Springs' top junk dealer because it was off the beaten path.

It was high time to correct that oversight.

"No time like the present, I guess." I tossed a twenty on the counter as I tipped my hat to her. "As always, it's been an experience."

"Anytime. Be sure to stop by soon. I'll keep my ears open for anything helpful."

"Ears and eyes both, if you don't mind." After all, I was going to need all the help I could get to prove Rambo's innocence.

CHAPTER THIRTEEN

B ACK IN MY truck, I pulled together some promotional materials I always kept on hand while the air condition-ing cooled the cabin. Even in February, parking one's wheels outdoors on a sunny day could lead to an environment inside that was as hot as Venus.

The stories about conditions getting hot enough to fry an egg on a sidewalk? I thought they were tall tales and nothing more until one sauna-like July afternoon. The humidity was thick enough you could practically drink it. Under a current-ly cloudless sky, the temperature hovered in the triple digits. While we waited for a thunderstorm on the horizon to arrive, I watched Goob do it on a dare. Then he ate the fried egg with a slice of sourdough bread and a lot of tabasco sauce. Nic recorded the whole thing on her phone and posted it on Instagram for posterity.

It was peak Paradise Springs.

I'd take the momentary inconvenience of a hot truck in-terior as it cooled off over the seeming hours spent shivering while the heater kicked in during the Midwest winters of my younger days. Any day of the week.

A short time later, I arrived at a three-way intersection east of town with a rusty signpost on one side and a bog on the other. The traffic sign on the post read TRIPLE R BOULEVARD. It looked to be something created with the belief that oversize blue lettering on a field of neon orange was an improvement over the staid green and white color scheme commonly found in street signs across America. An arrow as big as a six-year-old child, also in blue and orange, was affixed to the post right below the sign. It pointed to the right, thus confirming that Triple R Boulevard, as identified on the street sign, was to my right. As if the bog to my left hadn't made things clear enough.

Despite being designated a boulevard, the thoroughfare was not much more than a weed-choked pathway wide enough for one lane of traffic. The utility poles that ran alongside the lane gave me some comfort that at least I wasn't driving into an uninhabited swamp and was destined be swallowed up by a bog monster any moment now.

That's what I chose to believe.

After a hundred yards or so, and twice that many rib-rattling bumps, Triple R Boulevard widened and veered to the left. The road actually smoothed out—not much, but at that point I wasn't going to complain—and led to an ornate wrought iron gate. An arched sign above the gate spelled out PARADISE SPRINGS REUSE & RECYCLE in Old English–style script.

In blue and neon orange.

The impressiveness of the gate was diminished by the fact the facility was surrounded by eight-foot-high solid aluminum fence panels. At least the dull gray panels weren't topped with barbed wire. Instead, decorative owls were stationed along the top every ten feet or so.

"I don't think we're in Kansas anymore, Elmo," I said as I rolled through the open gate.

A cinderblock shed with a tin roof off to my left drew my attention. The structure's banana-yellow paint job made it impossible to miss, so I piloted the truck toward it. The brakes let out a little squeak when I came to a stop. A sign my trusty vehicle didn't care for the abuse I'd just subjected it to.

The noise the truck made must have caught the attention of the proprietor, because the largest, widest person I had ever laid eyes on emerged from the shed. Dressed in a purple satin track suit, they were seven feet tall if they were an inch, and as wide as two of me. This person made Rambo look small. With a shiny, bald head and dark sunglasses, they evoked images of Buddha spinning records at a hip-hop dance party.

They took a few steps toward me, smiled, and saluted. It was time to meet Big Baby live and in person.

I opened the truck's door and froze. I didn't know the individual's real name. As panic overcame me, I tried to recall if anyone had ever mentioned it. And drew a blank.

This was going to go well. Here I was, about to make a business pitch while asking about a murder suspect and I didn't even know what to call them. Holy smokes, sometimes I was such a doofus.

Well, it was too late now. I approached with a smile and extended my hand.

"Elmo Simpson, owner of Elmo's Critter Removal.

Thought I'd stop by to say hi, if you have a minute."

"Mr. Simpson, your reputation precedes you." My hand disappeared in theirs as they gave me a hearty shake that almost pulled my shoulder out of its socket.

"Big Baby, at your service. Welcome to my humble establishment." He stepped back, opened his arms wide, and bowed at the waist. Then he put one of his giant paws on my shoulder and guided me toward the shed.

"People don't cross my threshold by happenstance. They come here to discuss business. And so we shall."

The interior of the shed was as different from the outside as Oscar was different from one of Rambo's gators. The walls were drywall and painted a shade that reminded me of a chai latte. White pine planks, not store-bought laminate flooring, peeked out from under a gorgeous area rug in green, purple, and gold colors that called to mind Mardi Gras. Above our heads, a ceiling fan with blades that looked like palm leaves rotated at a languid pace.

"Nice office." I eased into a rattan armchair. "Love the rug."

"Thank you. Some people have said it really pulls the room together." We shared a laugh at the reference to the movie *The Big Lebowski* while they poured iced water into two tumblers from a glass carafe.

I took a drink while I sized up the person across from me. They'd seated themselves behind the largest desk I'd ever seen. Retro-style reading lamps on two corners of the desk provided ample light to the immediate area but left the rest of the room in relative darkness, thanks to a complete lack of windows. The light fixture in the ceiling fan offered modest illumination, at best.

There was no laptop or other digital device to be seen. It made me wonder if the abacus on a shelf behind Big Baby was for decorative or everyday use.

"What can I do for you, Mr. Simpson?" They withdrew a fountain pen from a drawer. Not a typical ballpoint. I bought that kind by the dozen at Target. This was a real live fountain pen with the fancy tip and everything.

"I wanted to talk to you about my rodent removal service, uh…"

"Please. It's Big Baby, nothing more, nothing less. Or *they/them* if you wish to refer to me in the third person." They arched an eyebrow, as if challenging me to call them by something other than their preferred moniker.

"All righty, then, Big Baby. It looks like you've got a large piece of property here. I'd be happy to conduct an inspection free of charge to see if you have any critter issues."

They took a quick look at the information packet I handed over.

"Far be it from me to be one to look a gift horse in the mouth, but I have a clowder of cats domiciled on the property. They quite enjoy hunting vermin, and I enjoy providing them a safe place to live. A rather symbiotic relationship we have, don't you think?"

"I can't argue with that. I have a cat of my own. In his prime, he was quite the mouser. I was thinking an inspection might show evidence of animals that the kitties can't get to, though, like burrowing rodents or bats."

"Well played, Mr. Simpson. I'll make you an offer." They leaned forward, their bulk casting a shadow across the desk. "I'll agree to your inspection proposal if you tell me why you're really here."

This wasn't a game of poker. Bluffing wouldn't accomplish anything besides wasting our time. Sure, new business was always welcome, but there were other important issues at play.

"I'm trying to figure out who's responsible for Fran Cohen's murder. I don't think Rambo Quigley did it. I've been told you might have information that could help my investigation."

Big Baby let out a long, loud laugh that sounded like a battalion of cannons being fired. It filled every corner of the room. It didn't seem menacing, though, so I chose to take that as a positive sign.

"An Indiana transplant to our fair shores has taken up the quest to uncover the truth behind Mr. Cohen's untimely, and dare I say gruesome, death. How splendidly quixotic."

"Maybe. But I made a promise. I work really hard at being a man of my word."

"Smashing." Big Baby rubbed their hands together and grinned. "I'll play along. What do you want to know?"

"It's about one of your regular customers, Abraham Longfellow. A lot of people know him as The Vampire."

They nodded. "I know him. It was a rather unkind prank to give the poor soul such a ghoulish nickname. I beseech you, do not use that pejorative term in my presence again. It's unkind and unbefitting of a businessman such as yourself."

Big Baby's cheeks had gotten redder with each word. They stood out against the rest of their pale complexion like a sunburn. Message received. No more use of nicknames.

"My apologies. It won't happen again. I understand Mr. Longfellow sells you aluminum."

"Indeed, he does. That and a lesser amount of steel in the form of cans and other food containers. He sojourns here on a regular basis. I make my purchases based on the weight of what he brings me. Then, I let the material accumulate until I resell it in bulk to a local smelter. Capitalism at its finest."

"It's great to see all that metal doesn't go to waste." I figured it couldn't hurt to butter up the guy and his operation.

"Indeed. Mr. Longfellow provides a valuable, if unsung, service. Without him, those valuable resources would go to waste in a landfill." They got to their feet. "Come with me."

I followed them back outside. We went past a long row of rusting automobiles from the sixties and seventies until we arrived at an intersection, where they stopped to toss a morsel formerly hidden in his pocket to one of the resident cats.

"It's important to keep the locals happy." They chuckled, their whole massive body jiggling at the little joke.

To my left, broken-down refrigerators lay on their sides, stacked five high. To my right, countless steel and wooden doors leaned against each other, protected from the elements by an aluminum overhang.

After a quick glance over my shoulder confirmed the truck was still where I left it, I cleared my throat. "You've got a lot of interesting things here. Are we going anyplace in particular?"

"Never fear, my friend. We're almost there." They flicked two bejeweled fingers on their right hand forward.

Another hundred yards farther along, we reached two dumpsters similar to the kind found at a construction site. They gestured for me to look inside them. One was half-filled with aluminum cans. The other held a smaller amount of steel containers.

"This is what Mr. Longfellow brings me. It's an arrangement that's totally aboveboard, I assure you. I trust this satisfies your curiosity?"

Not by a longshot. I showed them the pin I'd found. "Do you recall seeing him wearing this?"

"It looks vaguely familiar." Their eyebrows creased. "Why?"

"I found this near Fran Cohen's condo a few days after he was murdered. Do you know if Mr. Longfellow had any hard feelings toward the man?"

"Hard enough to commit murder? Highly unlikely. Though, I do know he expressed concerns about one of Mr. Cohen's latest gambits."

Now we were getting somewhere. "Did he elaborate?"

"It seems that Mr. Cohen wanted Paradise Springs to adopt a municipal recycling program. A corporate vendor he aligned with promised to offer every household a recycling bin free of charge and pick up said materials every other week. For a nominal fee, of course."

I traced a circle pattern in the dirt with my boot as I puzzled out possible motives. They all seemed too far-fetched. Then again, if someone had told me fifteen years ago that I'd be living in a trailer with an old tomcat, removing critters from homes and businesses, I would have said you'd been smoking too much weed.

"Hear me out on this." I put up my hands. It wouldn't help to make an enemy out of an information source. Or a potential client. "The Vamp... Mr. Longfellow makes a steady, if not sizable, income by recycling aluminum and steel picked from the trash. Things are going along just fine until Fran Cohen makes a proposal to the city that would effectively cut off that income stream. Feeling threatened, Mr. Longfellow retaliates and murders Mr. Cohen, thereby ending the problem before it starts."

Big Baby withdrew a peppermint from another pocket and slipped it into their mouth. They drew their own circle in the dirt with their sandal. After a minute or so, they pointed a finger at me.

"You should write mysteries instead of investigating them." They laughed. "I'll grant you, at its core, the scenario has merit. However, I must ask, if what you've proposed is true, how did Mr. Longfellow manage to entice an alligator much larger than he to enter Mr. Cohen's abode?"

"I don't know." It was true. And until I got a handle on that, answers would continue to elude me. "Any chance you helped him?"

Big Baby laughed and patted me on the shoulder. "Well played, Mr. Simpson. Alas, for purposes of your theory, I was on a series of conference calls the night in question."

"Didn't think so, but I figured it couldn't hurt to ask."

"Indeed. Had you not, I would have found your investigatory skills lacking. You know which path your quest takes you, then. Yes?" They rested their hands on their belly and we walked back to the shed.

"I should pay Mr. Longfellow a visit to get his side of things."

With a slap to my back that almost knocked my breath out of me, Big Baby let out yet another a long laugh.

"In the words of the inimitable Theodore Roosevelt, bully for you. Despite what I've heard, I can tell you're no burned-out slacker, Mr. Simpson. I wish you a successful quest. Feel free to conduct your assessment of my humble facility at your leisure. I am needed on a call shortly."

With their hands back on their belly, we strolled into their office. They had an aura that made me think we'd just chatted about cat videos instead of murder. When we reached the threshold, I cleared my throat.

"Big Baby, can you think of anyone who'd want Fran Cohen dead?"

"I can." They smiled. "Alas, for you, that figure exceeds the number of my fingers and toes combined. *Au revoir*, Mr. Simpson. And now that you've taken on the mantle of private investigator, do be sure to check behind you from time to time. You never know when someone may be sneaking up on you."

CHAPTER FOURTEEN

B IG BABY'S CRYPTIC warning propelled me out of there and on my way home as fast at the roads of Paradise Springs would allow. By the time I shifted into Park, the goosebumps that broke out mere seconds after the warning had subsided. My hands weren't trembling any longer, either.

I had to face facts. Reality was clear. I was in over my head. Though, to be fair, I'd never taken on a murder investigation before, so I think I was owed a bit of a learning curve. Regardless, I was going to have to learn fast. But first, I had priorities to attend to.

"Hey, buddy." I spent a few minutes on the patio scratching Oscar's gray ears, then under his tan chin. While I did so, he closed his eyes and started purring. The low rumbling sound, so reminiscent of the push lawnmower from my days growing up, made me smile.

Other people could say whatever they wanted. Chilling with my cat relaxed me way more effectively than anything else on Earth. And never left me with a hangover. Just clumps of cat hair that had to be vacuumed up on a regular basis.

And the sporadic hairball. But I preferred not to think

about those.

When Oscar had been sufficiently showered with attention, he stretched, went to the front door, and gave me an expectant look.

"I see. Dinner time it is."

I followed him to the kitchen, doing my best to whistle a Jimmy Buffett tune while I prepared his dinner. The fact that he pinned his ears back while I readied his meal had more to do with my lousy whistling skills than my feline-centric culinary skills. The only instrument I was even remotely adept at was the ukulele.

A fact Oscar, in his unique way, never hesitated to remind me.

Once my furry overlord had been attended to, I ate a quick dinner of week-old leftover sausage gumbo and took a shower. It was critical to be presentable for my regular Thursday evening chat with my mom.

Thanks to video-chat technology, my dear mother had decided she wanted to see her son while she talked with him. The first time we did that, I'd just come in from a long day dealing with a chipmunk infestation. Mom had been horrified at the disheveled, dirt-covered appearance I presented. She made it crystal clear that she missed the style of dress I employed back in my IT days.

Lesson learned. Since that night, I hadn't clicked the icon to join the call with her until my hair was combed, my teeth were brushed, and my shirt was clean. And pressed. Wrinkles horrified her more than Frankenstein's monster scared those poor townsfolk.

"Elmo dear, how are you? You look good." Mom's smile went from ear to ear, her brown eyes sparkling. Evidently, I'd cleaned myself up sufficiently.

I thanked her for the compliment and assured her I was taking care of myself. Don't get me wrong. I love my mom, Alana Simpson, with all my heart and soul. The sacrifices she made raising me after Dad died were too numerous to count. She managed to keep me out of trouble and on the honor roll while she worked her way toward a nursing degree.

She had often said she'd never been prouder of me than when I got my degree in computer science. That moment was eclipsed only when the tech firm I started with college buddies went public and I became richer beyond my dreams overnight.

Mom rushed to be by my side the day I had my break-down, too. She put her nursing skills to good use by taking care of me until I was back on my feet. And didn't bat an eye when I told her I sold my stock in the company and was putting the tech world in my rearview mirror.

I laughed along with her when she joked about how much she appreciated that I paid off the mortgage on the house I bought for her before I quit my job to become a layabout. She wasn't wrong, after all.

In the ensuing years, Mom had remained right by my side. Even when she thought I'd lost my mind once and for all when I sold my stuff, packed up the truck, and hit the road. We eventually reached an accord over that decision. It took her a while, but she came to understand that I was happy with my new life.

And had no intention of returning to the old one.

Now, for the first time since I'd set down roots here in the Panhandle a decade or so ago, I wanted her advice.

"I could use your opinion about something."

"Oh good. You haven't asked for that in ages. What's on your mind?" She gave me her half smile. It was the expression that let me know she was pleased I still needed her, but was reserving judgment until she heard what, exactly, I needed.

I licked my lips. During my shower, I'd debated leading up to my bombshell of a question with some small talk. I decided against that approach. She wouldn't like it. I was her only child. Better to get it over with.

Okay, Elmo, here goes nothing.

"There's been a murder here in town. The cops think a buddy of mine did it. He says he's innocent and asked me to investigate for him. What do you think?"

She stared at me with a blank face for so long, I thought the screen had frozen. Then she blinked once, opened her mouth, closed it, and blinked again.

"What do I think? I think it would be easier if you asked for suggestions on what show you should watch next on Netflix."

She had me there. So, I asked her.

"Either *Ozark* or *Longmire*. Both are totally bingeable."

"Great. I'll check 'em out." It wasn't worth the fuss to tell her I didn't have a Netflix subscription. "Now, about the other thing."

"I'm going to play along and tell myself you're not serious about this—"

"I am."

"Because it would leave me awake at night to think you'd willingly get yourself sucked into something so foolish. And dangerous. If anything happened to you, I'll never have a chance to have grandchildren."

The grandkids thing was a new move on the parental guilt-trip board. I had to tip my hat to her, she knew how to remind me she wanted grandkids. I'd made a promise, though, so it was time to play a little defense.

"Who said anything about being dangerous?"

"You did." She shook her head. "Murder, by its very definition, is a violent act. All you have to do is see how many true crime podcasts there are. I can barely keep up with them all. If someone was willing to take someone else's life, they won't hesitate to make sure you don't find out who they are. After the first murder, it gets easier, you know."

"When did you start listening to podcasts?" My mom was almost as adept with technology as I was. Still, it took me a minute to wrap my head around the idea that she listened to podcasts.

"When *My Favorite Murder* came out. I live alone. It pays to be prepared without anyone around to look out for me." She sniffed and even stuck her bottom lip out a bit in case I missed the message.

"You know, sometimes you can be as subtle as the drunk college boys who come down here during spring break."

"Because I have to make sure my point gets through that stubborn head of yours, which could use a haircut, by the way. Did you know I was in labor for twenty-seven hours with you?"

"I may have heard a rumor." Whenever Mom was annoyed with me, she reminded me of that fact. Which meant she reminded me of that fact two or three times a year. Minimum.

Her mention of true crime podcasts gave me an opening. I made my move before it closed.

"The reason I brought this up is because of your love of all things mystery and true crime. I figure if anyone could give me some unbiased, analytical insight, it'd be you." A little sucking up never hurt when dealing with Mom.

"Well, that's true. If I couldn't stop you from your Bohemian lifestyle, I suppose there's no way I can stop you from doing this."

"I knew I could count on you, Mom." I dove right into the case details before she had a chance to reconsider. The more I told her, the wider her eyes got. By the time I stopped, she was leaning in so close, she could have fallen right through the screen.

"Well, this one's easy." She pulled one of those elastic hair things from her pocket and used it to pull her long black hair into a ponytail. I couldn't escape the feeling that she was milking the scene.

"Your friend, Jumbo—"

"Rambo."

"Jumbo, Rambo-whatever. He didn't do it."

"What makes you say that?" It took all my self-control to keep my voice in a conversational tone. She was dragging things out to punish me for taking on what she saw as a fool's errand. I wasn't going to give her the satisfaction of seeing my frustration.

"From what you've said about this Mr. Cohen, he must have had his tentacles in a lot of things. When people like that get murdered, it's not a crime of passion like a lover's quarrel, say between you and your lady friend Nicola. It's not a power play, either, like a hostile corporate takeover. A case like this, it was about one thing—money."

My mom knew her true crime. All you had to do was ask her and she'd tell you. Whether her assessment of my situation was accurate was another matter. There was logic to it, though. Even without knowing Fran Cohen, she sensed he was the kind of person who lived by the Randy Newman song from my childhood, "It's Money That Matters."

"That means I should do what any private eye with half a brain would do. Follow the money."

"That's my boy." She put her palm up to the screen so we could exchange a virtual high five.

With the discussion of the ugly business of murder complete, we turned the conversation to more pleasant things. She'd met a guy through a friend at a concert featuring classic rock acts Blues Traveler and Big Head Todd and the Monsters. She liked him and was looking forward to having coffee with him some time over the weekend.

I told her I hoped she had a nice time. I meant it, too. When I was growing up, she went out on a few dates, but it was never anything serious. The men she met either wanted to jump in the sack right away or wanted someone to do the cooking and cleaning for them. She told people that she was more interested in making sure I was safe than she was in meeting a new partner. It was a nice way of saying her dates failed to meet her expectations, which was totally reasonable.

It wasn't that she didn't have many opportunities to date, either. She was only twenty-seven when Dad died, but going out wasn't a priority. Later on, she told me she was comfortable with who she was and didn't see the need to fill a hole that wasn't there.

Things had changed the last few years. After a close friend died of cancer, she started seeking out a guy to have in her life. I was pleased with the development. I loved my mom and wanted her to be happy.

I wasn't convinced that a dude she met at a concert featuring bands that hadn't had a hit in decades was the way to go, though.

On the other side of the coin, she had a solid argument that investigating a murder wasn't the most effective way of making friends and influencing people. Oh well, to each their own.

I brought the call to an end with my usual promise that I'd see her next Thursday night, same Bat-time, same Bat-channel.

With a beer in one hand and a bag of tortilla chips in the other, I headed back outside. The night sky above me was filled with tiny pinpricks of light. There were constellations up there that Nic could rattle off in half a second. Me? I was satisfied once I spotted the Big Dipper and could tell the difference between a waxing crescent and a waning crescent moon. Just seeing those heavenly bodies, so far away yet seeming so close, made me happy. That feeling helped me think.

And, boy oh boy, did I have a lot to think about.

Like, if The Vampire didn't murder Fran, what was his pin doing so close to the crime? Or was Fran really going to follow through on his threat to Claudine to reveal the alleged case of food poisoning? There was money involved with that question. No doubt about it.

What about the reverend? Did he and the departed Mr. Cohen get into an argument over reparations stemming from the fight and lose his cool? That was more of a crime of passion, not one that would have involved a lot of planning.

Then another thought occurred to me. That gator had plenty of time to finish off Fran. Why hadn't Minerva noticed anything before she called me? And last, but not least, was there anyone else out there whom Fran was targeting? If so, who?

I drained my beer and got another one. Over the course of the day, I'd learned a lot. The problem was, the way things were shaping up, there was a whole lot more I didn't know than what I did. And the colder the trail got, the greater the odds became that Rambo was going to be convicted of murdering Fran.

That was something I couldn't let happen.

CHAPTER FIFTEEN

THE ALARM CLOCK went off earlier than my liking the following morning. Which was the case most mornings, to be honest. In a perfect world, I'd work from ten until two in the afternoon. I was too young for a schedule like that, though. Maybe in another twenty years.

As I rolled out of bed, I was met with Oscar's inscrutable stare. He sat in the doorway, all prim and proper with his front legs together like a ballerina, and looked at me. Without blinking. I stared back, unwilling to admit defeat to a creature that lacked opposable thumbs. The seconds ticked by until what seemed days. He looked away first.

"Ha," I said in a raised voice, immediately followed a full-body cringe, as the memories from the previous day came to me. "Okay, you're right. I have no business investigating a murder. Doesn't matter. It's too late to turn back now. Rambo needs me."

Apparently uninterested in my rationalizations, he turned and walked away. No doubt straight to his food bowl in anticipation of the fish breakfast I'd promised him. It wasn't lost on me that his attitude reminded me way too much of Nic after I'd done something inadvisable. Like the time I decided to teach myself to windsurf and almost drowned.

A pot of coffee truck-stop style, black with nothing else, and a bowl of oatmeal later, I was as good as new. After giving Oscar some chunked-up grouper. I tried to be a man of my word, after all.

Fridays were billing days, so I spent a few hours in front of the computer sending, then paying, invoices. I always did the sending first. Starting the day doing something that resembled making money made me smile. And minimized the frown when I got to the paying part.

When I was finished, I tossed a treat to Oscar. "High fives all around, buddy. Another week in the black. Not too shabby."

The fact that he came over to rub against my leg after snarfing down the treat was a sign he agreed with my assessment. Not that he was angling for more treats. That's what I told myself.

Whatever gets you through the night. Am I right?

My phone rang while I was stuffing envelopes with paper invoices. The number wasn't familiar. Hopefully that meant it was a potential new customer.

"Simpson's Critter Removal. This is Elmo."

"Ah, Mr. Simpson. Greetings and salutations to you, sir. May I inquire as to your currently availability?"

The voice, and choice of grammar, was unmistakable. My heart began pounding against my chest. Maybe yesterday's sales pitch was actually going to pay off.

"I don't have anything on the calendar, Big Baby. How can I help you?"

"There is someone here with whom you would like to speak, I believe. If you can arrive before the top of the hour, I can arrange an assignation."

It was just past nine thirty. The recycling center was twenty minutes away. I'd have to forego a shave, but a shower was a must if I was meeting someone. I wasn't sure what the word *assignation* meant. I'd have to figure it out on the way.

I'd never been to Paradise Springs Reuse and Recycle before yesterday. Now, as I drove through the gates for a second time within twenty-four hours, I sat a little taller in the driver's seat. I'd managed to avoid the worst of the massive potholes that had almost devoured me the day before.

The sense of victory was short-lived.

A vehicle emerged from the conglomeration of Big Baby's inventory near the back of the lot. It was Longfellow's car. The 1964 Lincoln Continental sported a jet-black finish that was so clean, it could have just rolled off the showroom floor and that was even with the awful conditions of the road leading here. The chrome front grille was polished to such a shine I could see my reflection in it from twenty yards away.

The vehicle rolled to a stop a few yards away from me. The engine's low purr cut off and a moment later the driver's door swung open. The Vampire emerged from the car with a fluid motion I'd never be able to achieve while exiting an automobile.

I'll admit it. I was a little jealous of the gracefulness on display.

I'd never actually seen the man close up. He wore a suit that fit him so well it must have been custom tailored. All black, by the way. His shirt and tie were black, as well. The only color in the ensemble came from a royal blue pocket square and his two-toned wingtip shoes, which featured the same royal blue on the vamp parts of his shoes. That and a royal blue feather in the band of his wide-brimmed fedora. Once again, black.

The fact that part of his footwear was called *vamp* was not lost on me.

He removed his hat to reveal salt-and-pepper hair parted on the side that fell across his eyebrows, reminding me of photos of rock legend Keith Richards in his younger days.

The thing that answered any lingering questions about how Mr. Longfellow got his nickname was his pale white skin tone. It was like he hadn't seen the sun in years, or centuries, if you believed the stories.

I didn't honestly believe them. Well, maybe I did. In the Springs, one could never be too certain about anything.

Big Baby stepped out of their office and spread their arms wide.

"Welcome, gentlemen, to my humble office. I do hope you don't object to this little tête-à-tête I've taken the liberty to arrange. Please make yourselves comfortable."

Our host introduced us, then poured each of us a tall glass of ice water.

"What is the meaning of this, BB? You know how being out in the sun isn't good for me," The Vampire said.

"Which is why I brought you both inside." Big Baby gestured toward me. "Mr. Simpson is looking into the horrific murder of Fran Cohen. Yesterday, he came to me seeking to ascertain whether you had any involvement in the matter. I surmised since you were bringing me your business this fine morning, I would bring the mountain to Muhammad, as it were."

"What makes you think that?" The Vampire turned his whole body toward me. He stared at me with cold eyes so dark brown, they seemed to be black.

The question piqued my interest. Or the fact that the question didn't come with a denial is what piqued the interest. I was in luck. The pin I'd found was in the truck. I dashed out and returned a moment later.

"Because I found this near the crime scene." I held it out so both Big Baby and The Vampire could see it. "I have reason to believe your recycling route goes right past Mr. Cohen's condo. And that you were opposed to his plan for the city to start a curbside recycling program."

My two-part answer worked better than I'd hoped. First, it left him speechless for a moment. It also gave him enough to think about that he didn't come right back at me by asking how I knew about his route.

"A pin? Really? You think I murdered someone because you found that trinket. BB, I thought we were buddies. Instead, you've lured me in here to be subjected to this silliness. Aren't you better than that?"

Big Baby raised an eyebrow. "Steady on, my friend. Rather than behaving like a toddler unable to control their emotions, I suggest you respond to the allegations."

"They're not allegations." I'd done some homework after my chat with Mom. The Vampire had shown up at a city council meeting to voice his opposition to Cohen's proposition. "It's a matter of public record. Unless you want to call the report in the *Paradise Springs Palladium* a lie."

"That rag." The Vampire scrunched his hawklike nose as if he'd caught a strong whiff of dead skunk. "It's nothing more than a mouthpiece for business interests like Cohen."

"You don't deny it, then." I had him. It was a moment that would have made Kate Beckett from *Castle* proud.

"I do not." He lowered his gaze, his focus apparently on a ruby-encrusted ring he was spinning on his pinkie finger. Then he sighed. "That does not make me a murderer."

I mentally put a check mark into the Motive column. With the pin in my hand, I skipped over Means and went straight to Opportunity.

"What about this, Mr. Longfellow?" I held the pin out to him again. "Big Baby seems to think it belongs to you. Are they mistaken?"

He licked his crimson lips. His gaze darted back and forth between the mountain of a human behind the desk and the small, round collectible. That told me all I needed to know.

"No. How do you know that specific bauble belongs to me? Perhaps I have one exactly like at home and you're attempting to create evidence to fit a certain narrative."

"What do you mean?" His response threw me. Maybe I wasn't quite up to Kate Beckett level yet. Especially since I'd served up a softball of a question that was open-ended. He could answer it pretty much any way he wanted.

"I know what people—stupid people—in the area think about me. I've dealt with it all my life. Do you know I have a medical condition, Mr. Simpson?"

I shook my head. It wasn't tough to infer I was among the *stupid people* Longfellow mentioned, so I kept my mouth shut. It was like signing up a new customer. If I pushed too hard, he'd shut down and I wouldn't get any more out of him. Just like getting too aggressive in order to close a service agreement always blew up in my face.

"It's called porphyria, or more specifically *porphyria cutanea tarda*. Those with my condition commonly refer to it as PCT. Have you ever heard of it?"

Once again, I remained silent and shook my head. Maybe this was a situation where he, like a criminal mastermind, was about to go off on a monologue. If he kept talking, he might incriminate himself. It would make for an easy way to wrap up the case.

"Of course you haven't." He took a drink of his water. His hands were covered by form-fitting gloves, similar to calfskin driving gloves. "It's an uncommon genetic affliction. In my case, the most obvious symptom is an extreme sensitivity to sunlight. If I'm exposed to the sun for even a short period of time, my skin starts to blister, especially my face and hands. Remind you of a specific creature from folklore?"

"It does." It would be foolish to deny it. And insulting. "Can't you get any treatment?"

"Nobody wants to help the awful vampire. I'm the Creature of the Night." He leaned back and let out a long laugh.

The bitterness in it couldn't be missed. "There is no cure. The best thing those like me can do is tailor our lifestyles to make the best of the situation. Thus, the hat and gloves. If it wasn't cloudy this morning, I would have waited until after sundown to make my recycling delivery."

"Wow. I'm sorry. I didn't know."

"Perhaps," Big Baby said, with a gentleness, belying their massive size, "you could have asked someone. Like that fellow on the television says, *Be curious, not judgmental.*"

"You're right." I sat up straighter and cleared my throat. "I should know better. A lot of people prejudged me when I first came to the area. I didn't like it. I promise to do better."

They both gave me a quick nod. Evidently, my apology had been accepted.

Now that I knew about Longfellow's condition, a laundry list of questions came to mind. Here was a chance to put Big Baby's words to my advantage.

"If you'll allow my curiosity, it seems like you've chosen to lean into the rumors about you, what with the black car, which is gorgeous by the way, the clothing, only going out at night. Right now being an obvious exception. Why not try to get the truth out?"

"Isn't it obvious?" He gave me a long look. "People choose to believe what they want, regardless of what the truth is. I learned from an early age, there are certain benefits to serving as the Friendly Neighborhood Vampire. Especially in this locale."

"Ha, ha." Big Baby slapped a meaty paw on the desktop. "The most astute of observations, my friend. We should formulate a campaign for a new community slogan. Paradise

Springs, Where the Uncommon isn't Uncommon, or Welcome to Paradise Springs, Where the Extraordinary is Anything But."

"Those sound great." I rushed the words out before things could get even further off track. The Vampire had leveraged his alleged medical condition to avoid answering my question. "I'd like to circle back to my earlier question, Mr. Longfellow. Does this pin belong to you?"

"I'm afraid it's impossible for me to say." He removed his gloves and applied some lotion from a tube he'd taken from one of his blazer pockets to his hands and neck. "You say you found it near the crime scene. How can I be certain this isn't a ruse of some sort? Without some sort of official chain of custody to establish the provenance of the item, I'm afraid I can't help you."

"In that case, I believe our business here is concluded." Big Baby rose to their feet. "Thank you for your prompt response to my summons, Mr. Simpson. Please call on me in one week. At that time, I shall have a response to the proposal you submitted. Now, Mr. Longfellow and I have a transaction to complete."

Without giving me a second look, Big Baby and The Vampire left me. By the time I recovered from the abrupt dismissal and dashed outside, they were out of sight.

I scratched my chin as I mulled over my next move. It seemed as though Big Baby and The Vampire thought they were finished with me.

They couldn't be more wrong. I knew it down to my core that the pin belonged to the mysterious Mr. Longfellow.

All I needed was a way to prove it. Then I'd have him.

CHAPTER SIXTEEN

I SPENT THE afternoon responding to calls asking for emergency animal removals. They weren't exactly emergency situations in my book, but when someone is willing to pay crisis rates for me to remove a harmless blue-striped garter snake so they can proceed with their party, who am I to argue?

The upside to the busy afternoon was that it left me with little time to think about the case. When an animal finds a spot it likes, it prefers not to be moved. Especially when the change of scenery is forced by a human who is often accompanied by a stick and/or a metal cage.

And what's a critter to do when it's cornered? Bite the rude human disturbing it. Even an adorable little chipmunk will try to take a chunk out of you if it feels threatened. That's why I always wear gloves and long sleeves and give the task at hand 100 percent of my focus.

I am a literal example of the once-bitten, twice-shy cliché.

Once I finished stashing the removed critters in their temporary cages back at my place, my mind went straight back to the case. I didn't want to think about anything else for the rest of the day, so I dialed the one person on the planet who could make me forget about everything but her with a simple shrug of her shoulder.

"Five thirty's a little early for a booty call, Elmo. What do you want?" Nic asked after we said hi.

"Can't a guy call a woman who's his friend but not his girlfriend without it automatically being about sex?" I'd drunk-dialed Nic once, four years ago. The conversation hadn't gone well. And cost me a round of drinks at the Riptide when she told everyone the story.

"It's possible, I suppose, so I'll give you the benefit of the doubt. So, to that end, to what do I owe the pleasure of your call?"

"I'm in the mood for a nice dinner that someone else makes for me. I've got reservations at the Bayside for seven. Care to join me? I'd rather not dine alone."

"What's the catch?"

"There is none. I swear. Just you and me and the finest seafood on the Gulf Coast."

"You buying?"

"Absolutely."

"In that case, I'm in. Pick me up in an hour."

I pulled into a parking spot at the marina five minutes early. Nic and I may have been in an off-again phase of our relationship, but any minute I got to spend with her was a gift from above. Thus, the early arrival.

With butterflies flapping away in my stomach, I knocked on the door to her cabin. The nerves may have been caused by worry that I'd overdone things by getting her a small bouquet of flowers.

Or something else I preferred not to think about just then.

She opened the door and let out a low whistle. "Well, look at you. A suit jacket and everything. Not bad, Simpson."

"You're looking pretty good yourself." In fact, she looked fantastic in a little black dress that made her look like she'd just stepped off the catwalk at a New York fashion show. I handed the flowers to her. "For a lovely lady on a lovely night."

"Thank you." She batted her eyelashes at me, then with a laugh, turned and gestured for me to follow her. "You better watch out. Between the flowers and dinner, I might find myself falling for you all over again."

"I'm glad you like them." It was better to refrain from making further comment. If Nic wanted to get back together, she'd tell me. We'd talked about our relationship one night over a bottle of Puerto Rican rum and agreed that we were both too old to play games when it came to the heart.

While I'd always carry a torch for her, it was reassuring to know the lay of the land. And that land did not include us getting back together. Tonight was about a couple of friends spending some time together unwinding. Nothing more.

Well, mostly nothing more.

Normally, when I went to the Bayside, I parked in the lot across the street. It was free and the sixty-second trek to the restaurant was way better than paying to park in the restaurant's on-site lot.

The situation at hand called for a different approach. I

pulled up to the valet station and gave the attendant a salute.

"Mr. Elmo, Ms. Nicola, long time no see," he said as he facilitated Nic's exit from the truck.

"That it is, Sarge." The attendant's given name was William Harrison. Formerly a sergeant in the army, he lost the lower portion of his left leg during a fire fight in the Middle East. The limp caused by his titanium prosthetic was barely noticeable. Everyone else in town called him Billy. I called him Sarge to honor him for his service. My dad was a sergeant when he died. That connection mattered to me, but I kept it to myself. It was a subject that was a little too close to the heart for me to share.

When I exchanged my key for the parking stub, I slipped a fifty to him. "Were you working last Friday night, by chance?"

He eyed the bill, then glanced at the restaurant. "I was. Why?"

"Was the big boss here all night?" The restaurant was closed on Mondays. Unless she was out of town, Claudine was at work every other day of the week.

He ran a finger between his shirt collar and his neck. "She was, but now that you mention it, she left early."

I concealed another fifty in my palm as I shook his hand.

"Yeah." He nodded. "She left around nine and was back around eleven. Why?"

"No reason." I handed him a third fifty. "Forget I asked."

One of the advantages of providing on-site services to businesses in the area is that I get to know their floor plans as well as my own. In this case, that meant I'd been able to request a specific table at the Bayside. It was a window-side table for two overlooking the water. The nighttime view of the ocean from our vantage point was breathtaking.

It was also mere feet away from where Claudine liked to hang out when she had a free moment.

I made a point of saying hello to her on the way to our table.

She narrowed her eyes for a moment before raising her eyebrows. "Elmo, I apologize. For a moment, I didn't recognize you."

"He can be quite dashing when the occasion calls for it." Nic allowed me to pull out her chair and seat her. Normally, she thought it was old-fashioned. It was as if she was trying to score points on my behalf.

"This evening is a time for celebration, so what better way to do that than to dress up and share a meal at the finest restaurant around."

"That's very kind of you to say." Claudine actually smiled for a moment. It was a gesture normally reserved for big shot diners. "Please let me know if I may be of any assistance this evening."

She nodded to us and walked away as our server arrived. I made sure I ordered a bottle of the restaurant's finest champagne loud enough for her to hear. That would guarantee a return visit.

"Wow. You actually ordered a bottle of Dom Pérignon. What's going on? And what's with those questions you asked Billy?"

"Later. You only live once, my friend. *Eat, drink, and be merry, for tomorrow we shall die*, and all that."

Her eyes lit up. "Since you're holding out on me, then you won't whine when I order the surf 'n' turf? I missed lunch to accommodate a last-minute tour booking."

"Not tonight." To emphasize my point, when our server finished pouring the champagne, I ordered calamari for an appetizer.

"I didn't think you liked calamari."

"I don't. But you do." I lifted my champagne flute to her. "Cheers."

While Nic plowed through the appetizer like someone who hadn't eaten in a week, I enjoyed a warm dinner roll slathered in enough butter to clog my arteries. There was no doubt in my mind that Claudine, despite her disagreeable personality, knew how to produce mouth-watering food.

"Oh, my stars, I haven't had that in ages. It was so good." Nic took a long drink from her ice water. "I need to let you take me to dinner more often."

"My pleasure. Though next time it will be Riptide barbeque or pizza from Julio's."

"Works for me." She clinked her champagne glass against mine.

Sometimes it was good to leave things simple for the moment. Like a nice dinner with a friend. I had enough complicated things going on in my life, after all. To be honest, it was really only a single thing, but man, was this murder investigation complicated.

We were savoring our main courses, surf 'n' turf for Nic,

Cajun chicken fettuccine for me, when Claudine stopped by.

"I hope the dinner's been to your satisfaction." Even though she said it with a smile, there was an edge to her words. It was as if she was reminding me that the meal had been fantastic, regardless of what I might think.

"Wonderful," Nic said. "Can't wait to see the dessert menu."

"Same for me." It was time to make my move. "While you're here, Claudine, there's been a nasty rumor going around I thought I should make you aware of. You know, so you're not caught unaware if someone confronts you about it."

"Elmo, darling, in my business, rumors, especially the nasty ones, come with the territory." She didn't make any move to leave, despite her casual dismissal.

"It involves Fran Cohen. The story goes that he got food poisoning from something he ate here. Supposedly, he chose to blackmail you with a threat to go public and ruin the restaurant if you didn't pay him." I took a drink of my champagne to let the words sink in. "Anyway, wanted you to know."

Claudine's complexion went from a sun-kissed light bronze to white as the linen tablecloth as I spoke. She was a tough bird, though. After a moment, the color returned, and she let out a laugh.

That seemed way more forced than natural.

"Some of my competitors will stop at nothing to bring me down, Elmo. Even take advantage of a man's death."

"There's nothing to it, then?" I ran my fingers across my

brow to imitate wiping sweat from it.

"Of course not. The poor soul is dead. What purpose could possibly be served by dredging up, er, I mean *making up* something like that?" She messed with a button on her silk top. "Thank you for telling me, though. Enjoy the rest of your dinner. I'll make sure your server comps your dessert."

"How about that?" I straightened the collar of my dress shirt. "Free dessert."

Nic responded with stony silence and a glare that had been known to send drunken tourists to their knees begging forgiveness.

"What? You said you were looking forward to seeing the dessert menu."

"I cannot believe you've been lying to me all evening." She stabbed at an asparagus spear. "When I asked you what the catch was, you told me there wasn't one. I should have known better."

I gulped down the rest of my champagne. It was a dumb move trying to hide something from Nic and she saw right through it.

"See? There's your tell." She pointed her knife at me. "Don't bother denying it."

"Okay, you're right. I thought I'd try to arrange a chance for me to pump Claudine for info about Fran's murder. I didn't say anything to you because I didn't want you involved if it backfired."

"So you lied to me instead." She cut a piece of her steak with enough force to make me glad I was across the table from her. "As if that was supposed to make it okay."

I folded my napkin and dropped it on my plate. From the start, the gambit hadn't been without risk. I'd succeeded, yet let Nic down. Not exactly the result I'd been hoping for. Such was life.

"You're 100 percent right. I should have told you what I was up to. It wasn't fair and was an insult to your intelligence. I'm sorry."

With her arms crossed, Nic stared out the window. The waves rolled in and back out twenty times before she spoke. And that was to give her dessert order to our server. The waves rolled in and back out another fifteen times before she looked at me.

"Did you at least get the information you were looking for?"

Yes. I made a fist pump under the table. My punishment was over. Nic's curiosity about my mission had taken that spot.

"Partly." I told her about overhearing the conversation between Claudine and her assistant. "As you heard, she didn't actually deny it. I remember working with developers all the time who liked to parse their words when a project wasn't progressing as well as hoped. She gave me enough to make me think there was nothing to it, but that was all. When you combine that with the fact that she was gone for a couple of hours the night Cohen was murdered? I mean, she could have used the time she was gone to go see Fran. Use a discussion about blackmail as a cover to get inside his condo. There were no signs of forced entry—"

"Which means he must have known his murderer. He let

her in, she knocked him out somehow, and had her muscle bring in the gator. She'd probably been hiding it somewhere at her estate."

We paused long enough for our desserts to be placed in front of us. Nic had picked up on the fact that it was best for us not to be overheard.

"That was a good catch, Elmo. And how about the way she went as white as a ghost when you were talking? She must be into things neck deep."

"Agreed. The question is what things, exactly. I think it's safe to say her reaction confirms the blackmail scheme was true. That gives her motive for murder. Even though I still think a hundred grand is excessive for a single food poisoning claim."

Nic chewed on a forkful of double chocolate cake. Her eyebrows were furrowed, a sign she was deep in thought. When she was finished, she pointed her fork at me. The woman loved to use her dining utensils to emphasize a point.

"She's loaded. She could totally afford to pay someone to steal Rambo's gator and move it into Fran's place, drugging him in the process so he couldn't call for help. Maybe she did pay him the ten grand, then after stewing it over for a while, got mad and spent the remaining ninety on a hit squad to hide another secret."

"Bingo. That makes for two solid suspects now." When she asked who the other one was, I told her about my conversation with The Vampire. "He did a good job accusing me of being prejudiced against him. It put me on the defensive, so I didn't get as much out of him as I wanted to."

"You must have hit a nerve, though. I've never seen that guy except at night. And he's always super casual. Like nothing ever bothers him." She snapped her fingers. "Ask for the check. Elmo, I know what we're doing tonight."

CHAPTER SEVENTEEN

TEN MINUTES LATER, we were back in my truck heading out of town on Highway 30, the five-lane freeway that ran along the northern edge of Paradise Springs.

"Take a right at the intersection coming up." Nic was in the passenger seat, serving as navigator to a point she'd yet to disclose.

"Are you going to tell me where we're going?" I flipped on my blinker a few seconds before I took the turn. At times, it seemed like I was the only person under the age of eighty who used a turn signal around here. My Midwestern upbringing in action.

"Yes. In a quarter mile, there's a giant fork in the road. When you see it, take the left split."

I rolled my eyes but kept my mouth shut. This had to be Nic's payback for me not telling her about my sleuthing beforehand.

Until a giant metallic fork came into view.

It was the largest dining utensil I'd ever seen. I tapped the brakes, coming to a stop a few feet from the odd piece of artwork. Standing upright, with the four tines pointing toward the heavens, the sculpture was a good eight feet tall. The way it gleamed in the beams of my headlights indicated it was stainless steel or aluminum and polished to a bright finish.

"I gotta get a picture of this."

A few minutes later, Nic joined me while I was sending photos of the fork that was literally larger than life to my mom.

"I can't believe you've lived in the area for ten years and never heard of the Giant Fork in the Road." She shook her head. "I've failed you."

"Yeah, well, I guess we're even from the restaurant, then. I don't suppose there's a giant knife, spoon, and dinner plate around anywhere?"

"Afraid not." She stood beside the fork so I could take a few pics of them side by side. "This is Big Baby's first piece of public art."

"You mean the junk dealer?" I couldn't keep the high pitch of my surprised voice inside. "Of course you do. How many people are there in the world who go by Big Baby?"

She touched her index finger to the tip of her nose, then pointed at me, charades-style.

"They were an up-and-coming artist back in the day. This piece showed up out of the blue one day. They'd kept the project under wraps until people discovered it by accident."

"Wow." I let out a laugh. The levels of bizarreness that came with my adopted hometown were endless. "Did they get the owner's permission to put it here beforehand?"

"Yep. Which is why it's convenient you decided to stop. This piece of artwork stands on the edge of property owned by Abe Longfellow."

"The Vampire?" My voice had gone up yet another octave. "We're going to see him? Why?"

Nic headed back to the truck. "He held out on you earlier today. Can hardly blame him since he doesn't know you. He and I have a good relationship, though. I may be able to convince him to be straight with you."

My mind had officially been blown too many times in rapid succession for me to say anything. Instead, I kicked a pebble into the side ditch and got back in the truck.

We were both silent once I got us rolling again. After the sun goes down in the Florida Panhandle, if you're away from city lights, it gets really dark. It's a darkness unlike anything I experienced in Indiana. Maybe it had something to do with our proximity to the ocean. I didn't know.

I'd never asked anyone about it, though. I was afraid they'd laugh at the question. I already gave my friends plenty of material to laugh at. Shoot, since as often as not, I was laughing at myself, they were laughing *with* me.

That was totally okay.

As we motored down the narrow two-lane roadway, I found myself wishing I'd asked someone about The Vampire's home. Because it was like the darkness had wrapped us up in a black blanket and provided only enough room to see the next fifteen feet. After a quarter mile of creeping along at twenty miles per hour, I couldn't stand it any longer.

"It is just me or is it, like, really super dark around here right now?" I stole a quick look at Nic. The glow of her phone lit up her face and made her eyes seem like they contained liquid fire.

"It's just you." She took a quick look out the front windshield. "Okay, maybe it is unusually dark tonight. I'm sure it doesn't have anything to do with the person we're visiting. Unannounced."

I started to laugh, but the sound died in my throat when a house—no, an estate—materialized before us, revealed by a number of strategically placed security lights that had simultaneously turned on. A rambling structure full of large windows and ornate trim, it could be taken straight from the pages of *The Turn of the Screw*. There were even rounded turrets that extended skyward on either end of the house. A widow's walk spanned the gap between them. A wraparound porch with what appeared to be a wooden handrail softened the creepy vibe.

Or would have if the stone exterior hadn't been a dark shade of gray and the trim hadn't been painted in shades of forest green and crimson.

We crept up a gravel driveway that was smoother than most of the roads I drove every day. Regardless of what some people thought of Mr. Longfellow, the man took immaculate care of his property.

The silence after I shut the engine off made my skin crawl. There were no crickets chirping, no frogs croaking. It was dead silence. Evidently, we were far enough inland that even the low roar of the ever-present ocean waves could no longer be heard.

Holy smokes, I needed to get out of my head. I had a mystery to solve and freaking out over rumors wouldn't help.

"So, what's your plan?" Nic opened the passenger door.

"Um." I'd been so focused on not crashing into a tree that I hadn't thought about what to say when The Vampire and I crossed paths again. "I think he lied to me earlier."

"Then go with that. Let me see the pin." She gave it a close examination under her phone's flashlight. "Yeah, I've seen him wearing this. When I asked him about it, he spent the next hour telling me about the band Rush and their *2112* album."

"Excellent. You can back me up if he tries to deny owning the pin."

"Works for me. Let's go."

Before Nic could get out, I locked the doors. "You sure you want to get involved with this?"

"I already am."

"Okay, fine." I put up my hands. "At the risk of getting all dramatic, things could get dangerous from here on out. I'm not saying they will, but I'm the one who made the promise to Rambo. Not you. I don't want you to get caught up in something you didn't sign up for. In case things go south."

She looked at her hands for a moment, then took a deep breath. "At the risk of getting all dramatic, that may be one of the most thoughtful things you've ever said to me. I appreciate it. Rambo's my friend, too. And someone needs to look out for you. In case things go south."

"All righty, then." For the first time in a while, I grinned.

The front door was a solid piece of dark wood inlaid with a leaded-glass moon at eye height. There was no button to activate the doorbell. Instead, I had to use a tarnished brass door knocker. That was in the shape of a bat.

"When he told me he decided to lean into the vampire persona, he wasn't kidding, was he?"

"Nope." Nic pulled her sweater tighter around her shoulders. "He may be an oddball, but that doesn't make him a criminal. His money spends as well as anyone's. He's a generous tipper, too."

I was going to ask Nic what she knew about him when the door opened. With a creak right out of a classic horror film. Of course.

Bela Lugosi, star of the original *Dracula*, would have been proud.

"Good evening. May I help you?" The greeting came from a gentleman with a crazy head of white hair that was going everywhere at once, à la Albert Einstein. He wore round glasses with stainless-steel frames. Or silver, perhaps, for his own protection. His black tuxedo jacket had tails. Formal evening wear, apparently.

"Hi." I gave the man a little wave. "Is Mr. Longfellow at home?"

"Perhaps. May I ask who is calling?"

"Oh, come off it, Higgins," Nic said. "You know who I am. You've been going on my cruises for years."

"Indeed, Ms. Beecham. Your companion is not familiar to me, though." One corner of his mouth twitched. It was probably as close as this old man came to laughing.

"My name is Simpson." I handed him a business card. "I met the man of the house for the first time earlier today."

After giving my card a long look, he stepped back and motioned for us to enter. "The master will see you in the parlor. Please come with me."

The parlor had as much square footage as my trailer. Wood-paneled walls were covered by framed oil paintings in all shapes and sizes. Chairs upholstered in soft leather formed a semicircle around a wooden coffee table. The only light in the room came from candles placed in strategically located wall sconces.

"This can't be real," I said to Nic the nanosecond Higgins left us. "A butler who sounds just like the butler in *Downton Abbey*? A house with an actual parlor? That uses candlelight?"

"Focus, Simpson." Nic pointed at the door. "You're letting the surroundings get into your head. If you want answers, you need to act like it."

"Act like what?" The Vampire closed the door behind him. He'd made his entrance without a sound.

"Abe." Nic greeted him with a hug and a quick kiss to each cheek. Even when we were dating, she'd never greeted me with so much enthusiasm. "It's been too long. How are you?"

"My dear Nicola, to be graced by your ethereal presence makes me the most fortunate of mortal men." He took her hand and led her to a settee on the opposite side of the coffee table from the leather chairs. "What have you been up to? Tell me everything."

For the next fifteen minutes, they chatted like long-lost besties, holding hands and trading laughter. I wasn't completely forgotten, as right after The Vampire invited me to take a seat, Higgins entered with a bottle of wine and three glasses.

It was red wine. Dark red, like burgundy. Or blood.

Despite what he told me about his alleged medical condition earlier, Mr. Longfellow didn't cut any corners playing up to his undead reputation.

"A bottle of Chateau Montrose, as you requested, sir. Shall I pour?"

"Indeed, Higgins. Nothing like a glass of fine French burgundy with friends. Would you care to do the honors, Mr. Simpson?"

Higgins handed me a glass containing a small amount of the wine. Sure, a lot of times I come off as a bit of an uncouth slob. I hadn't forgotten my jet-set years, though. I gave the glass a swirl, then held it out to the light of the nearest candle. After that, I brought the glass to my nose and inhaled the fruity aroma. Lastly, I took a drink, let the wine linger on my tongue for a few seconds, and swallowed.

"An excellent varietal you have there. I get notes of blackcurrants and dark chocolate. Early twenty-tens?"

"Bravo." The Vampire clapped while Higgins poured for the group. "I didn't take you for a wine connoisseur."

"We all have a few secrets up our sleeves." I took a sip. Burgundy packed a punch that was not something to mess around with, especially on top of the champagne. If I was going to get any information from our host, I needed a clear head.

"Ah. I judge from the tone of your voice you're not convinced of my veracity during our earlier conversation." The Vampire leaned back and crossed his legs, as if daring me to challenge him in front of his friend, and in his own home.

"All right, boys." Nic took a big drink. She wasn't driving, so more power to her. "Stop acting like a couple of male gators circling each other. Elmo, this is a social call, so be nice. Abe, Elmo has some legit concerns that only you can clear up. Now, discuss like grownups so I can enjoy this glorious wine."

"Fine." The Vampire sniffed, took a drink, then held out his glass for Higgins to refill it. "I'll play along because Nicola has always been a dear to me and my friends. What is it you want to know?"

I placed the pin on the coffee table.

"Look, Mr. Longfellow. I've talked to a bunch of people who all say that pin belongs to you. It's over forty years old. It must have sentimental value, if not a ton of monetary value. Be straight. Is it yours?"

"And if it is?"

"Then tell me when you last remember having it." I took a moment to collect my thoughts. I had a narrow stream to navigate, and I didn't want to end up stuck on a sand bar. "Rambo says he didn't murder Fran Cohen and asked me to find the actual murderer. I believe him and that's what I'm trying to do. It's like putting together a puzzle and that pin is a piece in need of a home. You can help me find that home. And that will get me one step closer to figuring out who the murderer is."

"He's got a point, Abe," Nic said as Higgins topped off

her wineglass. "The sooner the killer's caught, the better."

"I take it that you don't think Quigley is the murderer, either. What makes you think your friend Simpson here is right and the authorities wrong?"

"Because I've known Rambo for ages. Sure, he can be a blowhard, but he's really not a bad guy. He just wants to be left alone to raise his gators. It's not unlike someone else I know."

The Vampire furrowed his eyebrows. "Young lady, you don't play fair. You know that, right?"

Nic laughed and raised her glass to him. "I'm a girl. Of course I don't play fair. Now, out with it. What's the deal with the pin?"

"All right. Since you seem to believe in Mr. Simpson's exploits, I'll be more forthcoming." He got to his feet and strolled to one of the windows. I couldn't help the thought that he was milking the moment. What a drama queen.

"Yes. It belongs to me. The last time I remember seeing it was a week ago. It was on the jacket I was wearing when I was making my recycling rounds."

"The night before Mr. Cohen's remains were found." I didn't want to make any assumptions.

"Correct. As you evidently know, my route takes me by the building where he lived. It must have come off when I was retrieving cans from a rubbish bin."

"Any idea how it ended up under a bush on his patio?"

"No. Perhaps I kicked it under there by accident." He brushed his hair to the side. "I'll give you that the timing is poor for me, but that's the truth, the whole truth, and nothing but the truth. I didn't kill Mr. Cohen. Believe me, if I had been driven to commit such a heinous act, it would have been done much more elegantly. Eaten by an alligator?" He shivered. "How ghastly."

"Okay." I joined him at the window. A heavy mist had rolled in making it impossible to see much of anything out there. A part of me couldn't help wondering if he'd gone to the window with the intent of calling the mist. "I believe you. Why didn't you save us all a lot of time and tell me this earlier today?"

"Big Baby is more than a customer. They're also one of the few friends I have around here. I didn't want them to think I was involved in this sordid affair in any way."

I grunted. It was a solid noncommittal response. It seemed to me that if Big Baby was his friend, he would have been honest in their presence. Once again, the desire to keep secrets seemed to be ubiquitous.

"Big Baby's an imposing individual. I can see how you'd want to stay on their good side." He accepted my verbal olive branch with a quick nod. "Do you have any thoughts about who might have been behind the murder?"

"I prefer to avoid gossip." He drained his glass and plopped back down on the couch next to Nic. "However, since you asked, in the spirit of cooperation, it wouldn't surprise me to find out that Sybil's your culprit."

"Seriously?" Nic had the word out before me. And I was thinking the exact same thing.

"Oh yes, dear." He patted Nic's hand as he emptied the contents of the wine bottle into his glass. "Now, the astute locals are well aware that Madame Seer is a total fraud. Are you aware of that, Mr. Simpson?"

"Yes." I brushed aside the verbal dart thrown at me. There were bigger things at stake than my ego. If there had been any of the burgundy left, I would have helped myself, though. As a matter of principle. Not as a childish way of getting back at him.

That's what I told myself.

"Then, we're all aware that her stock in trade are her psychic abilities, which, in reality, are nothing more than smoke and mirrors."

"What's the big deal?" Nic asked. "I've never heard anyone say anything bad about her in public. That's part of the Paradise Springs OG Code, after all. We stick together."

"But Cohen wasn't part of that group." A warm feeling coursed through me as a realization of where The Vampire was going came into focus in my head. And it had nothing to do with the alcohol I'd consumed during the evening.

"Very good, Simpson." He turned his focus on Nic. "He's not nearly the dullard I thought he was. I owe you an apology."

"Yes, you do. I wouldn't date someone without depth to them." Nic winked at me. "Elmo's full of surprises."

"Indeed." The Vampire put his hand up. "I'd rather not know more."

"You were talking about Cohen not having Sybil's back," I said. Keeping Nic and The Vampire on task was as challenging as getting Oscar into the dreaded cat carrier when it was time for a trip to the vet.

"Right. According to my sources, who shall remain nameless, Cohen overheard Sybil making unkind remarks about him. Evidently, she didn't know he was only three people behind her in line when the new ice cream shop opened. When he heard her comments, his complexion burned beet red, and he vowed to *Show her who's boss*."

"Sounds like Cohen being Cohen." I placed my glass on the coffee table. "I know for a fact he said worse things about me."

"Be that as it may, your business is more, shall we way, based in reality. When Cohen's comments got back to Sybil, she panicked, according to my source. She makes a good living spinning her tales for the locals and tourists alike. I imagine she didn't take kindly to having someone upsetting her apple cart."

"That's true." Nic tipped her glass side to side to hint she was ready for a refill. "I remember about fifteen years ago, the businesses got together to complain about some shady operations that had set up shop. There was a cell phone store that was selling drugs out the back—"

"And don't forget the surf shop that was spoofing credit card information," The Vampire said, pointing a long, pale finger at her. Then he snapped his fingers.

A second or two later, Higgins arrived with another bottle in a display of unbelievable domestic service. Like, to me, literally unbelievable. I had to make an effort to keep my mouth shut so my jaw didn't fall to the floor. The pause in conversation while the butler opened the bottle gave me time to come up with an important question.

"Is Sybil really the type to resort to murder to keep her business afloat? I mean, she could always have called Fran a liar if he ratted her out. And most people know fortune-telling's bogus anyway."

"I recommend against you saying things like that in her presence. She's as ruthless as they come." The Vampire filled our glasses. No ceremonial tasting this time around. "I knew her back when she was operating out of New Orleans. She's like a spider that's woven a web of deal making and deceit across the entire Gulf Coast. Trust me, Fran Cohen wouldn't stand a chance against her. She has resources that would make the CIA jealous."

"Wow. Okay, then. I appreciate you being so frank with me."

"Wait, if he's Frank, then who will I be?" Nic giggled at her joke, then took another drink of wine.

"You, my dear, may be anyone you wish to be." The Vampire gave her a peck on the cheek, then another one on her neck.

"Stop it, you tease." She gave him a gentle push. "I'm too young for you."

Things were getting weird. That was saying something when you lived in Paradise Springs. The Vampire, or Abraham Longfellow, or whatever his real name was, seemed to be in his late forties. Like George Clooney during the era of the Ocean's movies.

Like me, Nic was in her early forties. She wasn't too young for him. Unless he wasn't really a human living with porphyria. And instead, an actual vampire.

The wine must have been getting to me. I put down my glass and cleared my throat.

"If you don't mine my asking, Mr. Longfellow, have you gone to the police with your suspicions?" When he said no, I asked why.

"Let's just say the local constabulary excels in routine matters. In matters not so routine, they have a history of looking askance at me. If I presented myself to them this very moment, they wouldn't put much faith in what I had to tell them."

"I'm sorry to hear that. You deserve better. Before we go, the reverend's name's come up. What's your take on him?"

"Interesting." He tapped the rim of his wineglass with a fingertip. "Like too many men of the cloth, he's not what he appears to be, especially when it comes to monogamy. That's all I'll say on the matter."

"Fair enough." I dug my keys out of my pocket, wondering who the reverend was sleeping with. Revealing that would be scandalous, but reason for murder? I'd have to think on it. "Thank you for the information and the hospitality. We won't take up any more of your time."

Nic hugged The Vampire, then got to her feet. "Yeah, I have three tours tomorrow. I should call it a night."

"Then I will bid you both adieu. Good hunting, Simpson. Take care, though. One never really knows the source of what goes bump in the night, does one?" He shook my hand and smiled. It was a wide one that revealed abnormally long canine teeth.

I couldn't get out of that house fast enough.

CHAPTER EIGHTEEN

"WHERE TO NEXT?" Nic was suddenly all business as her seat belt clicked into place.

"I thought you were ready to go home." I pressed the accelerator a little more forcefully on our way from The Vampire's property than on our way to.

Okay, a lot more forcefully based on the gravel I kicked up on the way.

With a flick of her hand, she batted my response away. "That was all an act. Except for asking for more wine. That was delish. Abe's been after me ever since I moved to the Springs. I figured some harmless flirting would grease the wheels. I'd say it did the trick."

"Well, sure." I fought down the impulse to get all protective of her. She was a grown woman, after all. "Doesn't he creep you out, though? I mean, he's got fangs."

She laughed. "Lord, he really got under your skin. They're not fangs. Sometimes people with porphyria have receding gum lines. That can make their canine teeth look more like fangs. Case in point, Abe."

"I had no idea." I glanced at her. "You're really smart. You know that?"

"I like to think I can hold my own. Thank you for saying

so."

We passed the Fork in the Road. I didn't bother slowing down to give it another look. That could wait for another time. Like at high noon on a cloudless day. In July. When The Vampire was safe and sound behind the walls of his house.

"Okay, maybe he got to me. A little. Where are we going by the way? Pay Sybil a visit?"

"Not quite yet. I like the old bat." She chuckled. "Even though I could totally see her in charge of a meeting with a bunch of large men in suits with sunglasses and handguns telling them to take Philly Fran out."

The image made me laugh, too. A few months after I settled down here, I scheduled a consultation with Sybil just for fun. She gave me a tarot card reading and said I'd find my true path only when I stopped looking.

At the time, I thought it was standard fortune-teller mumbo jumbo. Telling enough to make me a happy customer, but vague enough that no promises were made. A couple of years later, though, I paid her a visit to see if she'd be interested in my animal removal services. When I was finished with my sales pitch and free inspection, she gave me a long look and smiled.

"I'm pleased you found your path. It takes some people longer, but Sybil the Seer is never wrong." She signed the service contract then and there. After insisting on a substantial discount, which she said was my show of gratitude for her guidance.

Yeah, the woman knew how to play the angles.

The intersection with the highway came into view. I loosened my white-knuckled grip on the steering wheel. Finally.

"Yeah. I'm with you." I pushed the turn signal lever down. "The repercussions of going after Sybil without rock-solid evidence scare me. If you know what I mean."

"That I do. Which is why we're going straight to the source."

The clock on the dashboard indicated it was almost eleven. "The Bayside's gonna be closed. Do you think Claudine's still there?"

"Not the restaurant, doofus." She picked up a white plastic card that had been rattling around in a drink holder. "The source of the mystery. We need to pay Philly Fran's condo a visit."

"Now that you mention it, I need to return that to the chief. It'd be foolish to give it back without taking advantage of it, wouldn't it?"

"Yes, it would." She turned the radio on. "I'm proud of you, Elmo, the way you're seeing this through. You're learning how to be devious, too. There may be hope for you yet here in the Springs."

We arrived at the resort with a plan in place. Well, sort of a plan. We parked under a palm tree a hundred yards from Fran's front door. I got flashlights and surgical gloves out of the truck's toolbox while Nic scouted the area to make sure the coast was clear.

When she nodded, we jogged to a black SUV parked about halfway to our destination.

"Put these on." I handed her a pair of gloves.

"Seriously? Do I even want to know why you have these? I mean, your leather ones, sure, but—"

"Sometimes I have to take a close look at critter dung to figure out what exactly I'm dealing with. That's why they come in handy. Not every animal I'm removing is courteous enough to stroll up and say hi."

"Studying chipmunk poop. I can't believe I never knew that." She slipped the gloves on. "And I thought my job got nasty at times."

"It's not exactly a topic for dinner conversation. For what it's worth, I'll take that over cleaning up after a tourist barfs on your deck anytime. Ready?" I handed the key card to her.

"Whenever you are, Reacher."

We raced to Fran's door. Nic arrived first and had the door open in time for me to dash inside without breaking stride. Once the door was closed behind us, we took a moment to assess the scene.

Nic went up and down the hall, sniffing. Moonlight streaming in through the patio door illuminated her sleek movements. "A vague bleachy smell, but that's it."

"No doubt Jolly Roger had a cleanup crew in here the second he was allowed to." I kept my voice low in response to her whisper. For all we knew, Minerva was at home. Even though her windows were dark, she might be home from a performance already. "What now?"

"You're the gumshoe. You tell me."

"But this was your idea." Yikes, we were sounding like David Addison and Maddie Hayes from the show *Moonlight-*

ing I watched with Mom growing up. "Never mind. If he had dirt on people, he would have kept it somewhere. Check in drawers for notebooks, a laptop, things like that."

I headed straight for Cohen's bedroom while Nic checked out the living room. She was way tougher than I'd ever be. Still, nobody should have to look at the scene where Fran was murdered. Even with the room cleaned, the mind was a powerful organ.

And Nic had an active imagination.

Don't ask me how I know that. Trust me.

I pushed open the bedroom door with one hand as I turned on my flashlight. The room was almost empty. No doubt all the furniture had been removed due to…what happened. A seventy-two-inch flat screen still hung from one wall. A vague outline of a headboard on the opposite wall indicated Fran watched TV in bed.

A lot of TV, judging by the size of the screen.

The Berber carpet had been removed, revealing a bare concrete floor. On my tiptoes, I moved to the closet. I gritted my teeth and slid one door open a few inches. When it failed to make a sound, I pulled it the rest of the way.

And was hit with a noxious blast of air. Apparently, when the room had been cleaned, nobody had bothered to air out the closet. I waved the gag-inducing stench away and shined my flashlight inside.

A handful of suits in various pastel shades hung next to at least two dozen floral-print shirts. Right by the shirts, freshly pressed linen slacks were ready to be worn.

They wouldn't be by Fran.

There were a few light sweaters on the shelf above the hanging clothes. Eighteen pairs of shoes were lined up next to each other on a ceramic tile floor. That explained the stench. With no carpet to remove, they probably hadn't opened the door. The dress shoes shined in the flashlight's illumination. Even a pair of flip-flops looked like they'd been recently washed. The odor came from shoe polish that must have been recently applied. I couldn't help wondering how recently.

Ignoring common sense, I tapped on the closet's interior walls. Since this was reality and not something out of a Sherlock Holmes story, there were no secret panels that opened up. Bowed, but not beaten, I retreated from the bedroom, making sure I left everything as I'd found it.

The bathroom and spare bedroom proved to be as unhelpful as the master. Even with the wall-knocking efforts. I headed down the hall to check in with my partner in this crazy caper.

Nic's efforts had been way more successful.

"Check these out." She handed me three composition-style notebooks. "I found them at the bottom of that curio cabinet in the corner, under a bunch of old *Time* magazines."

I flipped through the top one.

"Holy samolie, he was keeping tabs on everyone." There were notes on individuals from Rambo's grandfather to the police chief and countless people in between. "Talk about a gold mine. You rock."

"I know. It gets better, though. Check this out."

The piece of paper she held out for me to read was a letter from Sybil. The handwritten scrawl was tough to make out at times, but the message was as clear as the morning sky over the Gulf after a storm.

"She'd thought things over and was ready to play ball." I scratched my chin. "A little cryptic, but when you put this together with what The Vampire told us—"

"I know, right? Things don't look good for our friendly neighborhood fortune-teller. I can't believe the cops missed this."

I snorted. "You should have seen the crime scene investigation team. All of them looked green around the gills."

"Well, we haven't had a murder in Springs for a long time."

"Wouldn't surprise me to find out this was the worst scene they ever processed. And that they were too overwhelmed by everything to do a top-to-bottom search."

"Good point. Susan will eat them for breakfast if she finds out about this."

I looked at Nic. Her gaze met mine. We might not have been an item anymore, but there were times when we could still read each other's thoughts. Like now.

"Agreed. I'll keep this under my hat. When the time's right, I'll get them to her. Anonymously." I slid the notebooks down my shirt. It'd be easier to continue the search with them out of the way.

"Good idea...wait, what do you mean you'll keep this under *your* hat? It was my idea to come here."

"Yeah, and if the wrong people hear about this stunt, it'll

be a problem. I'm supposed to be investigating this, so if things go south, I should take the fall. Not you."

"I can take care of myself." She headed for the kitchen area, anger radiating off her like the heat from a lava flow.

"I know you can. But…" I reached for her arm. She recoiled like I'd shocked her.

"But nothing. This isn't the time for this conversation, Elmo. We need to focus on Rambo. We can talk about us some other time."

That's not what I'd expected her to say. I was ready for her to go off on me for not giving her proper credit as an independent woman. Instead, the vibe she was giving off signaled something deeper.

Did she have deeper feelings for me than she wanted to admit? God, what a cluster. Here, we were sneaking around a dead man's condo and all of a sudden, I was looking at her like a lovestruck teenager gazing at a crush who was totally out of his league.

Sometimes I could be really pathetic.

I shook my head. "You're right. I'm sorry. Let me help you go through the kitchen."

"I think not."

Nic and I turned toward the new voice. And found ourselves staring down the barrel of the biggest, scariest gun I'd ever seen.

CHAPTER NINETEEN

"EXPLAIN WHAT ON God's green Earth you're doing here." The man holding the assault-style weapon lowered his flashlight.

It was Jolly Roger himself.

The weapon in his hands needed no introduction. It was a Russian AK-47 rifle. Since my dad had been in the military, my mom thought it was a good idea for me to be familiar with guns. He taught her about responsible firearm use and she passed that knowledge and those practices to me.

The firearm with the business end pointed at my chest was one of the most fearsome ones I'd ever seen.

"Hold on a minute, Roger." I kept my voice low and neutral to evoke a sense of calm. Sometimes I was able to coax critters out of their hidey holes by using it. "I can explain."

"Put that thing away before you hurt yourself," Nic said as she stepped toward him. Evidently, she thought a more direct approach was the way to go. "Elmo and I have a legitimate reason for being here."

"And that is?" He kept the rifle trained on me. Though at least he lowered it enough that a bullet would take out my kneecap instead of my heart. I'd take any progress I could get.

"Critter removal." Nic and I hadn't discussed a cover story. When in doubt, I always brought up my business. Most folks don't want to hear any more after I uttered those two words.

I pulled the key card from my pocket, very slowly. Thank goodness Nic had returned it to me once we'd made it inside.

"The police gave it to me to remove the gator in Mr. Cohen's room." I swallowed and let the images speak for itself. "I wanted to give the condo a once-over before I returned it. I mean, there was no telling what vermin that whole...episode may have attracted without anyone noticing."

"Why didn't you check when you were still here last week?" He barked out the words but had lowered the gun even more. Now it was my big toe that was in trouble.

"The police," Nic said and went to take a seat on one of the stools at the bar that separated the kitchen from the living area. She was one cool customer. And an outstanding teammate.

"Yeah." I let out a weary sigh. "I did what I could, but it was an active crime scene. The best thing for me was to remove the gator and come back later after the cops were done."

He chewed on his lip, as if giving my story serious thought. So far, so good.

"The cleaners didn't say anything about bugs when they were here."

"And they did a bang-up job." I joined Nic at the bar. "But looking for critters isn't their job. With all the people going in and out, who knows what may have snuck in. Think about it. The cops cordoned off the area. That was to keep people out, though. Not anything attracted by the scent of blood. The patio door was left open for hours."

"Yuck." Nic grimaced. Whether it was real or acting was irrelevant. It was convincing enough that Roger put the rifle down.

"Okay, then. Did you find anything?" He took his phone out of his pocket. Maybe I was being overly paranoid, but my Spidey sense told me a wrong answer would lead to a call to the police.

"Not so far. Just need to finish the kitchen. The cleaners did a great job in Mr. Cohen's bedroom, by the way. I was worried they missed a spot here or there, which might have caused a problem. It all checked out, though."

"Okay, go ahead, then." He took a seat next to Nic. A little too close for my liking. Then he put the rifle on the countertop. His hand remained inches from the trigger. "I'll keep Ms. Beecham company while you finish."

The good thing about using my job for a cover was that I knew exactly what to do to keep the ruse going. There was no need to fake anything and risk getting caught in a mistake.

I started low, like I always do, checking the insides of the cabinets at floor level with my flashlight. I made a point of spending a little extra time under the sink. That area could be a haven for mice and other little critters.

When I was finished with the lower level, I got to my feet and stretched my back. A suit jacket and dress pants weren't the ideal outfit for this work.

It was better than getting hauled off to jail, though. Or worse.

Roger must have noticed my attire because his hand went to the gun. "You're dressed awfully nice for a job like this, Simpson. The same thing goes for your lady friend. What gives? You weren't really trying to burgle the place, were you?"

I let out a laugh. It may have been more out of panic than anything, but it reduced the tension a notch.

"It's totally my fault." I started going through the cabinets at eye level, as if he'd asked me about tomorrow's forecast instead of accusing me of a crime. "I promised the police chief I'd return the key card to her tomorrow. It's been a crazy week, and to be honest, I forgot to put it on my calendar. I remembered during dinner, and Nic was kind enough to come along and keep me company."

He stared at me for a few moments. It was a look that left no doubt he didn't believe me. But didn't have a way to disprove it.

"If what you're saying is true, why not call me to make arrangements for this inspection? I could have blown her pretty little head off."

I leaned on the granite countertop. "To be honest, it was my screwup, and I wanted to get it done without any fuss. That's also why I parked down the way a bit. I didn't want to take the chance of someone seeing my truck right outside this place's front door. It might lead to people asking questions and starting rumors."

"And you know how this town is when it comes to rumors." Nic stepped away from Roger. "About finished there, Elmo?"

"Yep." With a flourish, I closed the fridge door. "Nothing. I hope that brings you a little good news from this awful situation."

"I suppose." He rose and, with a casual manner, moved to a spot between us and the door. The man was good. Something had left him unconvinced.

"Don't worry. I'm not going to bill you for this. You're a victim, too, what with the crime being committed at your resort. I'm going to bill the city but waive my fee. I don't want to make any money on this. If you want, I'd be more than happy to send you a copy."

He stood there, rubbing his chin, as if conducting an internal debate about whether my story added up.

Nic cleared her throat. "Roger, I'm actually glad you're here. When we were going through the condo, we came across this."

He took the letter Sybil had written to Fran. "Where'd you say you found this?"

"She didn't." Nic had teed up yet another diversion. It was up to me to make sure it worked. "It was in the drawer of the end table by the patio door. A lot of times, critters will take refuge in a warm, dark space. I thought better to be safe than sorry and give the furniture over there a thorough check."

"Sybil's booked a few fortune-telling-themed cruises, so I recognized the handwriting." Nic took over. "The contents of that letter are disturbing. Do you think Fran would really expose some deep, dark secret she had?"

Roger turned his attention to the letter. I had to hand it to Nic. She was even quicker on her feet that I'd given her credit for. And I will give her a lot of credit any day. For a variety of unique skills she possessed.

"Anything's possible. It's a moot point now, though, isn't it? What with Rambo on the hook. I hear you bailed him out. Hope he doesn't take off on you."

"Here's a thing that's been bugging me for a while. Rambo cared about the alligator that was involved. Like, a lot. He had to know he'd be sentencing one of his prize animals to death. Why would he do that?"

"Beats me." Roger let loose on one of his signature laughs that had given him his nickname. "You should ask him that question. You're *investigating* this for him, aren't you?"

The air quotes he made around the word *investigating* made me ball my fists and count to ten. While I was counting, it occurred to me that Roger's lack of faith in my sleuthing efforts could work in my favor.

I shrugged. "I am, but I'm no pro. Just trying to help out a friend. That's why that letter might be important. What if Sybil's secret, whatever it is, is big enough to kill for?"

"It's worth looking into, don't you think?" Nic sidled up next to Roger and pointed at the document again. "After all, what does anyone really know about her?"

"That's a good point." He folded up the letter and slipped it into a pocket of his navy-blue designer pants. "I appreciate you bringing this to my attention. You've been a great help. I'll take it from here."

Cold panic ran through me. We couldn't let that letter get escape from our possession. Not until I confronted Sybil with it.

"Let me save you some time and effort. I can give it to Chief Eikenberry when I give her the key card and my invoice tomorrow."

"That's kind of you." He laughed again. "I have an appointment with her Monday morning. I'll bring it up then. The least I can do for Fran is to make sure the right person is brought to justice."

"In that case, we'll be on our way." Nic made her way to the front door.

"Uh, yeah." I stuck out my hand to shake. "Sorry for all the confusion. At least now you know you don't have to worry about any critters, right?"

"That's true." He took his hand in mine. It was a strong grip. One that belied his slight frame. "It's always a good thing to have one less worry instead of one more worry."

Nic and I didn't linger on the threshold. The rifle was still close at hand. It wouldn't take more than the blink of an eye for him to train it on us again if I said the wrong thing.

Our getaway was almost complete. Why test fate?

Especially when two large men greeted us when I opened the door. Dressed in black pants and gray polo shirts, they stood at attention, one on either side of the door frame, facing each other. The word SECURITY was screen printed in bold, capital letters on the sleeves covering the men's massive biceps.

They nodded to Nic and me as we passed. Other than that, they didn't move. So, we didn't stop.

We didn't speak until we were safely in the truck and on our way to Nic's place. At a red light, I gave the steering wheel a light punch.

"We were so close."

"To what?" Nic was messing around on her phone.

"Getting out of there with everything we need." I unbuttoned my shirt enough to pull out the notebooks. "It's great we got these, but I really wanted to keep my hands on that letter, too."

She gave my thigh a friendly squeeze. "Don't be so hard on yourself. We got more than we could have hoped for. Losing that letter isn't the end of the world."

I accelerated when the light turned green. "I know, but now we have to trust that the chief will actually follow up on it. I mean, it's not like I can go up to her and ask her if she's talked to Sybil about the letter we found in Fran's condo when we were doing a fake inspection that the police never asked for."

"Fine. How about this, then?" She held her phone out so I could glance at it. There was a document on the screen.

I grinned. "Is that what I think it is?"

"Yeah, man. I took a picture of it when I first came across it. Couldn't exactly do that with the notebooks." She tapped on her phone screen a few times. "Just texted it to you. Now, you can still pay your visit to Sybil."

"Nicola Beecham, you are a genius. I don't deserve to have you in my life." I let out a whoop as I started thinking about how I how I was going to confront Sybil about the letter. A copy would be every bit as good as the original.

"I know. On both counts. Think of it as payback for an enjoyable evening. This was fun. If a little nerve-racking. It's been a while since I had a gun pointed at me." She shivered. I got a sense it wasn't from the cool weather conditions. "What's your next move?"

"Homework." I pointed at the notebooks. "I want to make sure I'm prepared when I go see Sybil. It'll be my chance to confirm once and for all that she had a major motive for murder."

That was a dangerous scenario. And someone like Sybil wasn't going to give up without putting up a formidable resistance. Things were getting more intriguing with each passing minute.

CHAPTER TWENTY

B Y THE TIME I got home after dropping Nic off, I was wiped out. The notebooks were like sirens singing to me to just take a quick flip through their pages, though. No harm in that, right?

I knew better. If I opened one notebook, I'd be sucked in until I had given all three a solid once-over. With a full work schedule ahead of me over the weekend, the sirens would have to wait. Instead, I made amends to Oscar for being out way past my bedtime with bits of leftover baked chicken, then hit the sack.

Even thoughts about how Nic and I had made a better tandem than Jake Peralta and Amy Santiago from *Brooklyn Nine-Nine*, and what that might imply, didn't last more than a few minutes. Which was probably for the best. Because we were definitely not getting back together. Nope. I was sure of it.

At least, I was pretty sure of it.

I spent the next morning removing a bat that had been hanging out, literally, in an attic, then a duo of chipmunks who'd been burrowing underneath a homeowner's slab, and, finally, a snake who had been sunning itself regularly on a retired couple's back patio. I was ready for a breather.

I got in my truck, with visions of a tall glass of iced tea and a doughnut from Mary's Treats & Sweets making my mouth water. And then my gaze fell upon the key card.

"Sounds like an order to go instead of dine in." My next appointment was in an hour. It was looking like I'd be spending my break time visiting the police station instead of reading *Following the Equator*.

Spock was handling front-desk duty when I entered the station, a one-story building with a gray stucco exterior. We exchanged greetings, then he started telling me about how spending the morning doing paperwork and covering the front desk instead of being out on patrol wasn't a punishment. That it was really a way for the chief to test him on his ability to multitask while honing his administrative skills.

"That's great, dude." I extended my fist for a knuckle bump. More than likely, he was riding the desk to keep him out of trouble. He meant well and was trying his best, so I thought it was logical to encourage him. Being logical with Spock. That was a good one.

"Hey, I saw Chief Eikenberry's car out front." After five minutes of him talking nonstop, I cut him off. "Would you mind checking if she has a minute to see me?"

Susan Eikenberry held what she called *office hours* on Tuesday and Thursday afternoons from one to three. These were designated times when residents could stop by without an appointment and exchange a few words with Paradise Springs' top cop. Because of that, she wasn't accessible during other hours without an appointment.

My visit was a roll of the dice, but sometimes you had to

say what the heck. If she was busy, I'd give the key card to Spock with detailed instructions to have the chief call me before returning it to Jolly Roger.

My hand was in my pocket, ready to pull out a pen, when Spock returned. "The chief can see you right now, Elmo."

All righty, then. Things were looking up. I followed him down a hall to the last office on the right.

"She's in a mood," Spock said barely above a whisper. "Thought you'd want to know."

Maybe things weren't looking up, after all.

I gave the door three light knocks.

"Come on in, Simpson." She tossed a pair of reading glasses on her desk as I took a seat.

"Care for a green tea?" If I was going to bug her, at least I had the foresight to arrive bearing gifts.

"I shouldn't, but these reports give me a headache. There's an upward trend of arrests for possession. The mayor wants answers. Not your problem, though." She took a sip. "Mm, Mary makes a fine green tea. Thanks. Now, what do you want?"

Her abruptness caught me off guard. Instead of attempting to ply case information out of her, I went straight to giving her the key card.

"I've been meaning to return this to you. It's from Fran Cohen's condo."

"Thanks." She leaned forward with her elbows on the desktop and smiled. The expression reminded me of a barracuda going in for the kill more than anything else.

"Speaking of which, I heard a rumor that your truck was spotted near Cohen's place last night. I didn't know you had friends at the Sea Breeze."

My brain froze as my insides turned into jelly. Susan Eikenberry was a sharp woman, but how could she have known that? It was like she was Batwoman, who'd spent the previous night on patrol, guarding our beloved community from the shadows.

"I, uh, don't." My gaze went to the picture of palm trees on the wall to the printer on the corner of her workstation, to my bag. Then I had a brain blast that Jimmy Neutron would have been proud of. Hey, that movie appealed to college-aged kids, too.

"But you heard correct." I took the invoice I'd prepared before heading out to my appointments out of the bag. "Since everything was so crazy last week, I wanted to go through the condo to make sure it was critter free. That's what I was doing last night."

"Really?"

I gave her the invoice. "Yep. I thought it would be good to make sure there were no surprises for the next owner. You were there. You know how both doors were open for hours. Who knows what could have snuck in?"

"Hmm." She made a show out of putting her reading glasses back on and studying the document. "So, you inspected Mr. Cohen's condo for stray wildlife."

"Yes. Free of charge."

"How magnanimous of you." She brushed some strands of her blond hair out of her eyes. "Even though I don't recall anyone asking you to do this. You sure there wasn't an ulterior motive for these services rendered? Something to do with your friend Mr. Quigley?"

"Just trying to do my part to help out the community. It's like my mom says, *Be part of the solution.*"

"Uh-huh." She picked up a pen and twirled it in her fingers. "And my mom liked to remind me that a sucker was, in fact, born every minute. I'm no sucker, Simpson. Please don't tell me you were there on some harebrained detective scheme—"

"Then I won't."

"And to drag your girlfriend along, too. I mean, come on. Really?"

"She's not my girlfriend. We're just friends these days."

"Whatever. You're on the edge of becoming a pain in my backside. If Mr. Raines shows up for our meeting with even the most minor complaint about you, I won't be happy. Am I clear?"

"Yes." I raised my hand to ask a question.

"Do us both a favor and go away now. I have work to do." She pointed at the door and turned her focus to her computer monitor.

I wanted her to like me. Actually, I wanted her to think highly of me. If I annoyed her too much, those hopes would be sunk forever, like the secondhand Jet Ski I bought that turned out to have a leak in the hull and now resided on the Gulf floor.

I left without another word.

The weekend flew by. It seemed like everyone within

fifty miles had some animal or other that needed removed ASAP. The work was good for my ego. I tried to do a good job for my clients and for the animals I was moving. The fact that I continued to get business from new customers via word of mouth was proof that I did quality work.

The increased business was good for my bank account, too. The nest egg from my prior life was a welcome security blanket. The knowledge that I could tap into it if money got tight was a constant source of reassurance.

Still, I preferred not going there. The longer it stayed there, the better.

So, it wasn't until Sunday evening that I cracked open the first notebook. It didn't take long to figure out why someone wanted to murder Fran.

The man had used the notebooks to keep tabs on virtually everyone living in the Springs. Some of the notations were short.

For Spock, there was only a single line, A WELL-INTENTIONED DULLARD. NOT A THREAT TO ANYONE BUT HIMSELF.

Yikes.

I didn't think police work was the right profession for our local Leonard Nimoy lookalike. Still, it wasn't up to me. If he kept the chief happy, that was all that mattered.

I found the dirt on me in the second notebook. It left me gobsmacked. Two full pages were filled with Fran's research on me. It included information about my critter-removal business, who I hung out with, where I banked, and other facts. The volume of info he had on my current life was disturbing.

Toward the end of the section on me, there was intel from my old life. Some financial, some personal. All of it confidential. It was the kind of stuff only a hacker would be able to obtain. Or a government agent.

My blood began to boil as implications of the notebooks' contents fully hit me.

The man had personal, private information. A lot of it. The kind that he could use against people who wanted that information kept secret.

And kill to make sure it stayed that way.

A few hours later, I strode through the entrance of the Riptide with my laptop under my arm. The notebooks were back at the trailer, hidden away under lock and key.

I waved hi to Seven and took a seat in a corner booth.

"Heard you paid Big Baby a visit." She placed a tumbler filled with ice and an amber liquid on the table. "With the expression on your face, I thought we'd go straight to the hard stuff."

I nodded, then took a large drink. The Irish whiskey went down my gullet with a soft burn. Just enough to make me shake my head while still being enjoyable.

"Thanks." The only thing left in the glass was ice. "I could use another."

She pursed her lips and gave me a long stare. I couldn't tell if she was thinking about asking me about my deepest, darkest secret or throwing me out of the barbeque joint then and there, before I started causing her problems. After a long while, she raised her eyebrows.

"I've worked here long enough to know slugging down a shot of whiskey isn't your style. Between that and your pasty complexion, something's wrong and you're here to talk to Pops about it."

I nodded and turned my gaze to the glass in my hand.

"He's got the night off. Tell me what's on your mind. Maybe I can help."

Seven was the kind of woman your typical dude didn't say no to. She was the total package—smart, gorgeous, could drink a guy under the table, and mysterious enough to make said guy want to get to know her better. She was also way too young for me. And even if she wasn't, she was way out of my league.

Like, I was a musician busking for loose change on a street corner and she was recording albums with Coldplay and Lady Gaga, out of my league.

We had a few things in common, though. Among them, we were both mentioned in Fran's notebook collection.

"Okay, but you have to swear on Poseidon's trident that you'll keep this between us. You can't even tell your dad."

"Wowzers. This sounds like we both need a drink."

At the end of Paradise Springs Marina closest to the Gulf, a bronze statue of the mythical god of the sea stands guard. Legend says he was sculpted from the remains of a pirate ship that sank during a tropical storm. According to old news reports, he appeared out of the blue one Wednesday in 1923. The locals considered it a sign from a divine spirit and erected a pedestal on which he stands with trident in hand, guarding the town, to this day.

Over the years, it became a routine for crews of out-bound vessels to touch the trident before boarding as a way of asking for a safe voyage. While confirmation is impossible, the old seamen who hung out at Goob's claim that every captain who laid a hand on the weapon brought their ship home safe and sound.

Among the younger generation, Poseidon and his trident took on another function. He became an avatar for something of huge importance. So, when I asked Seven to swear on it, there was no doubt that our conversation was going to be significant.

She returned with another ice-filled tumbler and a bottle of Irish whiskey. While she poured, I tried to put my thoughts into order. It was vital that our conversation avoid devolving into a complaint session about Fran.

"Hit me with your best shot." She drained her glass in one gulp without the slightest hint of a grimace. Then she refilled it without a moment's hesitation.

"Recently, information has come into my possession. It involves Fran Cohen."

"Was said information obtained Friday night when you and Nicola snuck into his condo?" She took another drink, then smiled. "You should know by now that nothing stays secret in this town for long. Come on. Out with it. We can talk about how much time you and your not-girlfriend spend together another time."

"You might want to rethink that position after what I'm about to tell you." I spent the next ten minutes telling her about the contents of the notebooks. I even showed her the pictures I took of the entry about Wendell. "I only took this because I thought I'd be having this conversation with him. I'd never share this with anyone. You gotta believe me."

She downed her glass in a single gulp yet again, then gestured for me to do the same. When I did, it caused a little less grimacing this time. She refilled both glasses straightaway.

"Hell's bells, that man was a real piece of work. If he was still alive, I wouldn't mind feeding him to Rambo's gators myself."

From the sharp edge in her voice, I got the impression that Seven hadn't been joking.

"What do you think I should do?" I shrugged. "Sorry, this is usually the time when your dad imparts some of his patented Wendell Banderas wisdom on me."

"I may not be my father." She took a drink. This time it was only a sip. "I've been told he's not the only member of the Banderas family with the knack for offering prudent counsel."

I'd never heard anyone say that about the woman sitting across from me. When I did hear comments about her, it was mostly about how she could mix a mean cocktail and leave a man quaking in his boots with an arch of her eyebrow. At the same time. It couldn't hurt to hear her out.

"At the risk of sounding like a copycat, hit me with your best shot."

She barked out a laugh. "Well played. Here's what I think. If word got out about those notebooks, people would have been lined up around Cohen's building to have a go at him. The thing is, the only people who've seen them, that we know of, are you and your gal pal."

Even though Nic had only taken a token stroll through the pages, Seven's assessment was close enough. I nodded for her to continue, then took a sip of my drink.

A tiny one.

"I think the reverend's guilty of something, but murder's probably not it. That leaves you with Rambo, Claudine, The Vampire, and Sybil as your strongest suspects. That we know of. I agree that Rambo's not the guy."

"Which leaves me with the other four."

"Don't get me wrong, I wouldn't put it past Claudine to take him out if she felt threatened." She shivered. "That woman scares me."

I did a double take. "Somehow I find that hard to believe."

"I won't put up with drunks and I can hold my own in a fight, but that woman? I would *not* want to tangle with her. But the only hard evidence you have is that letter from Sybil. I'd lean on her first."

It made sense. And dovetailed in perfect formation with the conclusion I'd reached with Nic. I bumped my fist on the table.

"Sounds like I should pay her a visit tomorrow."

Seven clinked her glass against mine. "Good sleuthing. Just be careful. If she's within reach of her scooter and gets mad at you, be ready to bolt. She can be deadly on that thing."

I smiled but didn't feel it. Not only did I have to worry

about Sybil's potential shadowy connections coming for me, but I also had to keep an eye out to make sure she didn't run me over. As I took another sip of my drink, I decided that someday I was going to have to write a book about this insane quest of mine.

CHAPTER TWENTY-ONE

WITH SEVEN'S ADVICE in hand, I stuck around the Riptide for a while and feasted on a rack of ribs. With water to wash it down. The funky soul of JJ Grey & Mofro's "99 Shades of Crazy" kept me company while I motored through an ear of corn on the cob dripping with butter.

The song made me laugh and shake my head. Yep, I was probably a dozen shades of crazy pursuing this investigation. I wasn't an idiot, though. I'd never catch Fran's murderer if I got busted for drinking and driving. Fate had smiled on Nic and me during our Friday night adventure.

It would be foolish to tempt it again.

Which is why I leapt out of bed the second the alarm went off Monday morning like a man on a mission. Which I was.

It was Mission Get Sybil to Confess to Murdering Fran.

The woman was a member of the OG and she was a client. Because of that, I knew her workday schedule. After all, she didn't want me checking for rodents in the middle of one of her sessions. And who could blame her? She paid her bills on time and referred potential clients to me on a regular basis. The least I could was show her some respect.

Since it was Monday, her first appointment wouldn't be until ten A.M. From eight to nine, she hung out at the Springing Dolphin Coffee Shot. I'd catch her on her way out the door.

My chest swelled with pride when she emerged from the shop with a paper cup in her hand at twenty after the hour. All the efforts to know clients' comings and goings was paying off. In a way I'd never thought possible. I'd never imagined becoming a murder investigator, either. So, there you go.

She made sure her coffee was secure in the scooter's drink caddy, then put her helmet on. The glittery orange headwear with a four-inch lime-green mohawk clashed with her purple frock and brown handbag in eye-watering fashion. I still complimented her on the ensemble when I strolled up to her. The whole attracting bees with honey instead of vinegar thing again.

"Hey, I was wondering if you could help me with something."

"You can schedule an appointment like everyone else. Booking online is the most efficient option." She started the engine. It produced a mild *blurp, blurp, blurp* that paled in volume to Oscar's purr.

"It's not about…wait a minute. When did you start online scheduling?" Apparently, her age, whatever it was, didn't mean she was technology-averse.

"Rolled it out the first of the year." She held her phone out to me. "I've got an app that will be ready in time for the spring-break crowd. I had a vision these tech upgrades were needed."

I wanted to tell her the second sight wasn't needed to know folks used their cell phones more and more every day. I held my tongue, though.

"That's great. I wanted to talk about Fran Cohen, though."

"I got nothing more to say about him." She rocked the scooter off its kickstand and revved the engine. "The police came pounding on my door yesterday asking about him. I was in the middle of a session. The nerve of some people."

Before she could get away, I stepped in front of her. "You wrote him a letter begging him not to expose you. That was after he overheard you insulting him."

"Get out of my way." She nudged the black scooter forward, pushing me back a few steps.

"What happened, Sybil?"

"He came to me a while back. Claimed he was writing a history of Paradise Springs. We had a few drinks while I told him about my past."

I already knew what she told him. At least Cohen's version of it.

"Something happened, though. He learned something you didn't want anyone to know. Was that it?"

"Never you mind. If I find out it was you who sicced the cops on me, I'll put a hex on you that'll turn you into one of those chipmunks you love to trap." She gunned the scooter. It leapt straight at me, knocking me back.

I fell with my arms pinwheeling in a useless attempt to grab something. The back of my skull hit the asphalt with a *crack*, and I saw stars.

When the world came back into focus, Sybil was remounting her scooter. Had she taken a few seconds to check whether or not I was dead? Didn't matter the reason, she was still here. I staggered to my feet. The world started to spin so I grabbed on to her handlebars.

"It didn't matter what dirt he dug up on you. It was bad enough to cause you a lot of grief." I leaned against the scooter. One part of the move was to keep her in place. The other was to keep me upright. "You asked him to bury the information, didn't you? You offered to pay him, but whatever you offered wasn't enough. Am I getting warmer?"

"Get out of my way." She whacked my hands with a mag light that had been hidden in a pocket somewhere, while she cut loose with a string of curse words that would have won a world cussing tournament. "Keep your nose out of my business."

"What happened? Did you decide to kill him before your secrets got out?"

She glared at me. The hate in her eyes could have melted the coffee shop's concrete wall behind me.

"He had something on everyone. Including you." She jabbed her index finger at me. "I didn't kill him. I'd like to shake the hand of the person who did, though."

She tried to maneuver past me again. I gripped the handlebars tighter. "I know what he was holding over you. He was going to ruin your business once and for all. And he had a way to do it. Every chance he got, he was going to tell people that you're a fake. In order to protect the reputation of Paradise Springs, he was going to do everything in his power to run you out of business. And he was going to spill the beans about your sketchy past back there in New Orleans. That's powerful motive. He also knew about the cash you have stashed in an offshore account. There's your means to hire someone to do the dirty work."

"Watch your mouth, boy. You keep playing with fire you're going to be burned." She gave my knuckles another whack and sped off the second I yanked my hands away.

All I could do was watch as she motored out of sight. My hands ached. The back of my head throbbed. And my legs were still wobbly.

The sensible part of me insisted I had a concussion and needed medical attention. Of course, if I listened to the sensible part of me, I wouldn't have gotten involved in this whole messy affair in the first place.

Instead, I grabbed some ibuprofen from the truck's glove box. Engaging with live animals who weren't happy to see me had taught me any number of valuable lessons. A key one was the value of having something to help with the pain resulting from the occasional critter bite or bump on the head.

Crawl spaces are called crawl spaces and not standing spaces for a reason, after all.

With medication in hand, I eased into a corner table inside the coffee shop. I reviewed the confrontation with Sybil while I waited for my order of a Western omelet and green tea. It could have gone better. Like *having gotten a confession out of her* better. It could have gone a lot worse, too. Like *splitting my head open when I fell* worse.

"Quite the tussle you had out there. Good to see you survived." Minerva stood by my table. It was the first time I'd seen her since the morning she called me about the noise in the wall next to Fran's place. "May I join you?"

I gestured for her to sit. "Sybil's tougher than a wild boar. And scarier, too."

"Have you ever had to remove one of those?"

The server placed my order in front of me. I downed the pain reliever and chased it with the tea. The sooner the medication got working, the better.

"One time. A sow wandered into someone's barn and the door got closed before it escaped. If I never have to take on another one, it'll be too soon." I placed a napkin on my lap before I began eating. Minerva was a classy woman. I didn't want her to think I was a slob. "How have you been since…"

"That awful morning?" She wrapped her arms around herself as a shiver went through her. "It's been nightmarish. I simply couldn't stay in my condo, especially while the police were working next door. Thankfully, Roger was kind enough to let me stay in a vacant one until things settled down."

"I can only imagine." Minerva was known to be overly dramatic when the opportunity arose. And the opportunities seemed to arise a lot when she was around. This time, she seemed 100 percent sincere. Then again, she was an actor. "Is there anyone you can talk to?"

"Everyone at the theater's been marvelous. And when I'm on the boards, nothing else exists. The performances have been the perfect means of escape."

"That's good." I took a drink of my tea.

The throbbing at the back of my head had settled into a dull thudding if I moved too fast. My knuckles were scraped and sore, but nothing was broken. I let out a long breath in relief that I wouldn't have to reschedule my afternoon appointments.

"How long did you and Mr. Cohen live next door to each other?" Investigating while I recuperated seemed like a decent way to recover.

"Ever since he moved here from Philadelphia. Almost fourteen years." She looked out the window, as if she was going back in time to the day he arrived. "He'd been vacationing here for about ten years before then. The vacationers live in the part of the resort on the other side of the welcome center. Back then, we might see other once in a blue moon."

"Did he have any family who came to visit?"

She gave me a sly smile. "I heard through the grapevine you're looking into his murder. Are you interrogating me?"

"Nope. Just trying to get an idea of who the man was." I shrugged and leaned back in my chair, going for a nonchalant look. "I'm sorry. I shouldn't have brought him up."

"No need to apologize. It feels good to talk about it to someone who isn't wearing a badge. The thought of a killer running free among us has me on edge, I guess. To answer your question, though, he had business associates visit from time to time, but never family. I believe he was divorced and didn't have much contact with his children, two daughters."

"Any idea if there was any bad blood between Fran and his ex or Fran and his daughters?"

"I don't know. I got the sense that he was simply no longer a part of their lives. If I remember correctly, he mentioned one time that one of his daughters was an ophthalmologist and the other was in banking. I got the sense they're both successful in their careers."

My thoughts went to conversations with my mom. The idea that one could have done something so awful, or behaved so horrendously, that their children didn't want to have anything to do with them was heartbreaking. On the other hand, if Minerva's memory was correct, it didn't sound like Fran's family would have much of a motive for murder. I made a mental note to see if I could track them down. Confirm whether they had an alibi for the time of the murder.

Regardless, the conversation sure cemented the picture that the man knew how to make others angry with him, though. Angry enough to kill, even.

"The night before you called me, do you remember seeing or hearing anything unusual?"

"Like what? I mean, I've already told the police everything I remember."

That may or may not have been true. I hadn't seen Minerva in the notebooks yet. She was Fran's neighbor, though. I didn't doubt for a second she'd be there. Until I confirmed that assumption, I needed to lay a solid foundation for the questions to come.

"Whoever did it must have been waiting for you to leave to make their move. Do you remember when you took off that night?"

"My usual time, about five. Call time was at six for an eight o'clock curtain."

"And when did you get home?"

"Around midnight. I'm always exhausted by the time I get home after a performance, so I went straight to bed."

I scratched my chin. From six until midnight. That was a mighty big window for someone to drug Fran, move the gator in, and then get out. Especially since it was dark by six.

I couldn't bring myself to ask her any more questions. It would have been like throwing tomatoes at her onstage. She'd been traumatized enough. If we parted on good terms, that might leave the door open for me to circle back if needed.

"The bad guys must have done their work while you were performing. Thank goodness you didn't have to call off sick or something else unexpected."

"That thought goes through my mind constantly." She put the back of her hand against her forehead for a moment, as if she might faint. Or wanted to look like it.

"You're safe. That's what matters."

We sat in a comfortable silence for a while. Minerva sipped her coffee while I munched on a few of the vegetables from my omelet. I was dying to ask why she came over to my table but couldn't come up with a tactful approach. Thanks, muddled brain.

Then, I had an idea. I let out a laugh.

"What's so funny?"

"I was just thinking about my tussle with Sybil. It was embarrassing getting beat up by a tiny old woman. Did anyone in here see it?"

"Oh yes. We all did. I believe a few customers got footage on their phones. I'm sure you'll find it on social media soon, if it hasn't been posted already. It was quite the scene."

"Yeah." I rubbed my sore knuckles. "I have to ask. Do you have any idea why nobody came out to break us up?"

It was Minerva's turn to laugh. Whether it was real or acting, I couldn't tell, but it was full of mirth, with a musical quality to it.

"See that board over there?" She pointed at a small chalkboard on the wall behind the cash register. It was half-filled with hash marks.

I counted them up. There were thirty-seven little chalk stripes.

"Yeah. What about it?"

"Hassan, the man who owns the shop, started keeping track of the tussles Sybil's had in his parking lot."

"Wait a minute." I counted again. "She's gotten into over three dozen fights right here? In the parking lot?"

Minerva nodded. "Since he started keeping track. Sybil does love trying to run people down with her scooter. I think it's her way of letting people know not to mess with her."

"She's tried to run over thirty-six other people? That tiny woman?" The thought blew my mind. "Has she ever been arrested? Has anyone been hurt?"

"Let's see, so far, she's tried to run Chef Claudine over four times. And the police chief twice. The last time after the chief told Sybil she had to stop doing it. So, not thirty-six. Just thirty-two."

As if that makes it so much better. I kept the comment to myself. Minerva's tone of voice indicated she was taking way too much pride in Sybil's accomplishment.

That was Paradise Springs, where little old ladies on motor scooters were as dangerous as the gators. Maybe that should be the town's unofficial motto.

I made a mental note to ask Nic what she thought of it. If Sybil didn't run me down before I got the chance.

By the time I was on my way home from my last appointment of the day, angry fortune-tellers had dropped down on the list of current threats against Elmo Simpson, PI.

Around two o'clock, I'd noticed a silver sedan following me. They weren't very skilled at staying out of sight. They were persistent, though, as they stuck with me through three removals and one inspection. And that wasn't taking into account how long they'd been on my tail before I noticed them.

As I got out of the truck at home, I took a long look at the road. One conclusion was obvious. I had someone's attention.

And it seemed they wanted to know what, exactly, I was doing. That must have meant I was making progress on the case. It also meant I had a target on my back.

Good times, indeed.

CHAPTER TWENTY-TWO

"SIMPSON, DO YOU have any idea how many silver or gray sedans there are in the area?" Chief Eikenberry let out a tired sigh. "The only reason I called was to let you know Mr. Raines confirmed the story regarding your visit to Fran Cohen's condo Friday night. Not to talk about worries someone may or may not be tailing you."

Even though she was on the other end of a cellular phone call, Susan's tone was harsh enough to make me cringe.

"I'm sorry. I thought since I had you on the phone, it wouldn't hurt to mention it." Oscar jumped up on my lap and bumped his head against my free hand. The purpose of his appearance was to get head scratches, apparently, not offer moral support.

My life as a cat owner in a nutshell.

"If you were being followed by a black utility van or a black SUV with tinted windows, then I'd start to worry. A silver four-door, though? My guess is the driver was either lost or was following you to check out your work."

She was wrong on both counts. I could feel it in my weary and aching bones. And head. While I was taking my postwork shower, the bump on it from my fall screamed the nanosecond hot water touched it. Arguing with her was only going to make my head start pounding again.

Especially since she appeared to be giving me space to conduct my investigation. Whether she was doing Rambo and me a favor or was too busy to deal with me directly was a moot point. The best thing I could do was make sure I didn't incur the Wrath of Eikenberry and risk having my sleuthing brought to a screeching halt.

"I'm sure you're right, Chief. Thanks for the reality check." I let her know I appreciated her detective paying Sybil a visit. The message it sent that they weren't putting all their eggs in a basket named Rambo Quigley meant a lot. We exchanged a few pleasantries, then ended the call on good terms.

With the conversation concluded, Oscar made his way to his food bowl. He took a seat next to it and stared at me.

"Dude, I fed you like two hours ago." After all the day's strife, I was too tired to argue with him, so I dropped a few treats on top of the dry food he'd ignored. Good golly, I was such a pushover.

Too exhausted for any more conversation, I texted an update to Rambo. It was short and sweet. I was making progress and would call him as soon as I had something concrete I could take to the cops.

To his credit, he limited his response to a thumbs-up emoji. No questions, no suggestions, no request for details. My client was a practical man. I'd either find evidence to prove his innocence or I wouldn't. No amount of hounding or cajoling would change that.

Someday, when this was all over, I was going to have to

tell him how much I appreciated that faith in me. Come hell or high water, I was going to make sure that faith had been well placed.

I downed more pain reliever and dropped into my recliner. In bed, I sleep on my back, which is how Oscar likes it, of course. With my head aching, I wanted to keep it elevated a bit, so I kicked up the footrest, closed my eyes, and called it a night.

Or to be more accurate, part of a night.

Oscar woke me up by pawing at my face. I batted at him to get him to leave me alone, but he persisted. As I emerged from the dark well of slumber, something in my brain clicked.

He hadn't used his claws.

He only annoyed me that way when I was sleeping through an alarm. "Okay, buddy. What's going on?"

He leapt from the chair and bounded to the other end of the trailer. After a quick look over his shoulder, he climbed up onto the kitchen counter by the sink.

"Okay, then." My cat didn't move like that unless he was hunting or, given his age, trying to hunt. I glanced at my phone as I got out of the chair. It was almost three A.M. Nothing good happened at that time of night.

Oscar let out a low-pitched growl. His tail expanded out until it looked like a feather duster. Something had upset him. Big time.

I kept the lights off until I could see what, or who, the trespasser was. The critters who were staying the night were safe. If anything had gotten near their enclosure, the security lights would have come on.

Those lights were off.

A rustling sound by the back door made the hair on the back of my neck stand up on end. Even though that entry-way was closest to the bedroom, I rarely used it. More relevant at the moment, friends never came to that door.

Our interloper seemed to be casing the place. Keeping myself below the window line to remain unseen, I flipped the security light switch off. I didn't want the intruder to trip one and beat it before I found out who it was.

Then, I made my way to the bedroom to fetch Thunder, my trusty baseball bat. The roughened handle portion of the white ash beauty calmed me. I'd been an all-conference first baseman in high school. The bat had come from the summer I spent playing in the Cape Cod League. It had been by my side for over twenty years now.

This was the first time I'd called him to action in this manner.

With Thunder in one hand and my phone in the other, I opened the front door a crack. When nothing moved, I slipped out onto the front stoop. My thumb hovered over the flashlight icon as I tiptoed down the steps.

My heart was hammering against my rib cage with such force, I was convinced the prowler could hear it. It didn't matter. Somebody was paying me a visit without an invita-tion. With my investigation going full speed ahead, I wasn't taking any chances.

At the end of the trailer, I took a breath to steel myself and peeked around the corner. There was only darkness. A heavy blanket of clouds obscured the moon and any star-light. That meant no shadows. The visitor was sharp. It was a good night to slink around unseen.

In the distance, a frog croaked. The sound caused a massive adrenaline dump into my system. It was all I could do to refrain from jumping out of my skin. I backed myself against the wall right below my bedroom window and took a moment to pull myself together.

The split second I was ready to move, an unwelcome rattling sound came from around the next corner. That was in the vicinity of the back door. A flame of anger kindled to life in my belly. I was not in the mood to be messed with.

On the count of three, I leapt around the corner of my home. With the bat raised, I punched the flashlight icon.

"Hey!" My shout reverberated off the wall as the light revealed a small figure, frozen like a deer caught in the headlights.

This figure was no wild animal. It was a human being. One I recognized.

"What are you doing here, Claudine?" I marched toward her, the flashlight held straight out to blind her. Just like I'd seen on cop shows. The temporary vision loss would stop her from making a break for it.

She covered her face with her hands and crouched down, angling herself away from me to ward off the light. She was facing the trailer, though. There was no escape.

I stepped forward until I was practically on top of her. With the bat raised above my head, ready to come down on her if needed, I lowered my phone.

"Why were you breaking into my home?"

She winced at my shout. To be fair, it had been booming with fury.

"Please don't hurt me." She scuttled away a few feet, then stood. "I—I thought you were asleep."

"No kidding, Captain Obvious." I shook the bat at her. "Now talk."

"You won't hurt me." A touch of the Chef Claudine haughtiness had returned to her voice. She reached for her back pocket. "I'll tell the police you attacked me."

"Don't move." I used my height and reach advantage to snatch her phone away. "I'll tell the police I heard a prowler and responded in self-defense. The mayor will probably award me with a medal of valor."

"Fine. I'll talk. Do we have to do it here? And will you put that stupid baseball bat away before someone gets hurt?"

The ferocious Claudine the world knew and feared as much as loved was now back in all her glory. I couldn't help but smile at the woman's audacity.

"It can't be said I'm not a gentleman. We can talk on the patio." I motioned her forward with the bat. "If you try to run, you'll end up with a bonk on the head. It can't be said that I'm a sucker, either."

When she was seated, I took a risk by reaching back inside and turning the security lights back on. With a wave of Thunder, the light above the door blazed to life.

"Now, spill it." I didn't take a seat. Though I did lower the bat. It was the best I could manage.

"You're investigating Cohen's murder. Our conversation

the other night, shall we say, raised my curiosity."

"And?" I wasn't in the mood for games, but I also wasn't going to give away the info I had on her.

"By now, you probably know that wretched man kept track of every slight, every perceived insult, real or imagined, every misstep someone made that involved him, even tangentially."

"Something like that." She didn't know the half of it.

"Your questions gave me the impression you knew something important. I wanted to know what that was, so I followed you that night."

"You were tailing me all day. How long have you been keeping track of me?"

"I saw you and your girlfriend—"

"She's not my girlfriend." I winced. The words were a little too forceful to be convincing.

"You're so cute." She laughed. "When you and Nicola left the restaurant, I followed you. As I was about to say before you so rudely interrupted me, I saw you go into Cohen's condo."

"So? I was doing a follow-up animal inspection for Mr. Raines. If you don't believe me, ask him or Chief Eikenberry."

"No need. I like a good cover story as much as the next person. I found it intriguing that you tracked down Sybil so soon after being in Cohen's place." She got to her feet. "You found something in his condo. Something important. I wanted to see it."

Dang. She'd been following me for three days and I

didn't catch on until today. So much for my status as being a real-life version of Shawn Spencer from *Psych*. This discussion wasn't about me, though.

"And that made it okay to break into my home? To go through my stuff?"

"Well, I thought perhaps we could come to some kind of accord."

In reaction mode from the moment Oscar woke me, I hadn't thought about the motivation for Claudine's actions. Now that the adrenaline surge was playing itself out, my brain had started pondering that very issue.

What if Claudine was, in fact, the one responsible for Fran's murder?

She had the wealth to hire someone to commit the act. I'd have to double-check, but I was pretty sure the notebooks confirmed Fran's extortion scam.

The motive and means were enough for me. I dialed 911 and reported that I'd apprehended someone trying to break into my home.

"You may be a world-famous chef. You may have enough money to buy everything and everyone in Paradise Springs. That doesn't give you the right to break into my home just because you think I might have something you want."

She brushed some dirt from her gray chinos. Then she looked at her watch. After that, she let out a world-weary sigh.

"You realize, of course, that your choice to call the police was rash. It limits my choices. I don't like it when that happens."

"Are you going to fire me? Go ahead." It's not like I wanted to be associated with her if she was the one who had Fran murdered.

"Oh, I'll do much worse than that. I'll simply tell the police my car broke down and I knocked on your door asking for assistance. Instead of helping me, you went into a rage and almost bashed my head in with that baseball bat. Who do you think they'll believe?"

The rumble of a police cruiser turned our attention toward the road. A moment later, we were bathed in the vehicle's headlights as it turned into my driveway. Claudine got to her feet.

"Where were you the night Cohen was murdered?"

She furrowed her eyebrows. I'd caught her off guard.

"At the restaurant, of course. Fridays are my second busiest night."

"You weren't there the whole time. I know for a fact you were gone long enough to oversee his murder and get back to work. That should interest the cops. Unless someone else can give you an alibi."

"I hope you're finished. You may have won this battle, Simpson. You started a war, and not just with me. I won't stop until I've taken you apart limb from limb, roasted your remains on a pyre, and scattered your bones in the Gulf, where they'll never be seen again."

It was an impressive threat. The matter-of-fact tone of her voice made it all the more effective. And made it clear she'd delivered that kind of threat before.

As the door of the police cruiser opened, I gave her a

wide smile. She could threaten me all she wanted. I still had the notebooks. She wouldn't touch me until she figured out what I had. And had her hands on them.

Which meant I needed to solve this murder before she got a chance to do that.

CHAPTER TWENTY-THREE

B Y THE TIME the police officer took my statement, had a
look at the back door, confirmed the location of
Claudine's allegedly broken-down car, and told me someone
would be in touch, it was after five.

"So much for a good night's sleep, buddy. Here's your
reward for being the best guard cat ever." I gave Oscar some
treats and plopped back down in the recliner.

Unable to nod off just yet, I tried to make sense of Claudine's actions. From a rational point of view, which was
often in short supply in Paradise Springs, it made no sense. If
she really thought I'd found information on her at Cohen's
place, it would be dumb to try to get it herself.

It would be way more logical to have a lackey of hers
keep an eye on me and go through the trailer when I out on
my rounds. My job came with a decent amount of predicta-
bility. It wouldn't be hard to figure out a two- or three-hour
window when the trailer was empty. That routine thing cut
both ways.

Unless she was so desperate to find out what Nic and I
had found that she couldn't wait to make her move.

That sounded like panic-level desperation. Especially
with the whole threat of going to war, and not just with her.

Then another thought came to mind. How was she so sure we'd found anything? There were only three people who knew what we uncovered. I hadn't revealed anything. Nic hadn't, either. I was sure of it. Seven could keep a secret as well as anyone on the planet. How I learned that was a story for another time, though.

So, was Claudine simply playing a hunch? Or did she know about the notebooks' existence and somehow had learned the police didn't find them?

Now that my brain was running at full speed, I flipped through the notebooks until I arrived at the Claudine entry. I'd scanned it before, but now I studied it in minute detail.

The sun was up by the time I finished. Fran did, indeed, have an Everest-sized mountain's worth of dirt on Claudine. Ninety percent of it was tabloid material. It was the kind of information I had no interest in, but *TMZ* or the *National Enquirer* would pay top dollar for.

The other 10 percent seemed to be grounded in fact. The food poisoning episode wasn't the only issue Fran had with Claudine. There were four other issues that someone in her position wouldn't want to see the light of day.

Including one involving a certain man of the cloth. Huh.

Now that I gave it some thought, an affair with a minister seemed like it would be worth a whole lot more to a blackmailer than an isolated case of food poisoning. Could that have been the real reason behind Fran's cash demands? It was something I'd have to give some serious thought to.

My eyelids got heavy, and before I knew it, I was startled out of slumber by Oscar's howls. I checked my phone. It was noon and my feline buddy hadn't received his breakfast yet.

"Hold on. I don't think you'll die of starvation anytime soon." I gave him fresh water and more baked chicken morsels, his favorite. It was the least I could do after the events earlier in the day.

With the Boss of the House attended to, I made myself a peanut butter and jelly sandwich and pondered my next move. There was no doubt in my mind that Claudine had already been processed and released on her own recognizance. Here in the Springs, big shots tended to be given a level of deference average folks like me and Rambo didn't receive.

I had to move quickly. She'd chosen not to give me her alibi for the time of Cohen's murder. Instead, she got angry at me. Was that the behavior of an innocent person? Maybe, maybe not. Regardless, like the real Mr. Spock, the logical thing for me to do was move her to the top of my suspect list. If she found out about that decision, she'd get angry again. And like a wasp, she'd strike back by stinging me.

Hard.

By the time I finished my sandwich, I'd arrived at an inescapable conclusion. Despite my desire to leave Minerva in peace, I needed to talk to her once more. She was as close to a firsthand witness as I was going to get. And she had a few secrets of her own that Fran had made note of.

An hour later, I was knocking on her door. Thank goodness Tuesday was my day off.

"Elmo, this is a surprise." She'd opened the door but left the chain latched. "What can I do for you?"

"After our chat yesterday, I thought this might help you relax in the evening." I offered her a box of assorted flavors of herbal tea from Mary's Treats & Sweets. "Mind if I come in?"

After a look over her shoulder and then a glance over mine, she unlatched the chain. I followed her through the living area to the patio out back.

A four-foot-deep by ten-foot-wide concrete slab made up the floor. On either side, pebbled walls painted seafoam green extended out from the building's wall to provide Minerva privacy. A three-foot-high aluminum fence with a swinging gate completed the enclosure. From my current vantage point, I couldn't see Cohen's patio.

Two white plastic chairs sat facing the ocean. They flanked a small round drink table. Above us, a ceiling fan hung idle, awaiting the hotter conditions to come. The little courtyard-like area was cozy. I liked it.

"Would you care for a glass of water?" Her smile seemed forced for some reason as she gestured for me to take a seat. She was wringing her hands. If she was nervous, she was doing a lousy job of hiding it. Which seemed odd for an actor who'd performed on Broadway.

Allegedly.

"No, thanks. I don't want to take up much of your time. I came by because I need your help."

"What is it?" Like lots of people, Minerva couldn't resist the pull of being needed. She eased into the other chair. It was time for a little test.

"You've lived here a long time. What's your take on the

new development efforts the mayor's been getting behind recently?"

"To be frank, I don't care for them. One of the reasons I chose to live here was because of the peace and quiet. For most of the year, at least. By the time my career on Broadway came to an end, I was ready find a place where I could slow down."

"I hear you. That's one of the things that I like, too."

It was also one of the things Fran was trying to change. Which might make for some uncomfortable moments for Paradise Springs' preeminent thespian.

"Do you know a woman named Cheryl Long?"

Her eyes went wide for the briefest of moments. It was an almost imperceptible reaction that I caught only because of my days playing penny poker with my mom and grandmother. I lost a lot of change to those women growing up.

"I'm afraid not. Should I?"

"She's from Allentown, Pennsylvania. Happens to have the same birthday as you. A *devotee* of the theater, too, I understand. Does any of that help?" I used air quotes when I spoke the word *devotee*. *Member* would have been more accurate, but I wanted to see her response.

Minerva began chewing on the corner of her lower lip. She was busted. And she knew I knew it.

"I think it's time for you to leave, Mr. Simpson. I feel a headache coming on." With her white frock billowing in the breeze coming in from the Gulf, she looked like a wisp of smoke as she rose from her chair.

"I don't care about your identity, Minerva. Or should I

call you Cheryl?" I stayed seated. "Doesn't matter to me. We all have a past. What does matter is that Fran Cohen knew about it, too. And he knew that Cheryl's husband, your husband, died not long before you moved here. And left you quite a fortune. You spent time as an understudy for the real Minerva Longet back in the day. Is she still living a quiet life in the Adirondacks?"

"What do you want?" She practically spat the question at me.

"The only thing I want is to figure out who's really behind Cohen's murder. Somehow, he learned about your real identity. And your fortune. Those are a couple of pretty big secrets someone might want kept under wraps."

"I'm the one who called you. Why would I do that if I was the one who had him killed?"

"Misdirection's the obvious reason. You get out from under Cohen's thumb and let Rambo take the fall."

"Except for the fact that I was at the theater all evening. I don't have, nor have I ever had, a key to Cohen's home."

"Maybe not. But you sure knew where he kept his spare key card."

She waved her hands in front of her like an umpire calling someone safe. "We're done here. If you don't leave, I'll call the police."

"There's no need for that." I stood. "Thank you for your candor. Was he blackmailing you?"

She looked at the ocean. A tear ran down her cheek. "Not in the typical way. From time to time, he demanded other things from me, of a more personal nature."

Wow. I had thought Cohen couldn't have gone lower than his extortion of Sybil. And Claudine. I'd been wrong. Cohen had been a cancer on this community, using his foul notebook to destroy lives bit by bit.

With every day that passed, the argument that Paradise Springs was a better place without Fran Cohen became stronger.

"I'm truly sorry, Minerva." I made a motion of tipping an imaginary hat to her and made my way to leave. When my hand was on the door handle, she asked me to wait a moment. I turned to her.

"When you catch the person who did this, do something for me. Will you?"

"When? Don't you mean *if?*"

She shook her head. "I know things, too, Mr. Simpson. I know about your past. There's a lot of sorrow there. And I know you won't stop until the killers are caught. This mission of yours is a way for you to heal some of those emotional injuries."

After grilling the woman, the last thing I expected was a compliment. I was unable to speak, thanks to a dumb lump that had suddenly formed in my throat. The best I could do was give her a bow from the waist.

"So, when you do catch the ringleader, before you turn them over to the police, please tell whoever it is thank you. From all the people Fran Cohen hurt."

It was a dark request. One born of pain and anguish and nightmares. It was one I could empathize with.

Whether it was the kind of message I could live with delivering? At this point, I wasn't certain.

I was certain that I wouldn't stop until whoever was responsible was behind bars. Then I was going to permanently delete the photos I'd taken of the notebook pages and toss those vile notebooks into a fire and watch them turn to ash.

That way nobody would be hurt by the information they contained ever again.

CHAPTER TWENTY-FOUR

THE RESULT OF the visit with Minerva had left my head spinning. Was she still a suspect? Yes. After all, the dirt Fran had on her gave him control over her as well as a source of income from extortion. When you add the horrific sexual assault he committed against her, she became an even stronger suspect.

The same could be said, to differing degrees, for a lot of folks in Paradise Springs, maybe as many as a couple of dozen who were likely targets of his blackmail schemes. Who seemed to have more money than others, though? Who would he have kept bleeding if he hadn't been murdered? Claudine, The Vampire, and Sybil were among that group, along with any number of big wheels in town like Jolly Roger and even Wendell. So, it seemed that it all came down to two issues—information and money.

Cohen had information. The other folks had money. And Philly Fran wanted that cash.

Which made sense, except for the fact that I had a handful suspects with plenty of motive to want the man dead, plenty of capital to make it happen, and plenty of opportunity with no witnesses to be found.

Shoot, if I studied the notebooks in detail from cover to

cover, I'd probably end up with twenty or thirty people who met the same parameters as my main suspects.

Then, I had a brain blast.

Following a hunch, I scaled the stairs. Maybe the neighbors above Fran and Minerva could tell me something.

To my disappointment, nobody answered at either door, so I went to the front desk. The attendant was a brown-haired woman I'd gone out with twice. The spark hadn't been there, so we parted as friends.

"Hiya, Tickle Me Elmo. How are you?"

"Hanging in there, Gretchen, thanks." I gave her a grin but cringed on the inside. I wasn't a fan of the nickname. The toy by that name came out in 1996. It was an ideal time for bullies to use it against me.

"Hey, I was wondering if you could do me a favor." I leaned toward her and kept my voice low. "After what happened to Mr. Cohen, I wanted to offer a free inspection to both the folks above him and to Ms. Longet. I knocked upstairs, but nobody's home. Any idea how I can get ahold of them?"

"For security reasons, I can't give you their names." She nodded in the direction of the main office. The security guards from the other night were standing at attention by the door.

"I get it. Thanks, anyway. I'll buy you a beer next time I see you at the Riptide."

She held up a hand. "Hold on. I can trust you, so I'll tell you this much. The one above Mr. Cohen belongs to a snowbird couple. They aren't down here from Ontario yet.

The other one's owned by a family who only uses it from time to time. I haven't seen them since the New Year holiday."

"I'll check back next month, then. You totally rock. And I appreciate you maintaining their confidentiality. Professionalism at its finest." We exchanged a knuckle bump.

"Anytime, buddy. You can make it two beers at the Riptide and we're even steven."

"Deal." I appreciated the limited information, but was bummed on the inside, too. Oh well. Not every idea was a winner.

On the walk to my truck, I took a moment to reflect under the shade of a twenty-foot palm tree. Was there something that connected my main suspects? Something they all had in common beyond their status as blackmail victims? A piece of information that tied them all to Fran.

As the deep green palm fronds swayed in the breeze above me, a seagull glided across the sky, its wings out full to take maximum advantage of the air currents.

Then it hit me.

All of my suspects were folks, like me, who relocated to Paradise Springs. It was clear a lot of the transplants wanted to keep their reasons for moving here to themselves. That was one of the great things about this place. Wendell taught me early on that you never asked someone about their past. If they wanted to tell you, they would.

Fran was a transplant, too.

With excitement bubbling inside me, I went to Goob's to pick up some carryout lunch. While I was in line, I called Rambo.

"Dude, I'm onto something. I'll be there in thirty with lunch."

A half hour later on the dot, I rolled to a stop in his driveway. Sometimes I was pretty good.

Rambo jogged out to meet me. The way he bounced each time one of his feet hit the gravel, it was a wonder the ground didn't shake.

"Tell me you got good news." He yanked the truck's door open and pulled me from the driver's seat like he was a kid excited to see a parent who'd been away on a long business trip.

"I think so." With lunch in one hand and a drink caddy in the other, I followed him into the barn as fast as I could go without spilling everything.

While we ate, I told him about the notebooks and the connection I'd made among the top suspects.

His shoulders sagged when I finished my report. He was kind enough to withhold comment about my news apparently failing to live up to the hype.

"Look." I crunched down on a hush puppy. "I know it may not seem like a lot, but it's the first connection I've been able to make. Cohen kept tabs on tons of people, but, if I'm right, the only people he went after were fellow outsiders with cash."

He shrugged.

"Don't you see? You don't fit either of those categories. That takes you out of the suspect pool."

"Yeah, that's right." He sat up a little straighter and took a long sip of his ice water. "You still gotta prove it, though."

"Believe me, with Claudine after me, I know." I laughed, despite the grim situation. "It's too bad Cohen didn't keep an entry on himself in the Notebooks of Doom. I bet that would be interesting reading."

"You don't have to. A Web search will tell you all you want to know. It'll take some digging because he hid all of his operations under names of shell companies, but someone like you could find the info. That's what my granddad told me. And he's never wrong."

"Did he give you any details?"

"Not a lot. This was right after Cohen moved here full-time. Granddad said to steer clear of him. That he'd been neck deep in some shady real estate deals around Philly. Things like forcing folks out of their homes to make room for fancy new places to live."

"Kind of like he was trying to do here." I tapped a finger on the tabletop. "And you just got around to bringing this up now?"

"Sorry, dude. I've had a lot on my mind. Got my own problems, in case you hadn't noticed."

Really? In the past few days, I've been run over by a maniac on a scooter, almost been burglarized by a borderline sociopath who has more knives in her collection than I can imagine, and had the barrel of the biggest gun I've personally seen in my life pointed at me. And why did all of these things happen to me? Because I'm helping you with your problems.

That's what I wanted to say. It wouldn't have helped the situation, though, so I went with something more diplomatic.

"I may have heard a rumor."

Rambo stared at me for what seemed like ages. Then he barked out a massive laugh and slapped the table with his palm.

"You're all right. You know that, Elmo? I apologize. When I told my grandad what you're doing for me, he said I'll be okay."

"Really? I didn't know he knew anything about me." To have that intimidating man think I could make things turn out all right was the highest of praise, indeed.

"He didn't until after the hearing the other day. Told me if you get me out of this pickle, he'll make you a pot of his special alligator stew and give you a bottle of his special brew to wash it down with. That'll put hair on your chest."

I gave Rambo the best smile I could. Alligators were incredible animals. I had the greatest amount of respect for them. I didn't want to eat them, though. Growing up in Indiana, I'd been quite content to get my meat from cows, chicken, pigs, and even bison on a rare occasion. That hadn't changed in my decade residing on the Gulf Coast.

"That's really thoughtful, but I wouldn't want him to go to any trouble."

"Grandad don't make his gator stew for just anybody, Elmo. A bowl of that with one of his home-brewed beers is a meal to remember."

"I'm sure it'll be unforgettable." In more ways than I could imagine.

With my report complete and the dinner gone, I told Rambo I needed to get going to check out a potential lead. I lied.

It was either that or stick around and run the risk of more conversation involving consumption of various parts of large carnivorous reptiles. The choice to tell him a little fib was a total no-brainer.

By the time I got home, nightmarish visions of gigantic, mutant alligators rising from a nearby swamp to take their retribution on me for dining on one of their cousins had been replaced by something much better.

A vision of me on the front porch, sipping a cold drink.

Oscar must have sensed something special was brewing when I picked him up and kissed him on the head upon my arrival.

"I've got an idea, buddy. I think it's a good one."

He responded by rubbing his cheek against my hand. Then he gave me a quick and harmless bite on my thumb. Snuggle time was over.

I made us both dinner, brewed an herbal tea, and got settled at the patio table. While I snacked on some popcorn, I went through the notebooks and created a chart on my tablet. It consisted of two lists. They were the names of folks Cohen had made observations about. The one on the left consisted of Paradise Springs natives. The one on the right included folks who'd moved here.

It was painstaking work as I had to make certain I didn't put people on the wrong list. The effort was worth it, though. By the time I finished reading the last entry in the third notebook, an unmistakable pattern had emerged.

Fran had made notes on hundreds of people. And by that, I mean every person over the age of eighteen who resided in Paradise Springs and might have had money over the last fifteen years. The thing was, his observations about the area's natives tended to be fairly benign. Yes, they were often tasteless and offensive, like the entry about Seven, but they didn't include sensitive information. That data only appeared in his entries about the transplants.

People like Claudine, Minerva, The Vampire, and Sybil. Yeah, and me, too.

"This can't be a coincidence, buddy." Oscar had gotten comfortable in the chair to my left. I ran my fingers up and down his spine as I examined the two lists. "From what I can tell, Cohen didn't mess with the locals. If I'm right, that means I can disregard everyone on that list."

Satisfied I was correct, I prepared to delete the list of lifetime locals. Something in the back of my mind stopped me. I went through the chart, one name at a time. Almost eight hundred souls in all.

Thank goodness I was a fast typist.

When I reached the final name, a local teen who ran his own lawn maintenance service, a light bulb blazed to life.

The only people who were worthy of his interest were business owners, politicians, a couple of local activists. The movers and shakers of Paradise Springs and its environs. With the exception of one name.

Jolly Roger Raines. For some reason, the good resort owner had escaped being mentioned in Fran's journals.

"That's eyebrow-raising, don't you think, Oscar?" My cat gave me his patented unblinking stare. "Right, you don't have eyebrows. Sorry. But if you did, you'd have to admit

Roger's absence from these notebooks would make you raise at least one. Right?"

He kept looking at me. Then he blinked and followed that by licking a paw and rubbing his ear with it.

"I'll take that as a yes."

Our discussion was interrupted by an SUV coming up the driveway. It was Susan Eikenberry's ride.

"Evening, Chief." I gestured for her to take one of the two remaining seats while I closed the tablet. "Oscar and I were enjoying an evening outdoors. What can we do for you?"

As if on cue, my roommate climbed onto the table and sauntered over to her. When she put her hand out to him, he sniffed, then rubbed his head against her fingers and began purring.

The old tomcat was putting on the charm. He was going to get some treats at bedtime tonight.

"I was on my way home." She scratched under Oscar's chin. "Thought we could have a little chat."

"Great. I don't want to cause too much trouble for Claudine, but just because she's famous, she shouldn't be allowed to do whatever she wants."

"Yeah, about that." She raised her eyebrows when Oscar leapt onto her lap and demanded more scratches. "She's sticking to her story that you went overboard when she knocked on your door asking for help. That you almost whacked her over the head with that bat of yours."

"Is that so?" I looked up. The night sky was clear, the total opposite of the conditions when Claudine tried to break in. Thoughts about the vastness of the universe tamped down the sense of resentment the chief's words had triggered inside of me.

"It is." Susan took a page from Oscar's book and stared at me without saying a word more.

"That's it, then? End of story? The famous restaurateur goes scot-free while I get a visit from the police? Not seeing a lot of blind justice in this equation."

My use of a conversational tone was intentional. There was no need to shout at Susan. My pointed comments were every bit as intentional, though. I didn't like it when the little guy got trampled by the big shot.

"I reviewed the responding officer's report, along with your and Claudine's statements." She placed her police cap on the table. "It comes down to a he-said, she-said situation. The officer on duty found no sign of a break-in and you didn't report anything stolen. Without any witnesses to corroborate either your story or hers, there's not much for us to go on."

"I see."

"Unless there's something you want to tell me that you didn't include in your statement." She'd moved from scratching under Oscar's chin to scratching his belly. The one time I attempted that, he bit me, hard. What a traitor.

"Don't think so. Not that it would matter anyway." Under no conditions would I divulge the existence of Fran's notebooks to her.

"Come on, Simpson." She shook her head. "Fran Cohen's murder has my team stretched to the breaking point.

Most of them have never had to deal with a murder investigation. The overtime's going to destroy my budget. Given the current state of affairs, I suggested to Claudine that she should steer clear of you and your property. That's the best I can do."

"Fine, whatev—wait, are you all still investigating Cohen's murder?" I leaned forward in my chair. The resentment had vanished into the nighttime darkness, replaced by curiosity.

"We're still exploring all appropriate paths of inquiry. Mr. Cohen's daughters and ex-wife are proving to be difficult to pin down for interviews. I'm not at liberty to say anything more. Which leads me to the other reason I'm here."

Oscar had curled up in her lap and was purring away. The sucking up he was doing was causing me to have second thoughts about that kitty treat promise I'd made.

"I know Rambo asked you to conduct your own investigation. You have the right to do that. That said, the office has received some complaints regarding you and said investigation."

"Who from? Or are you not at liberty to tell me that, either?" I had a solid idea who the complainers were. If you made a Venn diagram of who my main suspects were and who the complainers were, odds were good you'd have a solid circle.

"It wouldn't be appropriate for me to say. And before you get all snippy with me about it, I'm doing you a favor telling you this informally." She traced a circle on the tabletop with her index finger. The yellow nail polish shined in the light by the outdoor lights. "While I don't have anything to support this assumption, I can't help wondering if your investigation is making certain people uncomfortable. For the right reasons."

"Really? That's interesting." It was true. Actually, more than interesting. It was energizing. Confirmation I'd made someone nervous enough to prompt a complaint to the police. No doubt, with the intention of scaring me off the case.

That wasn't gonna happen.

"Did you know Claudine doesn't have an alibi for the hours of nine to eleven the night of Mr. Cohen's murder?"

"That's a bold accusation."

"It's the truth."

She pushed a few strands of her blond hair that had come loose behind an ear. It amazed me that she could get so much hair into a tiny bun at the back of her head.

"I'll look into it. It's also my duty to remind you about the importance of not interfering with an ongoing police investigation. Do we understand each other?"

"We do."

Oscar decided the meeting was over, so he made a graceful exit from Susan's lap. As soon as her car was out of sight, I grabbed for my phone. There was no way I was making an exit, graceful or otherwise, from my investigation. The finish line was too close to quit now.

CHAPTER TWENTY-FIVE

WEDNESDAY MORNING BROUGHT clouds and scattered showers to the area. It was the kind of weather that led the lifelong residents of the Panhandle to put on jeans and sweatshirts and grumble about the chill in the air.

My Hoosier blood hadn't thinned that much yet. With my rounds to do, I wore long workpants with only a T-shirt on top. No heavy clothing for this guy.

"It's like fifty-five degrees, Elmo. Put on a jacket. You're making me cold." Nic was wrapped up in an oversize sweater that came down to her thighs. She pulled the sleeves over her hands and shivered.

"Back home, they're having sleet with a high of thirty-eight today. This isn't cold." Having said my piece, I shrugged into a rain jacket I kept in the truck's toolbox. I didn't want to get distracted by one of our all-too-common quarrels that were usually over nothing of significance.

"That's better." She climbed into the truck. "Where are we going? Your text message was awfully cryptic."

"That was on purpose." I filled her in on recent developments as I drove out of the marina's parking area. My report didn't end until we arrived at a public beach access area on the eastern edge of town.

"I wanted to talk to you someplace where we wouldn't be overheard, so here we are."

"Aren't you being a little dramatic?" She took the po' boy sandwich I'd picked up at Goob's without objection. "I mean, do you really think someone's trained a listening device on you?"

"No. That's a little over the top, even for this town. That doesn't change the fact that I was followed for three days before I noticed. I don't want to take any chances."

"Well, you weren't a real member of the OG Paradise Springs crowd until Sybil tried to run you down. With that hurdle crossed and Claudine following you, I'll indulge your paranoia."

"Thanks." I stared at my sandwich for a moment. "I think."

"Don't mention it," she said through a mouthful of toasted French bread, lettuce, and shrimp.

"When did Sybil try to run you over?"

"A while back. It was before she put that skull and crossbones sticker on the front of her ride. She was hosting a group of fortune-tellers and wanted to book a cruise. When I told her my price, she said that the spirits had ensured I'd give her a significant discount. When I told her the spirits were wrong, she called me a few choice insults and drove that scooter right at me. I stepped aside. She kept moving and flipped me the bird as she drove away."

"What happened to the cruise?"

"She paid full price. Now, what's your point?"

"What do you know about Jolly Roger?"

She stopped chewing to wipe the corner of her mouth. Then her brow furrowed as she pondered the question. "The usual stuff. Real estate developer, made his fortune a while ago, single. Why?"

"I think he knows more about the murder than he's letting on."

"It did happen at his resort. I'm sure there are any number of things he's having to deal with that nobody knows about." She dipped a French fry into a little plastic container of mayo.

"Sure, but what about this? I've gone through Fran's notebooks from front to back and there's no mention of Roger anywhere. You can look for yourself. There has to be a reason for that."

"I'm going to preface this comment by making it clear I'm playing devil's advocate here. Could it be as something as simple as Fran not wanting to make the guy who owns his building mad at him? After all, that's something Roger could hang over his head that nobody else could."

"That's totally possible. Let me ask you this. Those security guys we passed when we were leaving Fran's condo the other night. Have you ever seen them before?"

She shrugged. "No, but I don't get over to the Sea Breeze often. Roger hired them ages ago and had them keep a low profile. We're probably noticing them now because he's increased their visibility in response to the murder. You know, to show people there he's taking their safety seriously."

Nic was good. She had a reasonable answer for everything. Which was why I was having this conversation with her. I was far from done, though.

"What about the gun Roger had with him? That thing could have taken out a small village."

"True, but it's perfectly legal to own one in this state. Whether that rifle is his way of compensating for something else, I'll let someone else decide."

"He's one of your regular clients, right?" When she nodded, I barreled on. "What do you do for him?"

"I do a lunch cruise every Thursday for the residents and vacationers. It's a three-hour trip around Choctawhatchee Bay. There's a private island near Hogtown Bayou where we stop for lunch. The owner lets Roger show people around the place. It's great for wildlife sightseeing."

Fascinating. "And does Roger accompany the folks taking the tour?"

"Yep. He says it's a value-added personal touch. The break at the island comes in handy. I use the time to tidy up the boat. In the summer, it's a quick turnaround to prep for the afternoon cruise."

We sat in silence while we ate. I took the time to chew on the information, too. Something in a far corner of my mind was bugging me. Like when I get a mosquito bite on my back somewhere I can't reach and need to use a ruler to scratch it. For the life of me, I couldn't figure out what was niggling at me, though.

"What's with this sudden fixation with Jolly Roger?" Nic wiped her hands on a paper napkin. Her sandwich was gone. "Seems to me that Claudine's got to be the murderer.

Everything fits the profile, she doesn't have an alibi, and she was even stupid enough to attempt to break into your place."

"You're not wrong. It bothers me that that Roger's not in Fran's notebook. It's like back in the day when I'd be working on an app. If the code was missing a single piece of information, or if that information was in the wrong place, the program wouldn't run. Everything had to fit together, in the proper sequence, to get the desired result."

Nic nodded. "And Roger's that piece of missing code."

"Exactly." I'd barely touched my fries. I traded them for Nic's slaw, which she'd ignored. "Until I can figure out what's missing, I can't be confident about whether the murderer's Claudine, Sybil, or even Roger."

"What about the reverend?"

"I don't have anything solid beyond the fact that he grew up here and Cohen's notebooks barely mention him. It's weird that there are zero mentions of the guy's affair with Claudine. To be honest, I'm afraid he'll try to get me to join his church if I go talk to him. That would make it weird when I respond to that by asking if he's been sleeping with Claudine. I'd rather avoid that if I can."

"Whatever floats your boat. Okay, back in your tech days, what would you do when you ran into a roadblock like this?"

"I'd ask someone to look at the code."

"Except we're not talking about code in a literal sense now, knucklehead."

"Right. Then I'd go back to the starting point. To see if I could figure out what had been entered wrong or if something was flat-out missing."

She snapped her fingers, then pointed at me. "Then that's what you should do now. The notebooks are your one solid piece of evidence. Go through them one more time. Slowly, one page at a time. Maybe that way you'll find something you missed before."

My phone buzzed. I needed to be at my next appointment in an hour. On the way back to Nic's boat, she thanked me for lunch.

"It's the least I could do. I appreciate you taking the time to help me brainstorm. I'm getting closer. The answer's out there, almost within reach."

"Then keep at it. And if I can think of anything helpful, I'll let you know. I'm really proud of you, Elmo."

With Nic's encouraging words floating through my mind, I kept focused on my appointments throughout the afternoon. Whenever the case began to invade my thoughts, I pushed it into the background. It wasn't until I released the critters I'd been holding, two chipmunks, a raccoon, and a snake, that I let my mind go back to the question at hand.

Who was the person in charge of the plot to murder Fran Cohen?

After dinner, I sat at my desk and stared at the notebooks. Each one had a unique cover. One was red, one was green, and the other featured alternating white and black vertical stripes. Each one contained one hundred pages. I wasn't looking forward to flipping through three hundred pieces of paper. Like Nic said, before I did anything else, I needed to make sure I hadn't missed anything within the stout paperboard covers.

I was about a third of the way through the one with the red cover when I stopped. The answer to the nagging itch in the corner of my brain finally came through.

"Dude." I gave Oscar, who was curled up on top of a small stack of papers on my desk, a head scratch. "What if, instead of flipping through each of these pages, I count them. Maybe I'm missing something because it's really missing. As in gone."

He responded with a slow blink, then reached out to me with his right paw. Maybe he was only stretching. I chose to believe otherwise.

"I'll take that as an affirmative."

Ten minutes later, I had my answer. Two of the books had all one hundred sheets. The one with the red cover was missing four. I flipped through it at a turtle's pace, analyzing the center binding stitching for telltale signs the absent sheets had, in fact, been removed.

I hit pay dirt a third of the way in. It was easy to overlook, but scraps of paper no larger than one of Oscar's claw clippings remained along the spine's edge. With mounting excitement, I flipped through the rest of the notebook book until I came across a corresponding spot two-thirds through. With the gentlest of tugs, I pulled. Two sheets came free from the binding.

The conclusion was inescapable.

Someone had torn two pages out of the notebook. Due to the stitching-like binding of the booklet, two corresponding pages had been left behind. Those remaining sheets, which I had just come across, were no longer attached to anything. Did that mean someone had been in a hurry in his attempt to dispose of incriminating evidence? Or was it the result of something completely innocent? I scratched my chin, trying to force an answer to come to me.

Then, another idea popped into my head. According to Sybil, Fran had claimed to be working on a history of Paradise Springs. What if he'd used that same cover story with Roger? And in the middle of his research found out something really bad about Mr. Raines? I mean, so bad it ended up in murder?

"Time for more research." I dropped a kitty treat in front of Oscar. He was a stellar wingcat.

Roger owned the Sea Breeze Resort and Condominiums. You can find almost anything about a business on the internet if you know how and where to look. With that in mind, I determined that a corporation named RRPS, LLC purchased the property in 2009. A report in the *Palladium* said it was a cash deal and that by keeping the resort out of foreclosure, the LLC got it at a big discount off the original asking price.

If you considered a purchase figure of seven million dollars a discount price.

Roger was listed as the company's president. No other officers were mentioned in any Secretary of State filings. That led to my next question.

How did Roger come up with that kind of money?

"What now, Elmo?" Nic didn't seem happy to hear from me. Explosions were going on in the background. She must have been watching one of her favorite action-adventure movies.

"Did Roger ever tell you how he made his money before he came here?"

"Yeah." The sounds of mayhem ceased. "He said he made a bundle in the tech world right before the dot-com bubble burst. That he was lucky he got out when he did. Why?"

"Following a hunch. Did you know Roger paid cash for the Sea Breeze?"

"I did not. Must be nice to have that kind of cash lying around."

"No doubt. Thanks for the help. I'll let you get back to your guns and explosions."

I ended the call before she could ask any questions. The sinking feeling in my gut suggested the less she knew about my hunch, the better.

CHAPTER TWENTY-SIX

I WAS THE ripe old age of twenty when the dot-com bubble burst. Friends and colleagues went from the penthouse to the poorhouse in months. I escaped financial ruin because I was too young to have any money to invest at the time. Over twenty years later, memories of those dark days were still as fresh in my mind as if they'd gone down twenty days ago.

Very few people who'd jumped on the internet commerce wagon train escaped unscathed. A select few made money. Despite using all of my computer skills, after an hour of searching, I could find no evidence that Roger Raines was one of them.

In fact, I couldn't find any evidence of his involvement in the tech sector at any time.

Which was odd, because like I said, for me those awful times back in 2000 when I was studying computer science were seared into my mind. They were as vivid as my mom's memories of the 1983 Beirut bombing that took my dad's life.

I had no memory of Jolly Roger from the days of my tech-filled youth. The Web made no mention of him. It left me with one conclusion.

"Hey, Oscar, what's that thing your grandma likes to say about those Sherlock Holmes stories she likes? *When you've eliminated all the impossibilities, whatever you have left, regardless of how improbable it is, has to be the truth.* Something like that, right?"

He bumped his head against my hand. His encouragement was gratifying. Especially since most of the time, he ignored my musings.

That had to mean Roger was a big, fat liar about how he made his money.

The code in my head had revealed the problem. It wasn't a matter of the data in the sequence being entered incorrectly. Some of the data was flat-out missing.

I had, finally, identified the missing data. Now, I could start filling it in and once complete, it would reveal the person responsible for Fran's murder.

More Web searching unearthed another attention-getting piece of data. Prior to his purchase of the Sea Breeze, the man had kept a low profile. So low, I wasn't able to find anything about him. That issue wasn't unheard of. Gobs of people, in the interests of privacy, lived their lives without leaving a digital trail behind them.

Jolly Roger didn't fit that profile.

While he wasn't a publicity hound, his image often appeared in social media posts promoting resort activities. As one of the major employers in town, he wasn't shy about voicing his opinion about issues that affected the resort.

Like in a recent report in the *Palladium*. The article covered a development commission meeting. He'd attended to voice his opposition to Fran's push for the development of more resorts.

Most folks took his position with a grain of salt. He was only trying to keep the competition out, right?

What if it was really a move to keep the area's profile lower than the neighboring communities like Destin and Panama City Beach? That way Roger, or whoever he really was, could keep whatever suspect activities he was running under the radar.

I needed to talk this through with someone. It couldn't be Nic because I didn't want to put her in any more danger than I already had if I was right. She could take care of herself, no doubt, but I'd asked a lot of my ex-girlfriend. More than I probably had a right to.

Though, to be fair, she hadn't objected much. At the end of the day, it wasn't up to me to make decisions for her. If I crossed a line she didn't want me to cross, she'd let me know. Man, she was cool. I didn't want that coolness to lead to her being in someone's crosshairs, though.

Rambo wasn't right, either. He was too close to the matter at hand.

A look at the clock on the wall gave me the answer.

"Gotta go, Oscar. I have a vampire to track down."

If someone had told me two weeks ago that I'd approach the Springs' Lord of the Night for help, I would have laughed out loud. Then run away and hid to make sure it didn't happen.

My, how drastically things could change in a matter of days.

It didn't take long to find him. He was in the early stages if his route and had just picked up a plastic bag Goob had left for him. Dressed in black from head to toe, he was a living, breathing shadow as he glided toward his car. Though I still wasn't certain about the living part.

"Mr. Longfellow, could I have a few minutes of your time?" My mouth went dry. It took all of my self-control to stay where I was by his driver's-side door.

"Some would say I have all the time in the world." As he gave me a fang-filled smile, his trunk popped open. He must have pressed a button on a key fob concealed somewhere on his person. That was way more reassuring than assuming he opened it with his mind.

"Um, yeah. I need to apologize for my assumptions about you. They were hurtful and unfair. I promise to do better."

He looked at me. Despite my fear that he was going to hypnotize me, I maintained eye contact. Especially after his last comment.

"Thank you." He removed the surgical-style gloves he was wearing, also black, and offered to shake.

I took his hand in mine. It was as cold as the inside of a refrigerator. Despite my struggle to live up to my words, I forced a smile.

"Your wheels are amazing." I released his hand and pointed at his vehicle. Even in the dark of night, it had a mirrorlike shine. "Cars today don't have anything like the character of these babies."

"Indeed." He ran a black-painted fingertip along the

trunk's edge, then watched as it closed. Without any evident prompting from him. "It was a gift from my parents."

"That's too cool. Do they live in the area?" A little buttering up couldn't hurt.

"No. They moved away. A long time ago. They were originally from Europe and decided to return to their homeland."

That was it. No more small talk. Either the person in front of me was the world's greatest con artist or he really was a vampire. If that was the case, I had no desire to let the conversation go on any longer than necessary.

"I hope they're happy back home." I rubbed my hands together. "So, I could use your opinion about someone."

"This is related to your investigation, yes?"

"It is. I took your advice and talked to Sybil—"

"And almost paid for that encounter with your life, I understand." He grinned, revealing those fangs again.

"Yeah. The bump on my head still hurts. She confirmed everything you told us. I'd like to get your take on somebody else, though." I took a deep breath. "I think I know who's responsible for Fran Cohen's murder."

"Since you're here, alone, mere feet from me, after dark, I'm assuming you no longer consider me a suspect."

"That's correct."

"In that case, do tell." He opened the car's passenger door and gestured for me to get in. Like I had any real choice in the matter.

Once we were seated, he pressed a button to start the car. The only way I could tell it was running was a low-level vibration that hadn't been there a moment ago. "We can talk while I continue with my route."

I told him about what I'd learned since our last conversation, avoiding any mention of the notebooks. The Vampire was in there. And Fran's observations about him weren't kind.

"You were already living here when Raines moved to the area, right? Do you remember anyone talking about his background at that time? You know, things like his qualifications to run a resort, where he got his capital to buy the Sea Breeze?"

He drummed his fingers on the polished wooden steering wheel while Rush's Geddy Lee sang about the downside to living in the limelight.

"Those are thought-provoking questions, Mr. Simpson. As I recall, the powers that be were too excited about the purchase to ask many, if any, probing questions. The resort was suffering, occupancy was down, and maintenance was lax. That, in turn, led to the town suffering. His appearance was akin to a white knight arriving astride his charger, ready to lead the bedraggled forces to victory. I believe his purchase was in cash. That went a long way toward silencing any potential critics."

"How long did it take to get the resort back up to snuff?"

"Not long at all, come to think of it. He oversaw the renovation himself and hired labor from the area to complete it." He turned right and we came to a halt in front of an Irish pub called Cleary's. "This is my next stop. I shall return in a few minutes."

While The Vampire was gone, I studied the imaginary string of code in my head. The answer was still out of reach.

But my fingertips were brushing up against it.

I was mulling over what to ask next when, as if out of thin air, he was behind the wheel and had pressed the ignition button.

"That was fast. Get many cans?"

"Siobhan Cleary is kind enough to have instructed her staff to compile aluminum and steel cans for me. It only takes a moment to retrieve it. You must have been deep in thought if you failed to notice my return."

"That must have been it." I was creeped out enough for one evening. I could walk back to my truck, if needed. One more question and I was out of there. "Do you know anything about the two security guards that have been working there since Fran's murder?"

"As a matter of fact, I do. They are Mr. Raines's security staff. They arrived shortly after the purchase agreement was consummated. They did a lot of work overseeing the resort's renovation work. When they're not running errands for him, he prefers to have them stay out of sight. To avoid disturbing the residents and guests. That's clearly changed in light of recent events."

"Okay." I considered myself an observant guy. You had to be that way to succeed in my line of work. "Anything else?"

"Big Baby once commended the duo's work ethic, going so far as to note that they'd never seen the two of them away from the resort campus longer than a few days at a time. Why?"

The final piece of the code dropped into place. The program ran without flaw. I smiled and turned to face The Vampire.

"I know who murdered Fran Cohen."

Now, all I had to do was to prove it.

CHAPTER TWENTY-SEVEN

I DRUMMED MY fingers on the truck's steering wheel while I waited outside the Sea Breeze's main entrance. Roger would be emerging soon. Skies were clear and the forecast was for a high in the midseventies. Ideal conditions for a lunch cruise.

An ideal situation to confront a murderer, too.

Despite spending half the night trying to tie the man to illegal activities, I'd come up empty. He'd done an amazing job hiding it. The information was all there, though. Now, it was a matter of pushing a button to execute the program.

Well, almost all there.

The specific illegal operation he was involved in was still a mystery to me. Everything pointed toward smuggling, though. So, that was what I was going to go with.

I glanced at my phone. The resort's lunch cruise was due to launch in twenty minutes. The shuttle bus taking passengers to Nic's cruise ship was idling under the welcome center's canopy. The only thing remaining was for the man himself, Jolly Roger Raines, to join the group already on board.

My phone buzzed. It was a text from Nic asking if there was any sign of him yet. Earlier, I'd asked her to delay launching if Roger arrived with the group. She'd agreed, but only if I explained my scheming to her later. Over dinner at the Bayside. My treat.

If the murderer didn't turn out to be Claudine.

As I was typing my response, he made his way through the entrance's revolving door. I sent the affirmative with a request to stand by and leapt from the truck.

"Roger, hey! Got a minute?" I gave him a friendly wave as I jogged up to him.

"Not really." He frowned and switched his backpack from one shoulder to the other. "I need to get this group to the marina for a cruise."

"Right." I edged myself between him and the bus's entry door. "The weekly lunch cruise around the bay. A reliably popular event on the resort's activity calendar."

"Indeed, it is. I'm glad you know about it." He laughed and moved to go by me.

I put my hand on his shoulder. And applied a tiny amount of pressure. Just enough to get his attention.

"Oh, I know about it. I know about it all. The stop at the private island. The excursion on the island that you lead. The precious few minutes where you steal off to your drop site to exchange the cash in your backpack for the contraband that's been stashed there. You know, when everybody else is having lunch."

His eyes narrowed and he turned to face me head-on. One hand went into a pocket of his cargo shorts. The other tightened its grip on the backpack strap.

"Are you on something, Simpson? I have a busload full

of paying customers waiting to have a good time. You have no business showing up throwing around these baseless allegations right in front of them."

I stepped closer until we were within a foot of each other. "They're not baseless. They're rooted completely in fact. That's just the tip of the iceberg, though. I also know Fran Cohen found out about the operation you and your so-called security team have been running. That's why you had him killed."

"Okay, Elmo." He stepped back. "It sounds like you need professional help. Let me call someone to come pick you up."

He withdrew his hand from his pocket. It was holding his cell phone. "Is there anyone—"

He didn't finish the question. Instead, he cracked me on the side of the head with the phone. The roundhouse swing packed a wallop and sent me tumbling to the ground. My head hit the pavement and I saw stars.

For the second time in a week.

The uproar from the bus brought me to my senses. Passengers were shouting, taking video with their phones, and pointing. I looked in the direction most of them were aiming.

Roger was sprinting toward a black vehicle with a trident logo on its front grille. A Maserati, the kind of imported sports car that was fast and had unsurpassed handling.

In other words, a perfect getaway car.

I got to my truck as fast as my rattled skull would allow. In seconds, I was burning rubber out of the parking lot.

Roger's car had maneuverability for days. Most of the streets in the Springs area were straight lines, the result of the community being planned in a grid pattern.

That meant the massive engine of my truck could catch up and let me keep up with him. For a while at least. As I followed him down Gulfview Lane, weaving in and out of traffic, ignoring horn blasts from irate motorists, something surprising occurred to me. He wasn't heading for the highway interchange. He was going the opposite way.

Toward the marina.

It didn't take a genius to figure out what his plan was. And it was up to me to make sure he didn't pull it off.

I loosened my grip on the steering wheel when a yellow traffic light came into view. I'd catch up to try to reason with him there. As I eased off the gas pedal, the gap between us grew. He wasn't slowing down, even when the light switched to red. In fact, as he jerked to the left to pass a car in the middle turn-only lane, he was speeding up.

The marina was mere minutes away. If I gave up the chase and called the cops, he'd be long gone by the time they made it to the marina.

I gritted my teeth and floored it.

Fortune was with me as I charged through the intersection at sixty miles per hour. With Roger still in sight, I used the voice activation on my phone to call 911.

"A black Maserati sports coupe is driving at excessive speed toward the marina. The driver is Roger Raines. I think he's attempting to flee the country by boat with a large amount of cash."

I gave the dispatcher the license plate number and ended the call before she could ask questions. I couldn't stop Roger if I got in a crash.

I followed him through a bend in the road. Traffic began to pick up when we blasted past a sign indicating the marina was two miles away. Roger kept weaving among lanes to dodge motorists observing the twenty-five-mile-per-hour speed limit. I followed, conjuring up images of drivers racing toward the checkered flag at the Indianapolis 500.

At the sign indicating one mile to the marina, I voice-dialed Nic.

"Elmo, what in the world is going on?"

"Roger's the murderer. He's almost at the marina. He's making a run for it. Keep an eye out for a black Maserati. Once you do, don't lose sight of it. I'm right behind." Once again, I ended the call before questions could be asked. The pounding of blood in my ears overwhelmed the roar of the truck's massive V-8 engine. There was no margin for even the smallest of mistakes.

Masts from sailboats came into view. We were almost there. How we'd made it this far without causing a crash was beyond me. All I could do was stay on him and hope the luck held.

With a squeal of rubber on asphalt, Roger took the turn into parking lot too wide. He bounced over a curb, obliterated the welcome sign, and knocked over a trash barrel. The sports car was tough. He kept going, throwing the tires spewing gravel in the air as he accelerated toward the far end of the marina.

His mistake was costly. And not just in property damage. The error allowed me to cut his lead from fifty yards to twenty. I took advantage of the truck's stability and clearance to cut the distance between us even more by rolling over his crash site without slowing down.

I'd apologize later.

Hopefully, the apology wouldn't be made from behind bars.

The Maserati, now battered and dented, was almost to the end of the parking area when he slammed on his brakes, almost spinning out of control right in front of me. He leapt from the vehicle and sprinted away from me. Toward a group of cigarette boats that were moored safe and sound near the last berth.

In one hand, he had the backpack. In the other, he had a pistol.

"In for a dime, in for a dollar, Elmo." I got out of truck and scanned the area for a friendly face.

From the other direction, Nic was running toward me. I took her hand and we ran as fast as possible back in the direction she'd come from.

"He's got a racing boat. We need to cut him off. Come on."

God love her, Nic didn't ask any questions. She jetted away from me. By the time I arrived at her personal craft, sucking air from the physical exertion, the vessel was untied from its moorings and the engine was running.

The high-pitched wail of police sirens pierced the air as I joined her at the helm. She looked at me, her brow furrowed.

One hand was on the throttle, the other hovering over a two-way radio.

"We could call the Coast Guard." The lack of conviction in her voice spoke louder than her words. She knew the marina and the surrounding waters as well as anyone. If we didn't stop him from reaching the open water of the Gulf of Mexico, he'd be long gone.

"Hit it."

The thunder of the engine rattled me to my bones as the craft jumped away from the dock. While we powered through the choppy waves, I scanned the water.

"There he is." I squeezed Nic's shoulder and pointed to a low-slung craft bouncing up and down off our port bow. He wasn't moving very fast yet, but was definitely headed for open water.

She pushed the throttle to maximum and we surged forward, marina speed limits forgotten. A few hundred yards away off the starboard bow, a double-decker tour boat motored toward us.

"I'll try to cut him off there." She pointed toward a red traffic buoy, shouting to be heard over the din. "Be ready."

"For what?"

"I dunno." She shrugged. "Anything." We'd halved the distance to the buoy. Roger was getting his boat up to speed, though.

It was a game of high-stakes chicken. Nic kept her craft pointed straight ahead. She was trying to pinch him between her boat and a retaining wall on the far side of the marina. Roger cut through the water faster and faster with each second that ticked by.

Fifty feet from the crimson ball floating on the water, Nic adjusted course to cut between the buoy and Roger. A few heartbeats later, Roger corrected course to evade the noose that was tightening in on him.

He overcompensated, though, and the back end of his craft swung around, leaving him headed toward the retaining wall. The concrete structure was built to protect homes on the other side of it from rising water. The fiberglass hull of the speed boat wouldn't stand a chance.

"He's gonna crash."

He fought the steering wheel, letting off the gas to regain control. He got his craft pointed in the direction he wanted to go but with little thrust in his favor, Nic had the angle on him.

In desperation, he fired a couple of shots at us while he tossed the backpack overboard.

"Hold on, Elmo."

Nic yanked the wheel hard left and cut the throttle. Our momentum carried us toward Roger, while the abrupt change in the boat's orientation pushed a sizable wave at him. Before he could escape, the swell crashed over his boat, swamping the engines, and knocking him off his feet.

I jumped from the safety of Nic's vessel to the other and tumbled on top of Roger before he could get back on his feet. I used my size advantage to keep him down while I tied his hands with some mooring rope.

"Game's over, Roger. Time to face the music." I pulled him into a seat.

"I don't know what you're talking about." He looked at me and shook his head. "But you're going to pay for crashing my boat."

At that moment we bumped into the retaining wall, hard enough for the pistol to slide into view. He lunged for it. Without use of his hands or arms, all he accomplished was ending up facedown on the deck again.

I yanked him away from the weapon with one hand and grabbed it with the other.

"Dunno about that." There was a swim platform attached to the stern of the boat. A clip from one of the backpack's straps had gotten caught in one of the openings cut into the platform. Instead of drifting away in the water, the bag was dangling off the end of the boat, like a leaf on a branch. It was damp, but otherwise no worse from the wear and tear.

"What do we have here?" I held it out for him to see. "Think we'll find anything interesting?"

All of a sudden, I was cast in shadow. I glanced over my shoulder. Nic had pulled up next to us. She was sporting a wide grin. And had her flare gun pointed at Roger.

"The cops are on their way. You could turn that bag over to them when they get here. Or you could take a quick peek now. You know, to make sure there's not just sightseeing gear in there and this is one massive misunderstanding." Something on the deck of her boat caught her attention. She got down on one knee to look at it. "Oh wow. What do I have here? Sorry, Elmo, I need to look at this. Guess I'll never know if you look inside. It'll be your word against his."

There are a lot of things I don't know. One thing I do know is when to take a hint from my friends. I pulled on the zipper and looked inside. And let out a long laugh.

I'd been right. Holy samolie, I really had been right.

The bag was filled with stacks of bills. There were tens, twenties, even fifties, all wrapped in plastic and bound with rubber bands. I dug through it, my curiosity in overdrive. Among the bricks of cash, my fingers latched on to a passport. It had Roger's picture but a completely different name, Arnold Van Den Brooklyn.

"Hey, Nic? You up for a little adventure? Our waterlogged buddy appears to be a drug runner. In one more stop, I can prove his guilt. Whoever he really is."

CHAPTER TWENTY-EIGHT

"LET ME GET this straight." Susan Eikenberry stared at me, her jaw clenching and unclenching. "You're accusing Roger Raines of running a drug smuggling ring and murdering Fran Cohen."

We were back at the marina. Roger was secured in the back of Susan's cruiser. The money, passport, gun, and other items from the backpack were being held safely as evidence. Nic was giving Spock her version of how things had gone down.

"Yes. And there's no time to waste. You need to send officers to secure the Sea Breeze. Make sure nobody leaves until you have Roger's security guys in custody. They're probably working on their escape now."

"Why?"

"They're the ones who stole Rambo's alligator and carried it into Fran's apartment. I'll explain on the way." I took her by the elbow and guided her toward Nic's boat. "Spock, the chief needs a word with you. Come on, Nic. More adventure awaits."

I'd filled her in on what I expected to find on the island while we waited for the police boat to arrive and take Roger into custody. At first, Nic had been horrified. Then she got angry.

"I cannot believe I let that man manipulate me into helping him run drugs." She'd attempted her own end run around me to get to Roger. "Let me at him."

Now, with a chance to cool down, she couldn't wait to get going.

Once we were back on the water, the chief took over.

"Start at the beginning. Tell me everything, Simpson. Don't leave out even the smallest detail. Got it?"

As we motored to the island the tour stopped at, gentle waves provided the sensation of a kiddy rollercoaster. Up and down, up and down, up and down. Since we weren't at full speed, the engine produced a soothing rumble instead of its earlier eardrum-splitting racket. Overhead, wispy clouds rode the winds eastward at a casual pace, providing periodic respite from the sun.

On any other day, I would have found a comfy spot on the boat to curl up and take a nap.

My position between the boat's captain and my city's police chief was a stark reminder it wasn't any other day. I'd told my story and had been answering Susan's questions for a half hour when Nic cleared her throat.

"We're about halfway to the island, peeps. Do you want me to pull up to the dock or take a swing around its perimeter to get a look at the scene?"

"Tie us off at the dock." The chief was in full command mode. The forcefulness of her order left no doubt who had the final say in the matter. "Okay, Simpson. Tell me again what you think we'll find."

"A stash of drugs. Hidden in something watertight. Small enough to fit in Roger's backpack."

"And why, exactly, do you think this?"

I stole a glance at Nic. She rolled her eyes. This was going to be the second time in short succession for me to share my theory. I reminded myself that the chief was doing her job. Her insistence was no doubt a way to see if I could keep my story straight.

It was the truth, so that wasn't a problem.

"For a while now, Fran was going around asking to interview people for a book about Paradise Springs' history."

Susan nodded. "He talked to me about being the city's first female police chief. Go on."

"It was a cover story. He was really doing that to get dirt on people. You know how he could be at times. When he wanted to, he could turn on the charm. He'd get people to confide in him, reveal secrets without realizing it."

"So what if he was a rumormonger?"

"He was also a lawyer. He knew how to get information. He'd look into something probably shared in confidence and see if there was more to it. If it was big enough, he'd use the admission as part of a blackmail scheme. It was a despicable way to supplement his retirement income."

"You have proof of this?"

Before I could answer, Nic held her phone out to Susan. "Here's a letter we found when we were doing that final inspection. Looks pretty damning to me."

After a moment, the chief snapped her own shot of the photo. "Do you know where this letter is now?"

I jumped back in. "Roger took it. It's probably gone by now, but Sybil admitted she wrote it."

"One day soon, I will have a conversation with both of you about withholding potential evidence. For now, go on."

"Fran was blackmailing a lot of people. Claudine was another one of his victims. Somehow, she figured out Roger was smuggling drugs. My guess is she saw or overheard Roger or his henchmen, did some digging, put two and two together, and confronted Roger."

"Okay, but why use the alligator?"

"To pin the murder on Rambo. Roger was at the meeting where Rambo spoke out against the development proposal by his property. After that night, everyone knew how angry Rambo was. Roger had his security guys steal the gator. At the right time, on a night when Minerva was gone, he showed up on Fran's doorstep, knocked him out once inside, and had the gator set loose in the bedroom."

"Where'd they keep it? A lot of time went by between Rambo reporting it missing and Fran's murder."

"She's got you there, Elmo." Nic elbowed me in the ribs. Normally, I would have appreciated the friendly gesture. Under Susan's watchful eye, not so much.

"They kept it at the Sea Breeze. In a vacant condo. Probably next door to where his goons live."

"Some of the condos have adjoining doors," Nic said. "That would totally work."

"We'll see when I hear from my team." Susan's stubbornness was a touch frustrating. Then again, she needed evidence, not stories. Especially not stories from someone who'd been conducting their own investigation right under her nose.

To her credit, she'd given me space when I needed it. I owed her for that.

The island came into view. Roughly egg-shaped, it was about a mile long and a half-mile wide. An area by the dock the size of a basketball court had been cleared. A few picnic tables were scattered about, presumably to give tourists a place to sit while they ate their lunches. A trail at the far end of the clearing led off into the woods.

The moment was almost at hand. Once we were safely moored at the dock, I looked at Susan. She looked right back at me. I looked at Nic. She shrugged.

"Your story, Elmo. I think the chief wants you to lead the way."

Susan followed me around the clearing. When we came upon a picnic table, she'd look underneath. "I don't see any trash cans."

"Roger collected all the trash and brought it back on board," Nic said. "Clever ploy on his part now that I think about it. He kept trash bags in his backpack. A perfect reason for taking it with him onto the island."

"Who's up for a hike?" I gestured with my thumb toward the trailhead. "Roger kept his operation on the down-low for a long time. I'm sure the drop point was as far away from this spot as possible."

I turned and headed down the dirt path. Years of foot traffic had cleared it of any debris. The only trip hazards were the occasional tree roots that crossed the walkway. It was too narrow for two people to walk side by side, but comfortable for one person to take a leisurely nature stroll.

Or for one person to make an unimpeded sprint to the drop point.

After about ten minutes, I came to an abrupt halt. The hairs on the back of my neck stood on end. I made a 360-degree scan of the area.

"It's here."

I closed my eyes and took a deep breath to calm myself. At the count of ten, I opened them and began to study my surroundings. My gaze remained unfocused, absorbing everything—the leaves, grass, limbs, insects—on an equal basis.

"Elmo, what—" Susan's question was cut off when Nic shushed her.

"I've seen him do this before. It's weird but it seems to work."

First, I checked the canopy above. Nothing was out of place. Lots of green leaves and a few birds' nests. Next, I scanned my surroundings at eye level. Among the trees, ferns covered the forest floor, turning it into a sea of green. All seemed normal.

At ground level there was gap between two trees. It seemed off.

"There."

I waded through fifteen feet of undergrowth until I came to a tree that had fallen. The stump was about eighteen inches in diameter and at its highest point, a couple of feet from the ground. Upon initial inspection, the tree appeared to have been knocked over in a storm. When I looked closer, the break was a lot cleaner than what I would expect wind and rain to cause.

Nic and Susan gathered on either side of me. I got down on one knee and knocked on the stump. The sound wasn't right. It wasn't a solid *thunk*. It was more of a *whop*.

"It's hollow," Nic said in a breathless tone.

"Here. Put these on. There may be fingerprints." Ever the diligent law enforcement officer, Susan handed me a pair of rubber gloves. Someday, I'd have to thank her for giving me this moment.

When they were on, I gripped the stump with both hands and pulled upward. Nothing. Then, I twisted counter-clockwise, like I was unscrewing a lid. Again, nothing. I sat back on my haunches and studied the problem for a moment.

"There must be some kind of unique release system. The smugglers wouldn't want someone to find whatever's inside this by accident." Then it came to me. I twisted the stump clockwise, as if I was tightening said lid.

"Will you look at that? It's turning." Nic gave my shoulder a squeeze.

After four rotations, the top came off. I looked inside and let out a low whistle. "Chief, is it just me or does that look like a lot of contraband?"

She looked over my shoulder. "Well, I'll be, Simpson. That does look like a lot of contraband. Enough, in fact, to send Roger, or Arnold, or whatever his name is, and his associates to jail for a long time."

I got to my feet and brushed the dirt from my knees. Then I spread my arms wide and bowed at the waist, first to Nic, then to Susan. "Then my work here is done. Don't forget to tip your servers."

Nic burst out laughing. "God, you are such a dork."

"That's true." The chief cracked a smile. "But a dork who did okay today. Good going, Simpson. I'm proud of you."

Nic and I exchanged a look. The chief was known for her stoicism, not for any inclination to pass around praise as if it was candy on Halloween. To be told she was proud of me was about the highest compliment possible.

I grinned and kept my mouth shut. Why spoil a good moment. Know what I mean?

CHAPTER TWENTY-NINE

TWO DAYS LATER, I was sitting on the patio, my feet up in a chair and Oscar on my lap. It was February 29, Leap Day, that special day that came around only every four years. It was also my birthday. After a celebratory video call with Mom, I'd spent the day lounging around the trailer.

After all the private-eye craziness of the last two weeks, a day with nothing to do was the perfect present. The phone was turned off. My tablet and laptop were on my desk inside. That was one of the great thing about electronics. They didn't seem to mind if you ignored them.

"Forty-four years old, buddy." I scratched Oscar's undamaged ear as I took a drink of my green tea. "But only eleven in leap years. I like that one better. I'll live a long time that way."

My cat looked at me, then toward the street. Rambo's truck had just turned into the driveway. Nic was behind the wheel. He was in the passenger seat. As soon as the vehicle's wheels stopped turning, Rambo had the door open.

"There's the best gumshoe this side of Sam Spade." The second I got to my feet, he had me in a spine-cracking bear hug.

"I take it the charges were dropped," I asked before all

the air was squeezed from my lungs.

As soon as he let me go, he whipped off his suit jacket and tie. "Yep. I'm free and clear. I was kinda hoping the chief would apologize—"

"But we didn't want to push your luck. Right, Rambo?" Nic patted his arm like he was her ten-year-old son. Not a grown man three times her size.

She'd accompanied him to the press conference announcing the charges that had been filed against Roger and his two security guard accomplices. Yesterday, the chief had promised me that she'd make it known, beyond the shadow of a doubt, that Rambo had been cleared of all wrongdoing.

I'd declined the mayor's invitation to attend the press conference. My friend was free. That's all that mattered to me.

"Yeah. With that over, we got things to do. Come on." He led me to the truck while Nic took Oscar inside and locked the trailer. "Time to celebrate your birthday."

"I didn't know I had any birthday plans," I said as he urged me into the passenger seat he'd vacated only minutes before.

"Then call it a celebration in honor of solving your first case." Rambo squeezed himself into the back seat while Nic jumped back behind the wheel.

"What's he mean by celebration?" I asked her while we buckled up.

"You'll see."

Ten minutes later, we pulled into a parking spot at the Riptide. The lot was packed like a Friday night during peak tourist season, not a February Saturday afternoon.

"What's going on?" I looked at Rambo. "Are we celebrating your cleared name? I wish someone would have told me."

"Something like that." He practically yanked me out of my seat. "Come on."

I followed my buddies across the restaurant's threshold and was enveloped in twilight. The place was as quiet as it was dark. "Where is everyone? Wendell, you here? Seven?"

A moment later, the lights blazed to life, a banner with the words HAPPY BIRTHDAY on it was unfurled from the ceiling, and I was hit with a wall of sound. It was a single word.

"Surprise!"

Too overwhelmed to move, all I could do was watch as dozens of people streamed from hiding spots behind every nook and cranny of the restaurant to greet me. There were hugs, handshakes, and more than a few slaps on the back.

At some point, an Irish whiskey on the rocks was put in my hand. Right after that, JJ Grey & Mofro's funky Southern rock came over the speakers. As I waded through the crowd receiving well wishes, I caught the intoxicating aroma of Wendell's barbeque brisket and cornbread. Seven had just uncovered a buffet set up along one wall.

When I made eye contact with the restaurant owner, the man who welcomed me to the Springs all those years ago, and who'd become a great friend, he gave me a big hug. It was almost as spine-cracking as Rambo's.

"Happy birthday, buddy." He gestured to the crowd. "Folks wanted to do a little something to say thanks for catching Fran's murderer."

"And busting up a drug running operation at the same time," Seven said. "Way to go, Elmo Simpson, PI." She planted a big kiss on my cheek, then danced away, clapping her hands to the music.

"Wow." I put my hand to my cheek. It was burning. "It's going to take a while to recover from that."

"Well, she's always had a bit of a crush on you." With a laugh, Wendell guided me to a table marked with a paper sign that read, RESERVED FOR ELMO SIMPSON, PRIVATE INVESTIGATOR.

I stared at the sign. Then at the crowd. The party was in full swing. In my honor. A lump formed in my throat. I was about to take a drink when someone whacked me across the shin.

"Step aside, Simpson." Sybil had a plate that was piled six inches high in one hand. In the other, she held a wooden cane. "A woman's gotta eat. Besides, you wouldn't have caught Raines without my help."

I did as I was told, then took a seat. "Did she just hit me with a cane?"

"Sure did." Rambo, who had a plate as full as Sybil's, laughed and took the seat across from me. "And she don't even need one. I think it was payback for you accusing her of murder."

I shrugged. "Guess I won't be using her services anymore."

Nic slipped into one of the two open seats left. "Don't be so sure about that. If I know her, she'll be offering you a reading at half-price so she can say she's the seer to the Man Who Took Down the Mob, or something like that."

There was no point in arguing that what I'd done was far from that. In Paradise Springs nobody wanted the truth to get in the way of a good story.

As the party went on, I mingled with a Who's Who of my adopted hometown. The mayor shared a drink and a selfie with me, apparently our disagreement in the courthouse all but forgotten. Susan and Spock stopped by to chat and avail themselves of the buffet. They were on duty, so they had to decline when Seven offered them beers.

"How are things with Roger, I mean Arnold?" It had turned out that Roger Raines was the alias of Arnold Van Der Brooklyn, a scam artist who'd seemingly disappeared off the face of the Earth a few months before Roger showed up.

"He's lawyered up. His two security guys are singing like the proverbial canaries, though." She leaned in close. "I shouldn't tell you this because the investigation is ongoing, but what the hell, you cracked the whole thing wide open. Turns out, the security guys have been in the country illegally, working for Arnold. They've basically been slave labor for him. If they'd get out of line, he threatened to expose them to the authorities and take it out on their families in Colombia."

"Wow." I drained my drink. In the blink of an eye, Seven was there with a replacement. "You can add human trafficking to the charges, huh?"

"Yep." She chewed on a spoonful of baked beans. "I gotta hand it to you, Simpson. You connected the dots when we couldn't."

"Thank you. I'm happy it all worked out."

My thoughts went to Fran's notebooks. A search of Arnold's office and living quarters had failed to uncover Sybil's letter. The notebooks were the only pieces of evidence left that linked the deceased to his blackmail scheme.

I didn't like the deceased. His criminal behavior had been deplorable. Still, he didn't deserve to lose his life. Especially not that way.

People could say what they wanted about the man. I wasn't going to add fuel to that fire, though. I was going to do something a little different.

A bit later, I flagged Nic down and stepped outside with her. "Do you think anyone would notice if we made a quiet exit? There's something I need to do, and I'd like your help with it."

We looked around the restaurant. Rambo was holding court at the outside bar, telling tales about his time in the slam. His words, not mine. Claudine was perched on a barstool, a drink in her hand, giving him every bit of her attention.

She and I hadn't spoken. I wasn't quite ready to let bygones be bygones with her. In time, though.

"Sure. This is your day, after all. I'll make sure Rambo gets home safe. It was nice of him to let me use his wheels since he's too big to fit in my car."

We were almost at the truck when we stopped in our tracks. A familiar 1964 Lincoln Continental pulled into a parking spot. The Vampire emerged from the driver's side,

Big Baby from the passenger side.

"Holy samolie." They'd helped with the case. No reason for them to miss out on all the fun. I shook hands with both of them. "Thank you so much for all your help."

"Merely doing our civic duty," Big Baby said. "And now to enjoy a repast among the revelers. You're not leaving us, are you?"

"I'm afraid so. The last few days have caught up with me." That was true. "Please, go enjoy yourselves. There's plenty of food and the drinks are flowing."

"Indeed. The night is young, BB. Shall we?" The Vampire shook my hand, kissed Nic's cheek, and walked arm in arm with his friend into the party.

On the way home, I told Nic how much the celebration meant to me. "That was amazing. It seemed like everyone in town was there."

"Everyone in the OG crowd was invited. It was the least we could do. Goob wanted to be there. He said he's too old for shenanigans like that, so he was there in spirit. He wants you to stop by his place tomorrow to fill him in on what he missed."

I laughed. It was a tension-releasing, tear-inducing one that didn't stop until we got to my house. After all the stress and worry and fear, it felt good. Really, really good.

"Okay, you're home, Mr. Simpson, Private Eye. What do you need my help with?"

"Would you fire up the grill, please? I need to pop inside. Be right back." I fetched the notebooks and joined Nic as the third burner flamed to life. Sometimes you couldn't beat the convenience of gas.

She looked at the items in my hands. "Are those what I think they are?"

"Yep. First, if you haven't already done so, I'd like for you to delete the picture of Sybil's letter from your phone. I wiped all the case info from my devices this morning. Then, we're going to burn these babies. That way, they can't do any more harm."

"What about the victims of Fran's blackmail? These could help them recover damages from his estate."

"True. Do you think they want potentially salacious details brought up in a court proceeding, though? I think we're doing them a favor. All the secrets die here and now."

After a moment, she took one of the notebooks. "Let's do it."

We tossed the documents one by one onto the grill. First, the pages, and the awful information recorded on them, curled at the edges, then they caught fire. They burned until they were nothing more than piles of harmless ash.

As the smoke rose from the grill, a weight slipped from my shoulders. Two men who were hurting my community had been stopped. Like any real-life story, questions remained. Where had Claudine gone during that unexplained two-hour window? For an illicit rendezvous with the reverend or for some other reason she wanted to keep to herself? Was Rambo's farm safe from encroachment? Was Minerva going to keep up her charade? What did Sybil see, if anything, for my future?

Those were questions for another day, though.

When only a few embers remained, Nic took my hand in hers and gave it a squeeze. "Philly Fran can't hurt anyone now, can he?"

"Nope. And neither can Roger or Arnold or whatever his name is."

She chuckled and leaned against me. "That's good. We made a pretty good team, didn't we?"

I put my arm around her and drew her in close. The warmth from the grill's flames was nothing compared to the warmth coming from Nic.

"We sure did. You were an amazing Watson to my Holmes."

"Um, I think it was more like I was Alexa Crowe from *My Life Is Murder*, and you were Madison." She gave me a playful elbow to my ribs.

Whatever we were to each other, and to our odd little town of Paradise Springs, I had a feeling we were in it together for the long haul. What that actually meant for us? Well, I just have to stick by Nic to find out. And follow the clues wherever they might lead us.

That was the kind of mystery I couldn't wait to investigate.

The End

Acknowledgements

Many thanks go to my literary agent and friend, C.H. Armstrong, who saw something in Elmo and the oddballs of Paradise Springs and never gave up on them. I also want to thank the amazing team at Tule Publishing, especially my editorial team of Meghan Farrell, Kelly Hunter, Nan Reinhardt, and Beth Attwood. They took this story and helped me make it shine. Thanks to Lee and Molly for collaborating on a book cover that is absolutely fabulous.

Last but never least, I want to thank my wife, Nancy, who's my partner in crime and fellow beach lover. I'll take a trip with you to Margaritaville any time!

About the Author

J.C. Kenney is the bestselling author of The Allie Cobb Mysteries, The Darcy Gaughan Mysteries, and The Elmo Simpson Mysteries. He's also the co-host of The Bookish Hour webcast. When he's not writing, you can find him following IndyCar racing or listening to music. He has two grown children and lives in Indianapolis with his wife and a cat.

Thank you for reading

Panic in the Panhandle

If you enjoyed this book, you can find more from all our great authors at TulePublishing.com, or from your favorite online retailer.

TULE
PUBLISHING